MW00634660

FALSE CAST
FRANK BENNETT ADIRONDACK MYSTERIES
Published by S.W. Hubbard

Printed in the USA.

Cover Design and Interior Format

FALSE CAST

FRANK BENNETT
ADIRONDACK MYSTERIES

S. W. HUBBARD

CHAPTER 1

FRANK BENNETT PACED THE FRONT hall of his house, leaving faint footprints in the thin layer of sawdust on the floor. Neither he nor his wife had had the time to sweep up after the contractors who created havoc every day putting an addition on the small cottage that had been Frank's bare-bones bachelor home.

"Penny, come on!" he bellowed up the stairwell. "We're going to be late."

The only response was the accelerated tapping of his wife's high heels across the floorboards above his head. What could she possibly be doing? They were going to Earl's graduation from the police academy, not to the opera.

"I can't find my cream shawl anywhere. Have you seen it?"

Their lives had been turned upside down by the remodeling project, their possessions continually repacked and shifted as they moved themselves out of the path of the builders' saws and hammers.

"There's a scarf-y thing down here in the hall. Is that what you're looking for?"

"Cream?" Penny shouted.

"No, black. Can't you just wear that?"

"No, I can't wear a black shawl with this dress." Penny's voice had that "how dumb can a man be?" tone that Frank recognized all too well. It was a tone that had cropped up frequently in their discussions of where to live once they were married. Frank had favored buying a five-year-old ranch house with triple glazed windows and an energy efficient furnace. Penny had called that house's yellow kitchen "eye-scalding" and lobbied for a falling down American Gothic farmhouse with a termite-infested wrap-around porch and a claw-foot bathtub connected to poisonous lead pipes. Charming, Penny called it. So they had compromised on doubling the size of Frank's cottage, which was situated in a pretty spot above Stony Brook, with a new master bedroom, expanded kitchen and great room. The work dragged on, sometimes testing the strength of their six-month marriage.

"Relax. It only takes a half an hour to get there." A whiff of Penny's floral perfume floated down the stairwell with her words. "I'm almost done."

Frank could hear closet doors opening and shutting, drawers banging—not the sounds of almost done to him.

"Should we take two cars? I'll meet you there." His threat of last resort, designed to bring her running.

Instead, Penny laughed. "If we take separate cars, I guarantee you I'll be there first."

Too true. Penny's lead foot hadn't lightened since their marriage despite Frank's warning that it didn't do to have the Police Chief's wife seen speeding through town.

Finally, Penny descended the stairs, a sheer skirt with an uneven hemline swishing around her long legs.

Frank's irritation dissolved. "You look fantastic."

"Thanks, dear." She kissed him, and her lips were even with his. Frank looked down at her feet.

"What kind of shoes are you wearing? You're as tall as me!"

"Party shoes! I never get to wear them."

"Honey, the graduation party is in Earl's uncle's workshop. The North Country Stompers are playing. You can't dance in those."

"I know." Penny produced a pair of squishy-looking flats from her purse. "I'll make an entrance, then I'll change."

Making an entrance was what Penny did best. Frank still couldn't believe this lovely woman, fifteen years his junior, had wanted to marry him, a widower with a married daughter and two grandchildren. Penny would probably have been happy to live together, but Frank thought cohabitation unseemly. He felt during their courtship that people in Trout Run must be gossiping about him when they saw his truck parked in front of Penny's house or the library where she worked, whispering that he was a crazy old fool, or worse, a dirty old man. His imagination ran wild, hearing his sex life as the subject of conversation at Malone's Diner. "Frank must be gettin' lucky tonight!"

Once they married, Frank assumed the gossip must have stopped. At least, he hoped it had. What fun was there in commenting on the habits of a married couple? But he suspected people still murmured, "What does she see in him?" when they saw Penny and him together.

He asked that question himself every morning when he woke to find her long, slender arm flung across his chest, and every evening when he came home to find her singing off-key to the country music the workmen played. But when her eyes opened in the morning or she spied him approaching, her face lit up with undeniable pleasure. Despite his incredulity, Penny was just as delighted in him as he was in her. He had already won the lottery. Time to stop calculating how likely the odds were.

"What happened at the library today?" Frank asked as he navigated the mountain roads through Ausable Forks to pick up the Northway to Plattsburgh.

"I'm working on choosing the books for the kids' Summer Read-a-thon." Penny twisted in the passenger seat to face him. "Do you think ten-year-old boys will read a novel with a female protagonist?"

"I think your biggest hurdle is getting little boys through the door of the library during summer vacation. Once they're inside, I'm confident you could persuade them to read the phone book." A gust of wind pummeled the truck. "But summer sure seems a long way off."

"April is the cruelest month."

"It's nearly May and they're still predicting snow squalls for the weekend." Neither Frank nor Penny had been born in the mountains, but just like all native Adirondackers, they never tired of talking about the weather. "But once the snow stops, the blackflies will start hatching."

"Fishing season brings tourists. You and Earl will start getting busy again," Penny said. "Have you talked to Earl yet about his job prospects?"

"No, I wanted to wait until after the ceremony and the party. Why rain on his parade?"

"What did Lloyd say?"

Frank's foot pressed on the accelerator as he recalled the conversation. "He said what I expected the head of the Town Council to say. There simply isn't enough money in the Trout Run municipal budget to raise Earl's salary up to the level of an entry-level sworn officer in other departments in the region. As much as everyone loves Earl, Lloyd said he should look for a new position, and I should hire a new civilian assistant. That's all Trout Run can afford."

"That's depressing." Penny squinted out the passenger window, but there was nothing to see but the dim outlines of trees flashing by in the reflected glow of headlights. "Can't he just wear the uniform and keep collecting his civilian assistant pay?"

"Well, yeah—but that kinda defeats the purpose of going to the academy. He's tired of having to sneak around with the girls he dates, but he can't move out of his parents' house and live on twenty grand a year."

"So after all you've done to help Earl get through the police academy, now you're going to lose him."

Frank sighed. "Yeah, just when he was getting really good at his job. I'll have to break in some other teenager, I suppose."

"Do you regret encouraging him to go to the academy?"

"Of course not. I would never want to hold him back. I was hoping for a fairy tale ending where we could both get what we want, but life isn't like one of your story hour books."

They sank into silence until Frank exited the highway in Plattsburgh. It dawned on him then that he might have silenced his wife with a remark that came out more snappish than he'd intended. Frank had very quickly slipped back into the habit of being married. After spending twenty-two years married to Estelle before a brain aneurysm plucked her from his world, he now had picked up the thread of married life as if the six long years of unchosen bachelorhood had never happened. He didn't see Penny as a replacement for Estelle—God knew they were totally different. It was more that the reassuring comfort of being able to say out loud whatever thought passed through his mind had snapped back into place.

But maybe it shouldn't have. Penny wasn't high-strung—he wouldn't have been attracted to her if she were. But she wasn't yet inured to Totally Unfiltered Frank.

Frank took his right hand off the wheel and patted Penny's knee, as close to an apology as he could go.

She squeezed his hand briefly then twisted her head. "Turn there!" Penny pointed to a green road sign for the Division of Criminal Justice Services Training Center that Frank was about to sail past.

He took the corner on two wheels, and they pulled into the parking lot laughing.

Inside the packed auditorium, the Davis family occupied all of Row J, with two empty seats in the middle that clearly awaited Frank and Penny. Earl had finagled two extra graduation tickets from a fellow graduate with a small family. Even so, some of Earl's cousins had been excluded from the ceremony. But Great Grandma Gert was there, her cane propped against the seat, her blue eyes bright with excitement.

"I never thought I'd live to see this day," Gert said as the speeches ended and a recording of "Pomp and Circumstance" crackled over the sound system.

"She means she didn't think she'd live this long, not that she didn't think Earl could manage to graduate," Earl's mother clarified to Frank.

Gert was always predicting her own demise, but the 98-year-old looked remarkably spry. "There he is! There's Earl!" she shouted as the first row of cadets marched across the stage.

Antonini...Applebee...Bannister...Beyn...Bonkowski...Connor... Curnow... Frank gripped his armrests and leaned forward.

"Earl Davis," the commander intoned.

Row J erupted in cheers. Uncle Wayne blasted an air horn. Great Grandma Gert slashed the air with her cane. Down on the stage, Earl struggled to maintain a dignified demeanor. But as soon as he shook the commander's hand and accepted the diploma, a grin split his face. He looked up at them and it seemed he was exerting superhuman self-control to keep himself from waving.

Earl's mom leaned across her grandmother and grabbed Frank's hand. "I want to thank you for all you've done for Earl. I didn't think he should do this at first, thought he should train with my brother to install furnaces, but Earl just loves everything he's learned. He loves working with you."

Frank felt an uncomfortable thickening in his throat. "Right. Me too."

When Frank pulled up in front of Earl's uncle's house, the sound of bluegrass music echoed through the valley. Every neighbor in a ten-mile radius had been invited to the party, so there was no chance of complaints. Frank helped high-heeled Penny pick her way down the gravel driveway to the big workshop behind the house where all Davis family events were held.

"Look at the stars." Penny paused to gaze at brilliant canopy above them. "What a beautiful night!" Then she threw her arms around Frank's neck and kissed him, long and hard.

He responded, forgetting about the likelihood of other arriving guests. When they finally pulled apart, Frank tugged at his jacket fruitlessly. "Geez, Penny, now I have to walk into a crowded room."

"Oh, no one's looking at you." She took his hand and led the way.

Inside, the big open building was packed with friends and relatives. The band played on an improvised stage at the far end of the room, while folding tables covered with bright plastic cloths held enough fried chicken, potato salad, and venison stew to feed the entire county. Earl was in the center of a crowd of well-wishers, so Frank and Penny gravitated to their own best friends, Pastor Bob Rush and Edwin and Lucy Bates.

"How's business?" Bob was asking Edwin and Lucy when Frank and Penny showed up.

"No guests at all," Edwin complained. "But I've started a cooking class and I have six people signed up for that."

"March and April are terribly slow," Lucy complained. "We'd close the inn and go on vacation except that Olivia has school."

Olivia tossed her hair. "I could skip a month of school and still pass eighth grade. My classes are super easy."

Lucy and Edwin's foster daughter seemed to have shot up another three inches since Frank had seen her just a few weeks ago. She was straddling that awkward line between gangly and willowy, and Frank knew enough not to comment on her height. He remembered the days when Caroline towered over all the middle school boys and moaned about being what she termed "freakishly tall." Now, at twenty-eight, his daughter was a perfectly proportioned five-seven.

"I love that shirt, Olivia," Penny said. "You look so pretty in green."

Olivia barely lifted her head to acknowledge the compliment. "Thanks."

The Stompers chose that moment to launch into their biggest hit, "There's a Bear in my Trash (and he better git gone)." Frank's eyes lit up. "Hey, Olivia—they're playing our song! Wanna dance?" He held out his hand. The last time he'd been to a party where the Stompers played, Olivia had worn him out dancing the two-step.

Olivia shot him a glance that truly redefined the expression "if looks could kill." Then she spoke to Lucy. "Can we please go? This is so boring."

"Olivia, Frank asked you a question. You're being very rude," Lucy scolded. She took a breath to say more, but Olivia bolted away.

"Looks like you're stuck dancing with me, dear," Penny said as they watched Olivia plop into a folding chair and pull a paperback from her jacket pocket.

Lucy ran her hands through her hair. "I'm sorry, Frank. I don't know what's gotten into her. Yesterday she was all excited about coming to the party."

Frank laughed. "I've been turned down by plenty of girls in my time. I'll survive."

"Well, there's no excuse for being rude," Lucy said. "I'm going to make her come back here and apologize."

Frank reached for her arm before she took second step. "Relax, Lucy. Pick your battles. This one isn't worth having."

Edwin shook his head. "One day, she's playing with Legos, the next day, she's demanding pierced ears and eye shadow. Then she's back to Legos and wanting to be tucked in at night. My head is spinning."

"Welcome to the difficult 'tween years. It'll get worse before it gets better, believe me."

Edwin put his arm around Lucy. "We've figured out this parenting thing pretty well so far, right, Mama?"

Lucy's stern expression softened. "Just when I figure out one stage, we're on to the next. There's never a dull moment with that girl." She looked across to where Olivia sat, twirling a strand of her long brown hair as she read. "I can't even remember what life was like before we got Olivia."

The party rocked on. Frank joined in the fifty-person contra dance, and by the time it was finished, he saw that Olivia had disappeared from her reading nook. Edwin wasn't much of a dancer, so they had probably all gone home. Penny was dancing with Earl's uncle, leaving Frank to peruse the dessert buffet, when Trudy Massinay came up.

"Hey, Trudy—ready for a treat? That chocolate cake is not as good as it looks, but the banana cream pie will knock your socks off."

"Thanks for the advice. I shouldn't be eating any of it, but maybe I'll try one of these blondies." The sturdy social worker took a bar from an overloaded plate and nibbled around the edges.

"How's Mrs. Kepler adjusting to assisted living?" Frank had found the old woman wandering on a road two miles from her house and had called Trudy in to get her assistance.

"Hmm? Oh, pretty good." Trudy glanced up from her dessert plate. "She misses her cat, but she likes the food and the bingo." Her gaze returned to the plate and she fell silent.

Standing there like a post, Frank wished Penny would return from the dance floor. He'd never before had such a hard time making conversation with Trudy.

"Frank, I don't want to ruin the party for you, but there's something you need to know and I'd rather tell you in person." The sentence popped out of her in a rush.

He looked at her worried face and paused with a plastic forkful of pie halfway to his mouth.

"Anita Veech has been released from prison."

The fork tipped and the pie fell with a splat.

"What? She got fifteen years. She had to serve at least seventy percent of her sentence. She's not supposed to be out until—" He attempted to do the math in his head, but he'd done it many times before. Not until Olivia was over eighteen. Not until she was an adult. That's what he'd promised Edwin and Lucy.

"I know it's unexpected. But they've started this program to release nonviolent drug offenders early. Part of the movement to end mass incarceration and shrink the prison population. Anita applied and was approved. Apparently, she's been an exemplary prisoner."

"Well, she wasn't an exemplary mother."

A partygoer angling for the brownies frowned at Frank's sharp tone.

He lowered his voice and steered Trudy away from the buffet. "The court won't return Olivia to Anita, will they? Please tell me you won't let that happen."

"If she wants to regain custody, there will be a hearing in Family Court. Anita will have to show that she can provide a home for Olivia."

"A home! That tarpaper shack in the woods that they were living in before Anita was arrested doesn't qualify as a home, does it?"

Trudy pursed her lips. "Look, Frank—just because Anita won't be able to offer her daughter an antiques-filled Victorian doesn't mean that the court will let her stay with Edwin and Lucy. The court always favors the biological parent unless there are extraordinary circumstances. As long as Anita can offer a safe living environment, however modest, she may regain custody. And Anita was never violent."

Frank hurled the remains of his pie in the trash. "There's more than one way to abuse a child, Trudy. You know that. Anita neglected Olivia, physically and emotionally. That poor kid subsisted on junk food. Her teeth, her hair…she was skin and bones," Frank sputtered. "She couldn't focus in school and the other kids made fun of her. Now look at her. She's beautiful, and happy, and healthy and getting straight As. She's smart and creative, and Lucy and Edwin encourage all her interests." He grabbed Trudy's arm. "Don't tell me you're going to take Olivia away from all that."

Trudy sighed. "You don't have to tell me what a great job the Bateses have done as foster parents, Frank. I'm well aware. But severing the biological parental relationship is a huge responsibility. The State doesn't undertake it lightly."

"When is Anita getting out? Have you told Edwin and Lucy yet?"

"She'll be released next Wednesday. I'll inform them on Monday. But Frank, I need your support on this. That's why I'm telling you now. I want you to vent to me, not to Edwin and Lucy. Don't make a bad situation worse."

"But you said, 'if she wants to regain custody.' Do you know if Anita really does want Olivia back? Honestly, Anita didn't seem too cut up about being separated from her daughter when she was arrested."

Trudy shrugged. "I can't predict. It's true Anita had a very flat affect when I worked with her. But that might be a sign that she also was traumatized by her living situation."

Frank kicked the trashcan at the end of the buffet table. "Anita was an adult. She didn't have to live like that. She could have left with Olivia."

"And who raised Anita? A brutal, ignorant, paranoid old man. Is it any wonder she wasn't prepared to be a good mother?"

Frank felt a surge of anger toward Trudy, a woman he considered a friend. "I'm tired of these excuses. Where does it end? Anita should be held accountable for what she did to Olivia when she was little."

"Ah, Frank—life is not so simple. If it were easy for people to make good decisions, there would be no need for social workers like me."

CHAPTER 2

ON THE MONDAY MORNING AFTER the party, Earl walked into the office with Doris hot on his heels.

"Doesn't he look handsome?" the town secretary gushed.

Instead of his usual Carhartt work pants and blue shirt, Earl was wearing a khaki uniform to match Frank's, with his badge pinned on and his service weapon and handcuffs on his belt. Of course, he'd worn this during the graduation ceremony, but then it had seemed like a dress-up costume. Here in the Trout Run PD office, Earl really did look like a sworn officer. Frank remembered the first day he'd met Earl, nearly five years ago. As an eighteen-year-old, Earl had been scrawny and twitchy with insecurity. He'd bulked up some, although he was still lean, and had shaved off the goofy mustache. Mostly what had changed was his demeanor. Earl now faced the world with a calm confidence. Frank wasn't sure when or how that transformation had taken place. It had come over Earl gradually, he supposed, but the uniform illuminated the change.

Earl blushed as Doris fussed over him and Frank delivered a salute. But eventually the phone rang and Doris reluctantly returned to her post, and Frank and Earl were left alone at their desks. Frank busied himself reviewing the bulletins that had come in from the state police overnight, while Earl typed an accident report left over from yesterday. A day like any other, but a sense of waiting for the other shoe to drop hung over the room. Frank knew he should bring up the matter of Earl's title and salary, but he couldn't bear to face the kid's disappointment.

Unprofessional. He was Earl's supervisor and bosses often had to make hard decisions. Earl wasn't his child. The fierce papa bear protectiveness that welled up in him whenever anyone had the audacity to disappoint his daughter in any way was not called for here.

Frank resisted giving Earl the label of "the son I never had." He and Estelle had been far too young when their daughter Caroline was born. They'd waited five years before trying again…and nothing. They'd visited doctors to no avail, and then simply moved on. He hadn't been disappointed not to have a son. Caroline was enough for him. Yet he couldn't deny that Earl was far more than his subordinate.

And just as he'd blamed himself the time Caroline had been passed over for an exclusive exchange student program (surely if her dad had been a corporate big-wig instead of a cop, she'd have been selected), he felt partially responsible for the Town Council's refusal to promote Earl. He should've sucked up to them. For the past two years while Earl was at the academy, he should have been griping about how overworked he was in order to lay the groundwork for this promotion. But he was terrible at playing politics. And now both Earl and he would suffer.

He couldn't bear to tackle breaking the news today. Maybe tomorrow. Frank stole a furtive glance at Earl. Earl was looking right back at him.

"So?" Earl said.

"So what?"

"Did you get a chance to ask Lloyd about promoting me?"

Time to rip the Band-Aid off with one quick pull. Still, he couldn't meet Earl's eye. He tapped some papers into perfect alignment and stapled them. "Lloyd said there's no money in the budget to pay you the market rate for a sworn officer. You're welcome to stay in your current position, but….." Frank finally looked up. "I'm sorry, Earl. I tried, I really did. I hate disappointing you after all your hard work."

Earl pursed his lips and nodded. "That's what my dad said would happen. No way they'd ever raise taxes to pay my salary." He heaved a sigh and went back to typing. "Guess I have to put Plan B into effect."

Earl had a Plan B? That was news. "Which is…?"

"Send in my applications for the Saranac Lake and Lake Placid departments. And Plattsburgh, but that's not ideal."

"Do you know if they're hiring?"

"Lake Placid has two retirements coming up this year. Saranac Lake is expanding since the town got that new hotel and condo complex. One of the guys in my class has a dad who works for Lake Placid, so he'll get one of those slots. But I figure I have as good a shot as anyone at the other. Will you give me a recommendation?"

Frank ducked his head and coughed. This was no time to let Earl see the tears in his eyes. "Of course I will. I'll write you the best letter ever. Then I'll have Penny pump it up."

Earl grinned. "That oughta put me over the top."

The mood in the office had lightened. Earl had accepted the news much better than anticipated. It was Frank who still felt morose. Maybe Earl was actually happy to be moving on.

"You know, working in Placid or Saranac…in a bigger department… that could be good experience for you," Frank said.

"It'll be different, for sure."

"Having a new boss, you'll be exposed to other approaches, other methods."

"I suppose." Earl kept typing.

"You've probably learned about all you can from me. Time to learn from some younger guys."

Earl's gray eyes gazed at him without blinking. "I'd rather stay here. This is the best job in the world. But I knew when I started at the academy that it might end like this. I'm really going to miss you, Frank."

Frank rose and walked over to Earl's desk. "I'll miss you." He gripped Earl's shoulder, unable to speak.

Earl spun his swivel chair around. "Geez, Frank—it's not like I died."

Feeling that at least one of the burdens weighing on him had lifted, Frank headed out on the morning patrol. Light brushstrokes of chartreuse brightened mountains that had been gray and white for so many months. Still, the wind whipped fiercely. Shirtsleeves were still a long way off. He drove along Route 86 keeping the snow-capped Whiteface in view until, without consciously intending it, he turned and drove slowly past the Iron Eagle Inn. A cheerful spring flag fluttered from a flagpole on the wraparound porch. Edwin had recently touched up the gold paint on the eagle soaring on the inn's wooden sign. Lights glowed in the kitchen. Were Lucy and Edwin happily going about their day oblivious to the bombshell about to explode their world? Or had Trudy already stopped by to shatter their contentment? Frank longed to pull into the drive and let himself into the kitchen as he always did. But if they'd heard the news, he would not be welcome today.

And if they didn't know yet, he'd never be able to hold the secret.

So he drove on.

Frank took the short cut along High Meadow Road to get back to the center of town. As he came around the blind corner near the North Country Academy, he noticed that the body of the buck that had been hit by a car yesterday no longer lay in the weeds along the shoulder of the road. Frank had reported the road kill to the county public works department, but somehow he doubted they had removed the carcass so promptly. A far more likely scenario: that meaty beast was being ground into venison sausage by Walt Murphy. Murphy's Wild Venison Sausage had grown from being a local favorite to having a cult following among downstate foodies, and Walt had built himself a nice little sideline to supplement his income as a maintenance foreman for a hotel in Lake Placid. But Walt was hard-pressed to come up with enough deer after hunting season had ended, so Frank suspected he resorted to using fresh road kill. The practice of eating road kill might be unappetizing, but it wasn't illegal although selling the road kill to unwary customers probably ran afoul of some health code. However, the police chief of Trout Run wasn't charged with enforcing health regulations, so Frank turned a blind eye to disappearing deer carcasses. Frank supposed the ingredients in Walt's sausages weren't any worse than those in supermarket sausages. But he declined to eat them anyway.

Thinking about sausages made Frank hungry, so he decided to stop at Malone's for lunch. A nice beefy smell wafted out to him as he climbed the steps to the diner. Stew, meatloaf, pot roast? Whatever the special, it had attracted quite a crowd for a Monday in the off-season. Customers filled every table, so Frank took a seat at the counter in hopes that Marge Malone would spoon him up a bowl of beef stew as she passed. But Marge lumbered by three times without making eye contact, bearing armloads of plates for a large, noisy group who had commandeered three pushed-together Formica tables.

"A man oughta be able to do what he wants with his own land," someone said with greater volume than was necessary to be heard.

"Well, if you had a view of the covered bridge, you wouldn't want it blocked by a McMansion," a woman shot back.

"Who's that group in the corner?" Frank asked the man next to him.

"Monthly meeting of the High Peaks Historical Society."

"Kinda rowdy for a bunch of historians, wouldn't you say?" Frank twisted around to see a large, gray-haired woman stand up and tap her water glass with a knife to command attention.

"Please! We're here to plan our participation in the John Brown Farm reenactment. This discussion of Adirondack Park Authority regulations is totally off the agenda."

"Last month, they argued for an hour over whether it was okay to wear modern underwear under their Civil War uniforms," Rollie Fister said under his breath as he took the stool on the other side of Frank. "At least today's argument is worth having."

As the manager of Venable's Hardware and a hopeless gossip, Rollie always knew the scuttlebutt around town. Frank had only to raise his eyebrows to get Rollie to elaborate.

"The APA has made a final decision. They're not going to let the Gatrells sell part of their land to that luxury vacation home developer guy. Some people think Ronnie oughta be able to do what he likes with his land. Other people," Rollie glanced over his shoulder and lowered his voice, "don't want their own view of Stony Brook ruined."

"Forever wild!" someone at Historical Society table called out.

Rollie rolled his eyes. "Yeah, yeah. Fine for him to say. If I was a retired schoolteacher livin' off a fat pension, I wouldn't want any big, fancy houses built either. But those new houses would have brought some money and jobs into Trout Run."

Frank let the "fat pension" remark slide although he doubted anyone retired from the High Peaks school district was living large. "Refresh my memory. Who's Ronnie Gatrell? Where is this land?"

"Ronnie and Pam live just over the town line in Verona. He's got more than a hundred acres along the brook there. Land's been in his family since the first loggers came up here in the 1830s. They logged, and when the trees were gone, they farmed. But you know this land's no good for that, so then Ronnie's grandfather and father ran a metalworking shop, but there's not much call for that these days."

"So what does Ronnie do for a living?"

Marge crashed two cups of coffee down in front of them. "Ronnie Gatrell? He's doing something different every time you talk to him. You ready?"

Frank ordered the stew. He knew better than to ask if it would take long. Marge seemed particularly testy today, and requests like that would likely get him sent to the bottom of the queue.

"Marge is right," Rollie continued after she'd disappeared onto the kitchen. "Ronnie's always got some new plan. He's a damn fine carpenter, but you can't tell him anything. Doesn't understand the whole 'customer is always right' thing. You can't get repeat business with that attitude."

"So he wants to sell off some of his land?"

"Yep. Leon Shelby set up a deal to sell off some prime lots to this high-end developer. Woulda given Ronnie enough cash to live off forever, I guess. But the APA just put the kibosh on the deal. Obstructing the view of a scenic waterway—that's a no-go for those guys."

Marge hurled silverware and napkins in their direction, a promising development. Then she paused in front of a young woman with long braids and a pierced lip who kept opening and flipping her menu as if she expected it to sprout another page.

"Ready?" Marge asked.

"Do you have any gluten-free items?"

Marge rested her hands on her ample hips. "Bacon and eggs with hash-browns. I'll leave off the toast at no charge."

"I'm vegan?" The girl spoke in that plaintive, questioning voice that begged for parody.

Frank and Rollie stirred their coffee, waiting.

"Does the barley soup have meat in it?"

Here it came. Five…four…three…two….

"Of course it has beef in it! How the hell can I make a good barley soup without boiling short-rib bones?" Marge turned her back on the girl. "You want that organic tofu quinoa stuff, you go down to those fancy-ass cafes in Keene."

Marge kicked open the swing-door into the kitchen, leaving the stunned girl still clutching her menu. Rollie took pity. "Don't take it personal. Marge is a little crabby because one of the waitresses called in sick. You could get a tossed salad. I'll ask her to put some chick peas on it for you."

The girl shook her head, slid off her stool, and scampered out the door.

Rollie watched her go. "Who the hell was that, anyway?"

CHAPTER 3

FRANK EMERGED FROM THE DINER contentedly full, but still shaking his head at Marge's treatment of the vegan girl. Marge could certainly be prickly, but she usually saved her tart remarks for the regulars. The diner needed hikers, skiers and fishermen to stay afloat, and Marge was too smart a businesswoman to alienate tourists. Besides, he was quite sure he'd seen three-bean chili and veggie lasagna on the menu in the high season, so Marge wasn't above catering to her customers' preferences even if she didn't share them. Something else must've set her off today, and that poor girl had found herself in the wrong place at the wrong time.

As Frank crossed the green he saw Earl standing in front of The Store talking to two teenage boys who stood with their heads hanging, scuffing the dirt with their oversized sneakers. What could this be about?

He came up to the group in time to hear Earl say, "I'm just giving you a warning this time and I'm going to call your parents. But I better not catch you stealing anything again, or you'll get a summons and have to appear in front of the magistrate. Understand?"

The boys nodded.

"All right. Get on back to school, then."

Catching sight of Frank, they hopped on their bikes and took off in a blur.

"What was that all about?"

"Patty saw them in the mirror stuffing candy and soda in their pockets." Earl straightened his hat. "She called and I came right over."

"Why didn't you call me? You knew I was right next door in the diner."

"I took care of it. You wouldn't have done anything different."

True enough. But that was beside the point. "Shoplifting is not the same as speeding. If someone in this town is committing a crime, however small, I need to handle it."

Earl threw back his shoulders. "Why? I'm a sworn officer doing the job I've been training to do for two years. Aren't you sounding just like the state police when they say you should turn every case over to them instead of managing yourself?"

They glared at each other for a moment. Then Frank's fierce glower dissolved into a chuckle. Adjusting to Earl being a sworn officer was going to require a shift in his habits. "Okay, you made your point. Just promise me that in the unlikely event we have a murder before you go off to Saranac or Placid, you'll call me in on it."

"Deal."

CHAPTER 4

"YOU KNEW! YOU KNEW THIS was happening, and you didn't even warn me!" Edwin Bates had just slammed the door to Frank's office and turned the lock for good measure. He loomed over Frank's desk, his dark hair tangled, his eyes blazing.

"The police are always advised when a prisoner on probation is released in the community. I wanted to tell you right away myself, but Trudy insisted the news would be better coming from her. She's in a better position to answer your questions." Even though he'd been agonizing over Anita's release since the graduation party, Frank went into defensive mode in response to Edwin's attack. Thank God Earl was out getting a snack. Frank didn't need a witness to this showdown.

"Questions! My only question is, how did this happen? You told us Anita would be in jail until Olivia was at least eighteen. Who decided to let her out?"

Frank didn't have the heart to point out that Edwin, who was so liberal he made Frank look like Barry Goldwater, would normally be an enthusiastic supporter of prison reform and the end of mass incarceration. "Apparently, she's been a model prisoner. And you know they're trying to release more nonviolent drug offenders."

"Forget about the marijuana farm they had going on their land. What about all the other things she did? Selling her own baby.... Helping to sell Mary Pat's baby...."

"You know she was never charged with any of that. There wasn't enough evidence. And she was under the influence of her father."

Edwin spun around. "Anita was an adult. She could have walked away. She could have protected Olivia, and she didn't. And now the State of New York, in all its infinite wisdom, is going to give our little girl back to that woman."

That woman. Her mother.

"Nothing's been decided yet. Anita has to prove she's fit to take care of

Olivia."

"I won't let it happen." Edwin paced around the office. "We'll go to Mexico or Costa Rica. Open an inn there."

"Don't talk crazy, Edwin. Kidnapping is a felony that will get you sent to federal prison. How will that help Olivia?"

Edwin stopped moving and spun around. "It will help her become an architect...or a biologist...or a history teacher—whatever she dreams—not a waitress at Malone's diner or a cleaning lady at the Stop 'N' Buy. And I won't get caught. I'm smarter than those government paper-pushers."

"Like me?"

Edwin turned his back on Frank and stared out the window.

"Does Olivia know now that Anita is back in Trout Run?" Frank asked.

"We have to tell her today. We can't allow her to hear the news from someone else. Or worse, to just run into her mother on the street."

Edwin sank into a chair and propped his head on his hand. His shoulders shook. Seconds passed before he gasped for breath.

His friend was crying. Helpless in the presence of a sobbing woman, Frank was utterly vanquished by male tears. He froze, unable to speak, unable to touch Edwin.

"This is killing Lucy." Edwin lifted his tear-stained face, but he didn't make eye contact with Frank. "After the infertility treatments failed... after we realized we were too old to adopt an infant, we let go of the dream of being parents. We threw water on that fire and got adjusted. We were happy with our lives. Run the inn, travel, spend time with our friends and nieces and nephews—it was enough." He turned and gazed at Frank. "And then you re-lit the flame. You told us we could be parents, after all. You told us it wasn't too late, we could still make our dream come true."

Edwin stood up and shoved Frank's shoulder, his voice escalating. "You said there was no risk. You promised us that if we loved Olivia, we'd never lose her."

Frank stood still. If Edwin had pounded his head with a rock, Frank wouldn't have raised a hand to defend himself.

"The old pain was just a dull ache that surfaced every once in a while. To have her and lose her....this is torture."

"I'm sorry, Edwin. Believe me, when I suggested you take Olivia as a foster child, I never imagined that this could happen. I was certain Anita would be in prison until Olivia turned eighteen at the very least. I'm as shocked at her early release as you are."

"Well, you were wrong." Edwin's eyes blazed. "You made the mistake. But Lucy and Olivia and I have to pay for it."

After Edwin stormed off, Doris tiptoed into the office. "Earl went out to do the afternoon patrol while you were talking to Edwin. We didn't want to interrupt you for the patrol car keys, so Earl took his truck." She spoke as if she were at the bedside of a dying relative.

Frank nodded without looking at her. He knew damn well Doris had been listening to every word of the argument and probably couldn't wait to get on the phone and spread the gossip to her circle of clucking hen friends. If she knew what was good for her, she'd wait until she got home to start dialing.

From the corner of his eye, he could see her backing out of the office. "I'll hold all nonessential calls," she murmured.

Alone, Frank contemplated the wreckage of his relationship with Edwin and Lucy. They'd been his first friends when he moved to Trout Run. He'd gone from paying guest at the inn, to informal consultant on inn repair, to invited dinner guest, to friend. They were different from him, with their gourmet food and their arty pastimes, but he genuinely liked them both. He'd confided in them when he had problems, personal and professional. And Edwin had confided in him, telling him how he and Lucy had moved to Trout Run to take themselves away from Manhattan's temptation of endless fertility treatments.

Then Frank had effectively orphaned Olivia Veech by arresting her mother, uncle and grandfather. No one in Trout Run wanted anything to do with the half-feral seven-year-old. But Frank had seen a way to solve a complex equation with one single move: his friends longed for a child and he had produced one who desperately needed parents. Oh, how foolish he'd been to think that he had the power to make three people happy! What was that saying? Something like, if you want to make God laugh, tell him your plans. The Divine sides must be splitting today.

And to make matters worse, Frank knew that whatever happened next to Olivia, Anita, Edwin, and Lucy was entirely out of his control.

"Fra-a-a-nk?"

Doris's querulous voice intruded into his funk.

"I don't mean to bother you, but I'm worried Earl isn't back yet from the afternoon patrol."

Since when was Doris Earl's supervisor? Frank glanced at the clock:

nearly four, later than he'd realized. "So radio him."

"He's not in the patrol car, remember? I called his cell, but he doesn't answer. But I think I know where he might be, but really he shouldn't have gone there, which is why I'm worried so I wanted to tell you before I went home even though I said I wouldn't bother you, but—"

"Doris. Stop. Talking."

She stood before him, wringing her hands and gnawing on her lower lip.

"Where is Earl?"

"In Verona, I think. At the Happy Camper Day Care Center. That's the one run by Pam Gatrell."

Frank knew the place; he'd passed the sign many times. "And why would Earl be there?"

"Someone called, one of the parents, and said there was some kind of trouble there and I said Happy Camper is in Verona and that's not our jurisdiction and they should call the state police and they said they did but it would be forty minutes at least until they could get over there and couldn't we help and I said I'd ask Earl if he was nearby and maybe he could scoot over there, so I called Earl and that was half an hour ago and I haven't heard anything since and so I—"

Frank leaped up. "What kind of trouble, Doris?"

"She said Ronnie Gatrell was talking crazy and said he wouldn't let anyone pick up their kids until the bank promised to leave him alone about his mortgage."

Frank was halfway out the door when he shouted over his shoulder. "Does Ronnie have a gun?"

"I imagine so. Doesn't everyone?"

CHAPTER 5

FRANK TORE DOWN ROUTE 9 towards Verona, sirens blaring, lights flashing although there was very little traffic to push out of the way. What could Earl have been thinking to answer a call all alone, out of their jurisdiction, without even telling Doris to alert him? Once he passed the Trout Run town limits, he slowed slightly and cut the siren, keeping his eyes focused on the right side of the road for the sign that marked Pam Gatrell's business. Soon he saw a patch of color: Ronnie had used a jigsaw to cut the outline of three back-pack wearing kids in shorts and hiking boots, marching down a winding trail. Below their feet were the words, in electric blue, Happy Camper Day Care.

Not so happy today.

The patrol car threw up a spray of gravel as Frank careened down the long, sloping driveway. Trees crowded the drive on either side, and Frank slowed, unwilling to drive blindly into the unknown. He left the car parked in the middle of the drive so no one else could get by in either direction. Grabbing his binoculars, he crept through the trees to get a view of the house. He hadn't encountered anyone else and wondered what had become of the person who'd made the call to Doris. Where the drive leveled out and widened, a broad lawn surrounded a big log home with a wrap-around porch. Stony Brook rushed along behind the house. Brightly colored toy trucks and balls and dolls littered the porch. A swing set and a sandbox stood next to two Adirondack chairs in the yard. All were empty and unused despite the clear weather.

Earl's red truck was parked next to another pick-up and a minivan. Frank trained his binoculars on the red truck and could see Earl in the driver's seat with his phone pressed to his ear. He must've made phone contact with Ronnie or Pam inside the house. That's why he hadn't answered Doris's calls.

The anxiety gnawing at him was nudged aside by satisfaction. Earl was doing the right thing, stabilizing the situation until help arrived. Frank focused his binoculars on the house, but the afternoon sun shining on the front windows made it impossible to see inside. He worked his way through the trees until he was as close as possible to Earl's truck, still twenty-five yards away.

He stepped out of the shelter of the trees and ran toward Earl's truck.

A shot rang out, and the branch of a tree behind him exploded. Frank hit the ground.

Earl shouted to him through the open truck window. "Get back, Frank. Ronnie's threatening to shoot anyone who comes near the house. He's got Pam in there, and six kids. I'll stay here while you secure the area and watch out for the parents. They're sure to start showing up soon."

Despite the warning, Frank crawled forward on his elbows.

Another shot echoed through the valley. "Get the hell off my land," a man's voice yelled.

A woman's higher-pitched voice chimed in. "Ronnie, no! Don't shoot again. You're scaring the kids."

"Okay, Ronnie, okay. It's just Chief Bennett, my boss." Frank could hear Earl speaking calmly into his phone. "I didn't know he was coming. I'm going to send him away now, and we can keep talking, okay?"

Send him away? There was no way Frank was leaving Earl alone to deal with this lunatic.

"You called him here! I don't like being lied to." Ronnie screamed through the open window. "I been lied to enough."

"I understand you might think I wasn't being honest with you, Ronnie, but I was using my phone to talk to you, so I couldn't use it to call Frank. I'm going to send him away now."

Earl leaned out the truck window. "I just about had him ready to let the kids go when you showed up. You need to go back to the patrol car. Keep everyone away. He's all riled up because the bank is ready to foreclose on his house. He has no way to make his mortgage payments now that the APA ruled against him selling part of his land to that developer. I've been letting him talk about all his problems, building rapport, you know."

Rapport? Where the hell had Earl gotten that word? "I'm not leaving you here alone with him," Frank said, keeping his voice low enough that Ronnie couldn't hear.

"I know Ronnie. He's gone hunting with my cousins and me. He won't hurt me, but he's really mad at the government and the banks. If he thinks law enforcement is ganging up on him, there's going to be a showdown, and it won't end well for anyone. Please go back."

"He's nuts." Frank lifted his head just enough to make eye contact with Earl. "You can't count on him not to hurt you."

Another shot whistled above Frank's head. "I don't see him moving!" Ronnie screamed.

"Go back, Frank. He'll keep shooting until you do. It's the only way."

Frank edged away from the truck. "I have to be able to stay in touch with you."

"Toss me your cell phone. I'll use it to call Doris, and she can patch me through to your radio in the patrol car. Then you'll have an open line to what's going on between me and Ronnie."

It was an option, but hardly a good one. How could he leave Earl out here in clear range of an armed lunatic?

A bullet slammed into the dirt five feet from Frank's head. He threw the phone at Earl and scrambled into the woods.

He remembered a time when he and Earl been called to a home where a dog had gotten caught in a hole in a chain link fence. It snapped at everyone who tried to help it, even its owner.

Everyone except Earl.

Earl had sat on the ground just out of reach of the dog and spoke to it with that same soothing voice he was using on Ronnie. He'd talked for a good twenty minutes before he even tried to move three inches closer to the dog. Another ten minutes of talk before he held out his hand to let the dog sniff it. And eventually the dog ate some scraps of turkey from Earl's lunch sandwich while Frank used wire cutters to enlarge the hole. Finally, Earl had lifted the wounded and hurting animal and carried him gently to the patrol car for a ride to the vet.

Some scientists said animals didn't have emotions like people. But Frank knew trust when he saw it. And gratitude. And that's what he'd seen in the eyes of that mutt.

If Earl could pull off a rescue with that scared dog, maybe he could pull one off here too.

Of course, there was one difference.

The dog couldn't have killed him.

Just as Frank reached the patrol car, a beat up Ford Focus came bouncing down the drive. The driver slammed the little car into park and flung the door open so violently Frank thought it would snap off.

"My son! My baby! Where is he?" A large woman ran toward Frank, her jacket sliding off her shoulders, her hair streaming.

"Stop! You can't get any closer." Frank moved to block her, but she dodged around him.

"Henry! Mommy's here. Mommy's coming." She picked up speed as she ran downhill.

"Stop!" Frank chased after her, but he knew no words would halt her. He put on a burst of speed and pulled her down in a full body tackle. They both landed hard on the rocky ground. Frank's right leg twisted under her considerable weight.

Her face streaked with tears and dirt, she struggled to sit up. "I have to get my son."

"I understand." Frank kept her pinned even as he tried to calm her down. "How did you know something was wrong?"

"Janey, one of the other mothers, called me. She came to pick up her daughter and Ronnie wouldn't let her in. She said she called the police and then went to get her dad and her brother to help."

Frank took a deep breath. At any moment, more panicked parents and relatives would be arriving. "Listen to me. Your son is inside the Gatrells' house. Pam is taking care of the kids. He's okay right now. But Ronnie's got a gun and he's threatening to shoot anyone who approaches the house. He already took three shots at me. You can't get any closer."

The woman's eyes widened with fear. "What are you doing to get those kids out?"

"Another officer is negotiating with Ronnie right now. Earl knows Ronnie. He's trying to calm him down so he'll send the kids out. The state police are on their way. We just need to wait it out. I know it's hard, but you have to let us handle it."

She thrashed and bucked trying to break free of his grasp. "I can't wait. I have to get Henry."

"We're not going to let anything happen to your son, Mrs..... Tell me your name."

"Colson. Leandra Colson."

She had stopped struggling, but her shoulders trembled under Frank's grasp. He eased up a little, still wary that she might bolt. "Okay, Mrs. Colson. I know this is scary, but I need you to stay calm for your son's sake."

"You don't understand. Henry needs his pills. I can't wait hours for him to get out. He needs his pills." She squirmed a hand into her jacket pocket and pulled out an orange prescription bottle.

Frank glanced at the label: Clobazam. He didn't recognize the name, but it didn't sound like an antibiotic for an ear infection.

"He has epilepsy. If he doesn't take his anti-seizure drugs, he could die."

Frank and Leandra Colson sat in the patrol car listening to Earl chip away at Ronnie's resolve. Frank marveled at Earl's steady tone—never a shade of criticism or irritation. He himself felt like reaching through the radio and whacking Ronnie upside the head. Did the man hear himself, whining about all the ways he'd been wronged while six little children sat stoically, barely making a whimper?

"So what I'm hearing you say," Earl continued, "is you're feeling frustrated at how inflexible the bank is."

"That's right. Those assholes won't even give me a few more months to get the money together."

"You just want a few months."

"Yeah. Exactly. See, you understand. Why don't they?"

Mrs. Colson choked back a sob and shook Frank's arm. "He's not telling him to let the kids go."

"I know. We have to be patient. Earl has to get Ronnie's trust before he asks him to do something. Making demands will push Ronnie closer to the edge. We don't want that."

The young mother began to cry softly. "Why did I leave him there? I should have brought him with me to Plattsburgh. But it's so hard for him to ride in his car seat all day long. And he likes Pam...." Her sobs overtook her words.

Frank patted her hand awkwardly. "So Pam isn't your regular day-care provider?"

"No. I just use her occasionally when I have to drive up to Plattsburgh to run errands for my mother. Other than that, Henry is always home with me. Oh, why did I have to take him there today? And why did I leave him there without any extra pills? I was going to the drugstore today. I knew I'd be back way before he needed them. Oh, God!"

If only, if only... How often people blamed themselves for some inconsequential decision that changed the course of their lives. He hoped Mrs. Colson wouldn't have to live with terrible repercussions just for leaving her son with a babysitter for a few hours.

"How well do you know Ronnie and Pam?" he asked, more to get her to stop crying than for any desire to know.

"I went to high school with Pam. We're good friends. Ronnie is a few years older. She was crazy about him when they got married, but her life with him hasn't been easy. He's never been good with money. But I never thought he'd do something crazy like this."

Earl's voice returned. "You know what, Ronnie? I wonder if maybe you've been talking to the wrong guys at the bank. Who did you say your loan officer was?"

"Jerry Mayes."

"Uh-huh."

Thirty seconds ticked by and Earl didn't add anything to that uh-huh.

"What? What do you know about Jerry?"

"Oh, I don't know him all that well, just a little...."

Again, the long break.

Earl's voice, all the gentleness gone, suddenly commanded Frank over the radio. That meant he'd put his own phone on mute so Ronnie couldn't hear. "Get someone from the bank on the line."

Frank knew Earl didn't have long to talk. Ronnie couldn't suspect that they were communicating behind his back. He needed to tell Earl about little Henry. "Will do. But listen, Earl. One of the kids, Henry Colson, has epilepsy. He needs to take his meds by four-thirty or he could have a seizure."

"Pam knows about it," Leandra Colson chimed in. "But I told her I'd be back long before then."

Earl swore, but he didn't lose his composure. "Okay, I can use this. Just get me someone from the bank who knows something about Ronnie's loan. If Ronnie thinks we're putting something over on him, then all the trust I've built up will be lost."

Earl's voice was immediately replaced by Ronnie's. "That Jerry Mayes is a snake in the grass. He tricked me into signing those loan papers. He never told me I could lose my house. When the revolution comes, those bankers are all gonna die."

"Wow. That's a problem." Earl's voice had returned to a soothing murmur.

Ronnie continued to vent his rage while Frank used Leandra Colson's phone to call the bank. While Ronnie was on a long rant, Earl muted him again and Frank delivered the update.

"I've got a bank VP lined up to talk to Ronnie—Curt Blythen. Try for a deal. Tell him to send Henry out and he can talk to the banker."

"Okay, Ronnie," Earl interjected when Ronnie paused for breath. "I've found someone at the bank who's willing to talk to you. Curt Blythen. He's Jerry's boss's boss. He's a man who can make a deal, know what I'm sayin'?"

"Ha! I don't trust any of those bastards."

"Well…see, I'm thinking if you talk to Curt, you'll really show Jerry a thing or two. You'll show Jerry you're a man who goes straight to the top."

Long silence.

The seconds ticked on unbearably. Couldn't Earl goad him on a little more? But that's where Earl showed his talent. He knew the next move had to come from Ronnie.

They waited.

"Humph. Maybe."

Earl must be feeling the same elation that rose in Frank's chest, but he did a great job of keeping it out of his voice. Earl's next words were spoken ever so casually. "So I helped you out Ronnie. Now you gotta help me out."

"I'm not coming out just cause you say you got some banker on the line. No, sir."

"Of course not. I wouldn't expect that. But we need to cooperate to make this happen. I'd like you to show me a sign of good faith. Can you consider that?"

"Good faith? Like what?"

"I need you to send Henry Colson out. That little fella needs to take his medicine."

"That's a lie. You're trying to trick me."

"I wouldn't lie to you, Ronnie. Ask Pam about it. She knows about Henry's medicine."

There was some garbled conversation away from the phone, but Frank could distinguish the higher pitch of Pam's voice. Then Ronnie came back on the line.

"Pam says he's got some disease that makes him shake. She's worried he might have some kinda fit here."

"His momma is waiting for him up the drive. She's got his pills. So you just send him out and tell him to walk on up the driveway and his mom will be waiting for him. Can you do that for me?"

Silence.

"This could be a trick." Ronnie spoke with his usual belligerence, yet Frank could hear a hesitation, a longing in Ronnie's voice.

"Now Ronnie, you know me. Even on April Fool's Day I never can come up with any kinda trick that anyone would believe. Guess I'm just not a tricky person. I'm more like a problem-solving person. 'Member that time we had a problem dividing up that bear that you and my cousin both shot?"

"Ha! I forgot about that, but you're right. You were the one who figured the best way to do it. Me and ol' Ralph had too many beers to think straight."

Another stretch of silence. Frank was ready to crawl out of his skin. The clock inched closer to four.

"So what would happen?" Ronnie finally asked.

"You've been telling me all about your issues with the bank, so I figured, let's get someone at the bank who can fix it all up, right?"

Frank thought Earl's voice sounded as soothing as the music his dentist played in the waiting room.

"Right. And I can talk to him if I send Henry out?"

"Yes."

"But don't you go getting' outta that truck, you hear me?" Ronnie's voice escalated to a screech. "If anyone comes toward me, I'll shoot this kid, I'll shoot 'em all!"

A moment later, a tiny figure in a red striped t-shirt stumbled onto the front porch. He looked around in confusion, then spotted his mom waving from the driveway. His little legs pumped furiously as he ran up the hill.

Ronnie's gun was trained on him.

CHAPTER 6

LEANDRA COLSON CAUGHT HER SON in her arms.

One safe.

"Hello, Mr. Gatrell. Curt Blythen here, senior vice president at Adirondack Savings and Trust." The bank vice president stepped up to do his part. Frank had coached him on what to say: no trying to explain the bank's policies, no extravagant offers to forgive the entire loan. Neither would go down well with Ronnie. Blythen's job was to listen and reassure. Then, when Earl judged the time was right, they would make an offer that Ronnie could get only if he released all the other hostages.

The man had clearly spent years in sales and customer service. He had a smooth, confident patter would make anyone believe their problems were history. Soon Frank felt secure enough to turn his attention to the mob forming behind his patrol car. There were now five kids inside the house, but a gaggle of parents, grandparents, siblings, and neighbors had gathered, some in concern, some in morbid curiosity. The two state troopers who had finally arrived were having difficulty containing them.

"What about our kids? Why did you let him get away with releasing just one?'

Mothers clung to one another weeping and fathers shook their fists. One man had a Glock in a holster at his waist. Frank knew there were rifle racks in some of the pick-ups parked along the drive.

"This is a negotiation, folks. We have to give a little to get more in return."

"Why are you up here and letting a twenty year old kid handle the tough work? I read in the Mountain Herald that Earl Davis just graduated from the police academy last week."

"I'm tired of waitin'! We should just charge down there and storm the house."

"Don't talk like a damn fool." Another father shoved the last one who'd spoken. "He'd kill us and kill the kids too. Earl got Henry out. Let's see what he can do with the others."

"A vice president from the bank is talking to Ronnie on the phone. Soon, we'll offer Ronnie a deal," Frank said. "Try to be patient just a little longer."

Frank heard another car screech into the driveway. Soon, state police Lieutenant Lew Meyerson elbowed his way through the crowd to Frank's side. He kept moving, pushing Frank away from the parents. Frank backed up, but every step added to the knot of tension in his gut.

"What the hell is going on here, Bennett?" Meyerson's hot breath scorched Frank's ear. "I hear you let that rookie of yours go rogue. Get him outta there." Meyerson intentionally raised his voice. "I've got the state hostage negotiation team on the way."

"Thank God!" someone in the crowd cried.

That rookie of yours. Lew knew damn well what Earl's name was. "How long 'til they get here?" Frank asked. "Because Earl's already managed to get one kid out. A sick kid."

Meyerson shifted his weight and glanced at his watch. "Maybe forty minutes."

Frank knew it would be more than an hour. The team was based in Lake George, seventy-five miles away.

"Forty minutes!" a mother shrieked.

A father pushed his way into the discussion. "We can't sit on our asses doing nothing for forty minutes. He's got our babies in there."

"An untrained rookie is not qualified to manage this situation. It requires a team of expert—"

Leandra Colson stepped forward, Henry clinging to her leg. "Henry says Ronnie keeps talking about shooting his gun. He says the other kids are crying and that makes Ronnie mad." She stroked her son's hair. "He says you have to help his friends."

Just then, Ronnie appeared on the front porch. He had Pam in a chokehold with a gun pressed to her temple. "Come on out here, kids," he shouted through the open front door.

No one emerged.

Pam squirmed in her husband's grasp. "You're scaring them, Ronnie. They won't come out."

"Well then, you better find a way to make them come." He shook her by the neck so that her feet left the ground. "You're the big childcare expert, right?"

She scratched at his powerful arm.

"Let Pam go in the house and bring the kids out, Ronnie," Earl called out.

"I'm not lettin' her go. She's stayin' with me. This is her home too. It's her duty to stand by me while I fight for what's mine."

Frank watched the struggle on the porch through binoculars, Meyerson silent beside him. Pam's face was red and her hands clutched at her husband. Suddenly, she went limp in his arms.

Frank tightened the focus. Had she passed out? Had he cut off her air supply?

The change startled Ronnie and he glanced down. His grip loosened.

Pam gulped in some air and rubbed her neck. Then she used the opportunity to speak to Ronnie. Frank could see her lips moving but no one could hear what she was saying. Ronnie appeared to be listening, and eventually he nodded his head. He stepped to the side of the front door and let go of Pam, but he kept the gun trained on her head. He was out of sight of anyone indoors, as Pam stood in the doorway.

"Ava," she called. "Ava, I need you to help me."

"Ava is the oldest of the girls Pam watches," Leandra Colson volunteered. "Pam calls Ava her little mother's helper. If she can get Ava to come out, the others will follow."

Pam got down on her knees and spoke through the screen door. They couldn't hear what she was saying or see if Ava was on the other side of the door. Minutes ticked by.

Then Pam stood up. Ronnie tensed, using both hands to steady the gun pointed at her. The screen door opened, and a little blond head peeped out. Pam had positioned herself between Ronnie and the child. She pointed up the hill to where the parents stood waiting.

"You're going to play Follow the Leader, everybody. Ava is going to lead the way up the driveway to your parents' cars. I need everybody to follow her, okay?"

Pam leaned forward to hear something one of the kids said. "Yes, I know the rule is that you're not allowed to leave the yard unless you're with an adult, but we're changing the rule for today only. Today, you can leave with Ava. Ready?"

Ava stepped out and extended her right hand behind her. Another little hand reached forward and grabbed it. Ava tugged and a kid with a mop of red curls followed. He clutched a little blue bag of cookies in his other hand.

"Look up the hill, kids. Look at the moms and dads." Pam was clearly trying to distract them from the sight of Ronnie and his gun. Ava marched forward, but one of the little boys who came out made the mistake of glancing to his right. His mouth formed a perfect O of terror and he froze.

These were kids who knew about guns. Their fathers were hunters. If they'd been raised right, they learned at an early age that you never point a gun at anything unless you intend to shoot it.

Frank's hands squeezed the binoculars. He found himself praying because there was nothing else he could do. Please, God, let him keep walking. Give him the strength not to cry.

Ava chose that moment to look over her shoulder. "Teddy, move. Stick with me."

And Teddy moved.

The two minutes required for the kids to march up the hill felt like an eternity. When Pam saw the last of the kids embraced by their parents, she turned and picked something up from the porch floor.

It was the phone Ronnie had been using to talk to Earl. In a moment, they could hear Earl's phone ring, and then Pam's voice piped into the patrol car.

"I'm walking out of here, Ronnie. You can shoot me in the back if you want to. But just consider this: once you kill me, those cops are going to strafe this house with bullets. You won't have a body left to bury, just parts. And your son will be an orphan. And he'll know his dad murdered his mom. And no one will want a kid whose father is a crazy murderer, so RJ will have to go live in a group home, probably in Albany or Plattsburgh or maybe even New York City. And RJ'll know it was you who sent him there."

And then Pam tossed the phone onto a porch chair, turned her back on Ronnie, and started walking.

"Pam? Pam! You get back here!" They could hear Ronnie's voice both in real time, and a fraction of a second later coming through the radio.

Ronnie had his gun trained on Pam's back.

Time stopped. No one spoke. Parents turned their children's heads and backed away from the scene.

Would talking to Ronnie now make the situation better or worse? The decision was all on Earl. It wasn't fair. Earl had done a magnificent job, but now if he acted—or didn't act—and Pam was shot, Earl would blame himself.

Utter silence. Even the birds were still. Pam walked steadily up the hill with no more urgency than if she were going to get the mail.

Don't speak, Earl. Watching Pam, Frank suspected that maybe she knew what she was doing. She'd been unwilling to take any chances with the kids' lives, but she must have been fairly sure that the threat of their son being sent to a group home would get to Ronnie. Still....

She kept walking at an even pace, her tightly pressed lips the only indication of her fear.

Don't walk in such a straight line. Weave back and forth. You'll be harder to hit. Frank willed the message to her, but she continued on a direct path.

Ronnie kept his gun trained on her. The further up the hill she got, the less likely he would be to hit her with accuracy. Frank wondered how good a shot Ronnie was. When he'd shot at Frank, had he deliberately missed?

The radio was silent. Earl had clearly decided not to risk provoking Ronnie.

Good.

Pam was just twenty feet away from the safety of the trees when the shot rang out.

Everyone screamed.

A staccato burst of gunfire reverberated through the valley.

"Get back! Get back!"

Pam put on a burst of speed and sprinted like an Olympian toward them.

But Frank had seen Ronnie's gun as he fired the shots. It had been pointed up in the air. That last blast was just a blast of bravado. One last, childish, "you're not the boss of me" display.

She sank to her knees in the grass. Frank helped one of the EMTs lift her onto a stretcher.

"She's in shock. We need to check her out," the EMT said.

But Pam grabbed Frank's hand before she was wheeled away. "I want Ronnie kept away from me," Pam said. "I can't take this anymore."

"Don't worry, Pam. They'll take him to the hospital for a psych evaluation."

If the state troopers don't shoot him. If he doesn't shoot himself.

"And he won't get out after that," Frank continued. "He's going to jail."

Her grasp on his hand didn't loosen. "That's not enough. I want one of those, whattya call it? Orders so he can't come near me or our son."

"A restraining order."

"Yes. He's ruined my life. Taken everything and wasted it…my love, my house, my money, and now business, my reputation. I never want to lay eyes on him again."

CHAPTER 7

AND THEN THERE WAS ONLY Ronnie.

"We have an hour until sunset. I'm not letting night fall on that house so that Ronnie can slip away into the woods," Meyerson said. "We're done playing this game. Shoot a tear gas canister in there and be done with it."

"I'd prefer for him to come out of his own free will," Earl insisted over the radio.

Meyerson scowled, but he was hardly in a position to disregard Earl after all his successes. "Try one more time. Then we're going in."

"Ronnie, we're making progress toward a good outcome here," Earl said. "It's time for you to come out of the house and lay down your weapon."

"No way. They'll shoot me. I know they will."

"I won't let that happen, Ronnie. I promise. But you need to lay down your weapon and come out with your hands up in the air, you understand?"

"I did everything you asked. I let the kids go, and Pam too. You can't arrest me," Ronnie screamed.

Meyerson smacked his forehead with the heel of his hand. "For God's sake, the man fired at law enforcement officers, fired at his wife, held seven people hostage at gunpoint. Does he honestly think we're going to let him order a pizza and go to bed?"

"I can't live in jail. I can't be inside all day. I'll die."

"Ronnie, you need help. That's what we're going to get for you."

"Whattaya mean, help? I ain't going to the nut house."

"Look, Ronnie. I've done all I can for you," Earl said. "If you don't come out in the next ten minutes, the state police are going to shoot a tear gas canister into the house. Then they're coming in after you. If that happens, I can't protect you.

"I haven't lied to you ever. Not once through this whole day. So I'm telling you now just what's going to happen. If you ever want to see your son again, you'd better walk outta that house like a man."

Silence stretched on. Every passing second made it seem more likely they would hear one last gunshot, the sound of Ronnie ending his life.

Meyerson shifted his weight like a racehorse at the starting gate.

The front door opened.

The state police raised their weapons in unison.

Ronnie stepped out on the porch. He looked at the guns aimed at him and his weapon clattered to the ground.

He raised his hands.

It was over.

When Earl emerged from his pickup truck he was met with a chorus of cheers. The crowd engulfed him, patting his back, hugging him, slapping him high fives. His mother threw her arms around his neck.

Frank stood back. He thought Earl looked like a guy he'd once seen who'd been plucked from rough surf by lifeguards at the Jersey Shore: stunned to have come so close to death and survived.

When the crowd thinned, Frank walked up to Earl. Earl smiled weakly and extended his right hand.

Frank ignored the offer to shake. He pulled Earl into a tight embrace. He didn't care who saw or what they might think.

Earl's shoulders trembled.

"You're coming home with me," Frank said. "You need to decompress."

CHAPTER 8

EARL DIDN'T SAY A WORD on the ride home.

Penny rushed out to the front walk to greet them when she heard the car pull in. Frank hugged her briefly. "We're all fine. No one hurt at all. Earl did a fantastic job, but he needs to unwind. Give us a little time alone, okay?"

She looked miffed for a moment, but she must've sensed how much Earl needed the space. She watched them go into the living room, while she retreated to the kitchen.

Earl sat on the sofa and stared into space. "When it was happening, I felt like I knew what I was doing. Now I can't stop thinking of all the things that could've gone wrong. What if Henry had had a seizure? What if little Teddy had started screaming when he saw the gun? What if Ronnie had killed Pam in front of all those kids?" Earl shuddered. "I could have screwed it up. I could have screwed it up bad."

"But you didn't. Your training kicked in. You did what you had to do."

Earl put his head in his hands. "Thinking about it makes me feel like I wanna puke. One of the troopers told me I oughta apply for the hostage negotiation team. Are you kidding me? I don't ever want to do this again in my whole life."

Frank sat down next to Earl and handed him a glass half full of Irish whiskey. He'd never known Earl to drink more than a couple of beers, but the occasion called for the calming effects of something stronger.

Earl swallowed a mouthful and made a face. "Ever since I can remember, I've wanted to be a cop. Maybe I was wrong. Maybe I'm not tough enough for this job."

"You know what makes you a good cop, Earl? The fact that you're having these doubts. The fact that you're not drinking at the Mountainside right now bragging about how you captured Ronnie Gatrell single-handedly."

Earl looked up at him. "You've had doubts? I mean, I remember how upset you were after you had to shoot Oliver. That's understandable. But, did you ever think you couldn't do the job because, you know, the responsibility was too much?"

"Do you know why I left Kansas City, Earl?"

"You wanted to be closer to your daughter," Earl said.

"That was part of it. The part I told you. I never wanted to tell you the whole story."

"Story? What story?"

"I screwed up an investigation, Earl. I screwed up so bad that a guilty man walked free because we couldn't get the evidence to charge him. I was so certain I knew who was guilty and who was innocent. But I had the whole case wrong. They encouraged me to take my pension. I planned to come here and just sit on my ass till I died."

Earl smiled. "You're not very good at ass-sitting, Frank."

"I know. Edwin knew too. He encouraged me to apply for the Chief's job here. I figured I couldn't screw up directing after-school traffic. And then we got hit with the Janelle Harvey disappearance. I was spooked. I'd lost my confidence. I didn't trust myself." Frank stood and put his hands in his pockets. He crossed the room and looked out the window into the black night.

"Really? You didn't seem that way to me. You always seem like you know just what to do. How did you get your confidence back?"

Frank turned to face Earl. "I guess you could say I learned how to doubt constructively. Never to take anything at face value. Never to believe that there are people who can commit crimes and people who can't commit crimes."

He came back to the chair where Earl sat. "You have to walk a fine line between trusting your own judgment but never thinking you know it all. I think you did that very well today." He put his hand on Earl's back. "Very well."

Earl stared into his glass for a while. "If I drink all this whiskey, you'll have to drive me home."

Frank clinked his glass against Earl's. "We're both going to drink all this whiskey. And Penny can do the driving."

CHAPTER 9

WHEN FRANK ENTERED THE TOWN office after finishing the morning patrol on Wednesday, the first thing he saw was Doris's "Out to Lunch" sign propped up on her desk. Immediately, he felt a flash of irritation. He'd told Earl to take the day off after yesterday's ordeal. Would it kill Doris to delay her lunch for ten minutes so the office wasn't unmanned? His irritation increased when he saw a woman sitting on the hard bench in the waiting area. He could hardly stride past her without offering assistance, even if she needed a building permit or some other thing he was entirely unqualified to help with.

Frank paused in front of the woman. She was in her mid-thirties, with a tired face and a shapeless figure. "Doris is out to lunch," he said unnecessarily. "I'm the police chief. Not sure I can be of any help, but I'll try."

She rose, gazing at him with unblinking steadiness. "It's you I came to see, Chief Bennett. Don't you recognize me?"

There was something familiar about her hoarse voice, but he couldn't place the face. She had an odd smile with very white teeth that seemed too big for her mouth. Probably some mother whose teenaged son he'd arrested for drinking in the park or smoking weed under the covered bridge come to plead with him to drop the charges. Could he be expected to remember them all?

He shook his head with a smile. "Sorry, you'll have to refresh my memory."

"Anita Veech."

She watched him, grinning when his eyes widened and his mouth dropped open.

"Yeah, I've changed, right? Lost 250 pounds on that prison food. Didn't have anybody to put money in my account, so no snacks from the commissary for me. Ha! Let the student dentists practice on my teeth. Gave me implants." She bared her teeth in a mirthless grin. "Come back to my hometown and nobody recognizes me."

Frank continued to stare, trying to find in the nondescript person before him the shadow of the grotesque woman he had arrested five years ago. That Anita had weighed over four hundred pounds. Her features had been so sunken in fat that he honestly couldn't have described the shape of her nose or the turn of her lips or the color of her eyes. She'd had several missing and blackened teeth and straggly, colorless hair. He knew that she was in her early thirties when she was sentenced, but she had appeared neither young nor old, just an unfortunate example of the effects of bad nutrition and limited education.

The woman before him was far from beautiful, but she had achieved ordinariness. She could walk down the street without people turning to stare and shake their heads. Quite an accomplishment.

Frank had never known anyone to be so improved by a stint in prison. He didn't know what to say. Somehow "Congratulations, you look great," didn't seem appropriate. "I heard you'd been released early," he finally stammered.

"Yeah, I'm a nonviolent drug offender. Not dangerous, right?" She gave him that unpleasant smile again. Frank had his doubts about the free prison dentistry.

Anita continued talking. "Can we go in your office? What I got to say, I don't want the whole town to hear."

Frank opened the door and ushered her in. He felt like he was wearing a blindfold and couldn't imagine what he would see when it was torn off. Not for the first time, he marveled that Anita Veech had given birth to Olivia. Charming, funny, smart, pretty Olivia.

Anita sat in the chair across from Frank's desk and looked around. "Place hasn't changed one bit. Even that half-dead plant's the same."

Frank glanced at the yellowing philodendron. It really was time to put the thing out of its misery. His gaze shifted to Anita and he waited. She had requested the meeting. Let her talk.

Anita took a breath. "First off, I gotta thank you for a few things."

"Thank me?"

"I'm thirty-six years old and I'm finally free of my wacko family. I don't look like a freak anymore."

"You're saying you're glad I arrested you?"

"I'm glad you arrested all of us. Pap died his first month in jail."

"I'm sorry—"

Anita held her hand up. "He's burnin' in hell, which is the only place built to hold him. And my brother ain't never gettin' outta Attica, not the way he keeps makin' trouble in there. So like I said, I'm finally free of those two. They made my life a living horror movie. I got to Albion, I slept through the night for the first time since my mother died when I was six."

Frank took a breath as if to speak, but what could he say? What was the proper response when someone told you her family life was so terrible that prison was a welcome relief?

Anita didn't mind his silence. "And, I got some job skills that don't involve pushing a broom. I got you to thank for that, too."

"Oh?"

"I took a computer class in prison just to pass the time. Learned to code. Turns out, I'm good at it. Now I got a job with Gage Shelby. You know him?"

"I know Leon Shelby, the real estate broker."

"That's his dad. Gage has his own software company. He runs it out of his house, over near the covered bridge."

"That's great, Anita. Finding a job can be hard when you have a felony conviction. I'm glad it hasn't held you back." The words sprang from his lips spontaneously. Every cop had to be glad when an ex-con got a job. Employment kept that person from cycling back through the criminal justice system. But then he remembered this was Olivia's mother. A job would improve Anita's chances of getting her daughter back.

They sat in silence for a moment. Where was Anita going with all this? Surely, she didn't consider him a long-lost friend she was eager to update.

Finally, she resumed speaking. "So all-in-all, I gotta thank you for what you did. Turned my life around. Except for one thing. You gave my girl to those people, those fancy friends of yours."

"The Essex County Department of Child Protective Services placed Olivia with Edwin and Lucy Bates. They've been excellent foster parents to her."

"Yeah? Well maybe they were nice to her, maybe they weren't. I'll find out soon enough. All I'm sayin' is that woman isn't Olivia's real mother. I am. And I aim to get her back. I served my time. I finally got free of the crazy family that abused me and Olivia. I got a good job. Now I plan to raise my girl."

Anita stood up. "And you're not going to stop me. So don't even try."

CHAPTER 10

ANITA VEECH'S VISIT LEFT FRANK feeling morose, and with Earl at home, he had no one to cheer him up. He glanced at the time on his phone: Penny would be in the middle of her morning book club. Then his finger hesitated over the CONTACTS icon. He scrolled to his daughter's number and pressed call.

The phone rang and rang. He cut off the call without leaving a message; he knew she never listened to her voicemail. A few minutes later, a text message appeared on his screen: Hectic day. No time to talk. Will call tomorrow.

Would she? He hadn't had a full conversation with Caroline in weeks. She was always just about to get in the car, or dealing with some catastrophe, or having a bad day. Sometimes she handed the phone over to his grandsons, but she never seemed to call him back. He'd asked once if something was wrong and she'd snapped "of course, not." He was afraid to ask again.

Now he was doubly despondent. Surely there was something he could do to set his world back on track. He toyed with the idea that had come to him in the middle of last night.

Why delay?

Lloyd Burlingame's law office had a separate entrance on the first floor of his rambling old red brick house with forest green shutters. Frank walked in to an unattended waiting room and tapped lightly on the door to Lloyd's inner sanctum.

"What are you knocking for, Marie?" a cranky voice answered from within.

Frank opened the door a crack. "It's not Marie, Lloyd. It's Frank Bennett. Am I bothering you?"

The head of the Town Council sighed. "If Marie isn't back yet, you're not. Once she brings me the papers from Leon Shelby, I've gotta get cracking on a real estate closing. What's on your mind?"

Frank supposed he should have called for an appointment so he wouldn't be rushed, but the idea bubbled up in him and demanded immediate action. "I have something important I need to talk to you about."

Lloyd made a sweeping gesture of welcome.

"I suppose you've heard about how Earl saved those kids at the Happy Camper Day Care Center," Frank began.

"I heard that you and Earl spent hours of your time—time paid for by the tax dollars of the citizens of Trout Run—taking care of a problem that should've been handled by the state police." Lloyd tapped a pencil on his desk. "But Earl certainly did admirable work."

Normally, Frank would be irritated by Lloyd's penny-pinching ways, but this was just the direction he wanted the conversation to take. "Yeah, you know that's not the first time we've been called upon to help out in Verona."

Lloyd's brow furrowed. "You need to keep a tight rein on those activities. Just say no."

"The last time it happened, Father Tim from St. Margaret's called me directly because there was a vagrant sleeping in the back pew of the church and he and the Altar Society ladies were afraid to go in and prepare for Ash Wednesday mass." Frank knew Lloyd's wife was a devout Catholic and a member of the Altar Society at St. Margaret's, the nearest Catholic church. "I would've felt terrible saying no."

Lloyd coughed. "Yes, of course, some discretion is required."

"And then there was the time I chased a speeder from Trout Run clear to Verona and it turned out it was the guy who'd been dealing pills right there in the Stewart's parking lot behind the Dumpster. The manager of Stewart's had called the state police four or five times over the past few months, and they never got there in time to catch him."

Lloyd's eye's narrowed. "What are you getting at, Frank?"

"Last week's incident with Ronnie Gatrell proved once and for all how totally inadequate the state police coverage is for Verona's needs. You should talk to the mayor of Verona—"

"I will. I'll tell him he'd better be prepared to pay your and Earl's overtime on this latest intervention."

"That's all well and good, but the bottom line is, a community has to pay for its law enforcement. While Earl and I were over there tending to Verona, anything could have happened here in Trout Run."

"But it didn't."

"My point is, Verona needs to step up to the plate. They're always ballyhooing their low taxes. Well, anyplace can have low taxes by skimping on essential services and then relying on the good nature of other towns when an emergency arises."

Lloyd frowned. "True."

Frank leaned across Lloyd's desk. "I have a proposal to make. Why not hire Earl as a full-time deputy and have the two of us take over the law enforcement needs of both municipalities: Trout Run and Verona."

"Preposterous!" Lloyd tossed his pen across the desk. "Where's the benefit to Trout Run?"

"Let Verona pay Earl's salary increase. We get an experienced, well-trained officer instead of losing him to another town and replacing him with green teenager with no skills that I'd have to train."

"But you and Earl would be patrolling twice as much territory with no additional manpower."

"Ah, but Verona has a fantastic administrative assistant. She could do a lot of the paperwork Earl does now, and that would free Earl up to do real policing, not just traffic enforcement."

Lloyd cocked his head. "Hmm. We'd have to work out an appropriate division of expenses. It would take a while."

"I'm sure Earl would wait if he knew the promotion was coming."

Lloyd narrowed his eyes. "Did Earl and his father put you up to this?"

"No, no. The idea just came to me yesterday. I haven't even mentioned it to Earl. I wanted to run it by you first."

"Are you sure Earl would be interested? I know he's been applying to the Saranac Lake department. He'd probably get a broader range of experience over there. And I'm not sure we can match what they pay, but we can try."

"I don't want to speak for Earl, but you should definitely make him the offer. I'm pretty confident he'll take it."

"Before I talk to Mayor Abernathy, I'll need a plan that shows who will cover what and exactly how much of your time you'll spend in each town."

"I'll write up a plan." Frank rose and shook the mayor's hand. "You'll have it by tomorrow."

As soon as Lloyd's office door closed behind him, Frank picked up the phone. "Penny, I'll be late for dinner. But wait'll you hear why."

CHAPTER 11

TWO DAYS HAD PASSED SINCE the hostage crisis at Happy Camper Day Care. Ronnie Gatrell had undergone a twenty-four hour psych evaluation and had been moved to the Essex County Jail in Lewis. Today he would appear before the magistrate in Verona for his felony hearing. Earl would have to testify.

At three in the afternoon, Frank and Earl sat in the magistrate's office in the Verona municipal building waiting for the sheriff's deputies to deliver Ronnie. The district attorney and Ronnie's attorney were also there.

"Are you nervous?" Frank asked.

Earl sat staring straight ahead. He'd chosen to wear the tie with his uniform and fiddled with the tight knot. "No, I'm fine."

They had already discussed the likelihood of Ronnie's making bail. Neither of them knew the Verona magistrate personally, but the fact that Ronnie had endangered children and that his own wife was seeking a restraining order seemed to call for very high bail or no bail at all. Frank was fairly certain that at the end of this hearing, Ronnie would be returned to the Essex County jail to await trial.

The minutes ticked by and the judge checked his watch with a frown. Then the Verona town secretary stuck her head in the door. "They just pulled up."

Tension rippled through the small room. Everyone sat at attention.

Suddenly, the secretary screamed from the foyer.

"Shit!" a male voice shouted.

"Stop, or I'll shoot!"

Frank and Earl bolted out of the room, followed by the lawyers and the judge. Outside, in front of the municipal building, pandemonium reigned.

The sheriff's prisoner transport van was parked at the curb, the sliding door wide open. One deputy stood with his weapon drawn and aimed at the grocery store parking lot across the street. Another ran through the lot, dodging cars and shopping carts. A yellow school bus idled in front of the elementary school next to the market.

A flash of black and white stripes appeared at the corner between the school and the market.

"There he is!" Earl pointed. "He's heading toward the woods."

The deputy shifted his aim, but Frank grabbed his arm. "Don't shoot. There are too many people. School is letting out for the day."

"He's getting away!' Earl started to follow the other deputy, but Frank could see they'd never catch up on foot. He jumped into the Trout Run patrol car and sped around the corner, hoping to head off Ronnie behind the store before he reached the woods. But when Frank reached the loading dock that backed up to the thick woods behind the store, no one was in sight but the panting, heaving, overweight deputy.

Ronnie Gatrell had escaped.

CHAPTER 12

THE FIRST SIGN APPEARED THE day after Ronnie Gatrell's escape.

Run, Ronnie, Run painted in big red letters on the side of the old falling-down barn in the field on Gaston Road. Frank saw it on the morning patrol, and made a quick detour up the driveway of Jack Nesbitt, who owned the property.

"Somebody's been vandalizing your barn." Frank pointed over his shoulder in the general direction of the barn when Jack answered his knock.

"Ha, ha! I saw that. Wouldn't call it vandalism, per se." Jack grinned and took a swig of coffee from a mug that said THIS HOUSE IS PROTECTED BY THE GOOD LORD AND A GUN.

"Did you paint it?"

"No." Jack kept chuckling as he stepped out onto his front porch. "But I wouldn't say there's any call to investigate. I won't be pressin' charges."

"So you know who did it?"

"Naw. Just some kids being funny. But it is funny. That Ronnie surely did pull one over on those deputies. Put a little scratch on his own arm. Demanded a lot of bandages so they couldn't get the cuffs on him. Limped like a cripple. Then took off like a cheetah the moment he saw his chance. Gotta admire that ingenuity."

The details of Ronnie's escape had dominated the local news for the past twenty- four hours. Everyone now knew how Ronnie had gotten into a fight in jail. How he'd claimed his ankle was sprained and his hand was cut, so the nurse had to tape him up. How the deputies discovered the shackles and cuffs wouldn't fit, but decided to transport the prisoner anyway since he was barely able to walk. How no one had known that Ronnie was a track star in high school who'd run the mile in 4:10.

Frank was still stunned by their incompetence. Ronnie was over six feet tall. Strong as hell. Had they thought a deputy could just hold him by the elbow while they walked him to the hearing? It certainly seemed as if Ronnie had planned the escape although Frank didn't see Ronnie as a planner. Taking the kids hostage—he'd pulled that stunt out of his ass. But Frank wasn't about to agree with Jack that the deputies had been inept. How many times had he heard this man pontificating on the virtues of executing drug dealers and castrating rapists? Now Mr. Law-and-Order was soft on prison breaks? "Earl and I don't admire Ronnie. He's dangerous. He held six children hostage at gunpoint."

Jack tossed the dregs of his coffee into the grass. "Aw, Ronnie wouldn'ta hurt those kiddos. He was just pissed at the APA. And who can blame him? Stupid government bureaucrats in Albany tellin' a man what to do with his own land. And then the bank threatening to take it all. Why that land's been in the Gatrell family since Civil War times. It ain't right."

Frank knew better than to wade into the quagmire that was the politics of Adirondack Park Authority regulations. Still, he couldn't believe even the fiercest supporter of private property rights could endorse terrorizing little children and their parents. He took a step closer to Jack. "Ronnie Gatrell is dangerous and unstable. If you know where he's hiding—"

"Oh, calm down, Frank. I don't know where he is. Someone just used my barn as a billboard, is all. But lotsa folks around here hope ol' Ronnie makes it to freedom. I mean, first the banks take his land, then the government says he can't do nuthin' to save it, then they go and lock him up. A man like Ronnie can't live in a jail cell. He loves the mountains."

"That's just it. Where would he run to? He's lived in Trout Run his whole life. His wife says he's never traveled further than Plattsburgh. So he must be nearby."

"Maybe he is. But he sure is giving those state troopers and their damn dogs a run for their money. Why, they've got a hundred guys and twenty dogs combing the woods between Verona and Trout Run. They got so many roadblocks set up you can't drive anywhere without having to stop and show there's no Ronnie in your backseat. All that manpower, and still they can't find him."

Jack's assessment was true enough. The state police were in charge of hunting Ronnie down, but so far they hadn't found a trace of the man. But how long could a guy in a striped prison uniform with no warm coat possibly stay in the woods? The temperature at night still dipped below freezing. "That's why I think someone must be helping him."

Jack raised his hands in a show of innocence. "Not sure Ronnie needs much help. He knows how to live off the land, that's for sure."

The next sign appeared overnight: Run, Ronnie, Run painted on an old white sheet and strung off the side of the bridge over Stony Brook. Earl cut it down.

Unbelievably, there were people in town who complained that the artist's handiwork had been destroyed. Earl's uncle reported that his coworkers at the county road department were vowing to look the other way if they spotted any traces of Ronnie's presence.

On the third day, the message was condensed, but distribution expanded. Someone photocopied R^3 in fifty-point type on neon green paper. Hundreds of the signs popped up all over Trout Run and Verona: on light poles, the supermarket bulletin board, the gas station restroom door. Penny pulled one off the entrance to the library. When one went up in the window of Malone's Diner during business hours, Frank had enough.

He waited until the crowd had peaked at lunchtime, marched into the diner, and made a show of yanking the flyer off the window. Then he ripped it into bits and tossed it in the trash as the crowd watched.

Marge emerged from the kitchen with her hands on her wide hips. "Just whattaya think you're doing, Frank? That sign is my property, posted on my window."

"How is it that last week Earl was a hero for rescuing six kids from that maniac, but this week everyone in law enforcement is a stooge and all of you are cheering for a dangerous nut to stay on the loose?"

Every eye was on the showdown. No one even stirred a cup of coffee.

"Ronnie isn't a nut. He had a legitimate grievance. He was just pushed too far." Marge extended a plump arm toward her customers. "How many of us might do the same thing if we were faced with losing everything we hold most dear? I might take some hostages if someone came along and tried to steal this diner away from me."

"That's right." Someone behind Frank shouted out. "Ronnie just wants to hang onto his home. How can anyone blame him for that? He wouldn't have hurt those kids. He just got pushed to the limit."

There was a low murmur of approval. Frank spun around. Several people refused to meet his eye, taking a sudden interest in their BLTs and meatloaf platters.

"We appreciate all you and Earl do, Frank. Really we do." Iris Keefer spoke in the plaintive tones of a peacemaker. "It's just...well, Ronnie is a hometown boy. No one wants to see him locked up. Going to prison would kill him. We just want him to know that we're with him. We care what happens to him."

Frank looked around at the faces turned toward him. They were all people he knew, people he liked. This was Trout Run, not the Bronx or South Central LA. They didn't despise him. He knew that. Still, their support for Ronnie was infuriating. How could he not see it as a slap in the face for the work he did every day? What good was community policing if your community wanted you to fail?

"Ronnie is not harmless." Frank made a superhuman effort to keep his voice calm and steady. "The episode at his wife's daycare center was not a little temper tantrum. If you had been there to see how terrified those kids were, how desperate their parents were, you wouldn't be rooting for Ronnie. Ronnie could be a danger to himself and others. What he did at his home, he could do again."

Marge turned on her heel and headed back to the kitchen. She spoke without looking at Frank. "Ronnie doesn't deserve to be in jail. His wife and son don't want that either. Just let him be."

The lunchtime chatter resumed. Frank had been dismissed.

He left the diner, silently vowing to pack his lunch every day until Ronnie was captured. In fact, he might never eat at Malone's again.

After he crossed the town square, he looked back at the diner.

Through the steady drizzle he could just make out a spot of vivid green in the window.

"Why aren't you angry about this?" Frank sat at his desk eating Mrs. Davis's leftover bear chili that Earl had generously shared with him. "You risked your life negotiating with Ronnie. You went out there unarmed and talked him down. And this is how the town thanks you?"

Earl jerked his head. For years, he'd worn his hair long and flipped his bangs out of his eyes when he was nervous. Now his hair was cropped short, but the tic reappeared at times of anxiety. "I don't agree with them. But I understand where they're coming from. You know how some people feel about the APA. I don't take what they're doing personal."

"Okay, so I get that people think Ronnie got a raw deal and don't think he deserves a long jail sentence. But this cheering for him to stay on the run—that, I don't get. What about Pam and the kids? Doesn't anyone care about their safety?"

Earl crunched a Saltine. It was impossible to eat his mother's chili without something to cut the heat. "It's the slogan. Whoever painted it on the barn started a movement that's kinda gone viral. Pam and the kids don't have that. The louder voice gets all the supporters. People pile on the bandwagon without even thinking."

"Viral…Hey, you're friends with everyone on Facebook. Has it shown up there?"

"Yep, there's a meme. A roadrunner with Ronnie's face Photoshopped in."

"Can you tell who started it? Someone's gotta be helping Ronnie. The state police are getting nowhere because they don't know Ronnie's friends and neighbors like we do. If we figure out who, maybe…."

Earl grinned as he tapped the keys on his computer. "Why Frank—you're not suggesting we get involved in investigating something outside our jurisdiction, are you?"

"The Internet is the Wild West. Let's see who supporting Ronnie there." Frank rolled his chair next to Earl's and looked at the Ronnie-as-roadrunner meme his assistant had called up.

"One hundred twenty seven likes and comments," Earl said. "Marge Malone, Rollie Fister, Charlie who runs the dump, Ken, the track coach—it's not like these people are low-lifes. They might be sympathetic to Ronnie, but it's hard to believe they risk getting in trouble themselves to help him."

"Un-freakin'-believable," Frank muttered as he reviewed the list of Trout Run citizens supporting Ronnie. "Who's Boris Letmov?" he asked, spotting an unfamiliar name.

"Beats me." Earl clicked on the name and a profile popped up. "Whoa! Looks like he's one of those nut-case survivalist types. Look at this picture of the bunker he's got built on his property."

Boris, a beefy guy in camo gear, stood in front of a ten-foot high wall of canned goods. Ten semiautomatic weapons were lined up beside him. Another picture showed snow-capped mountain peaks much higher than any in the Adirondacks.

"Where is that?" Frank asked. "He's not local."

"Nope. Idaho," Earl said. "I've heard that whole 'be prepared to fight the government invaders' mindset is big out there. Ronnie probably connected with him on some survivalist website or something."

Frank shook his head. Clearly there existed a whole world of insanity he was totally unfamiliar with. "I wonder if Ronnie has any survivalist buddies a little closer to home. You know anyone like that around here?"

Earl leaned back to think. "I dunno. Most people in the Adirondacks have a lot of food on hand in case of a storm. And most people own a few guns. Hard to know when being prepared crosses the line to being crazy." Earl clicked out of Facebook. "This has been fun, but I've got the afternoon patrol to take care of."

After Earl left, Doris buzzed Frank with an outside call. "Some guy with a vacation home over on Mallard Pond is on the line. He said someone broke into his house and ate all his food. I asked him was he sure it wasn't a bear, but he said, no the food was cooked. So I guess—"

Frank cut her off and snatched up the call. He listened as an outraged man described a Goldilocks scene: his bed slept in, his canned soup heated on the stove, his vodka consumed, even his spare toothbrush used.

Mallard Pond lay wholly within the boundaries of Trout Run. "Don't touch a thing. I'll be right there."

The pondside cottage was a charming little bungalow with cedar shake siding and a wrap-around screened porch. Surrounded by balsam trees on three sides, the house offered total privacy. Only the side that faced the pond was visible, and that only to canoeists or kayakers out on the water. At this time of year, they were few and far between.

"I can't believe it," the agitated homeowner said. "I've owned this place for fifteen years and never once had a problem. Why, once I accidentally left the door unlocked for a month, and when I came back not a thing was missing."

He trailed Frank into the house, still talking. "He didn't take my TV or my DVD player or my laptop, but my brand new backpack is gone. I hadn't even cut the tags off it yet!"

Clearly not a thief looking for items he could sell. But a backpack would be useful for staying on the lam in the backwoods. Frank scanned the living area. The sight of a tall cabinet triggered an alarming thought. "You keep any guns here?"

"Nah. I'm a hiker, not a hunter."

So if this had been Ronnie's only refuge, he wasn't armed.

"How about warm clothes? Any missing?" Frank asked. The homeowner was short and wiry. Ronnie Gatrell was six-two and over two hundred pounds. Ronnie might be out of luck if he'd tried to switch out of his jail garb here.

"Underwear, hiking clothes, fleeces are all I keep here," the man said. "It's mostly old stuff I know I won't need at home. I checked the drawers in my bedroom. It doesn't seem like anything's missing." He opened a closet in the hall. "Looks like he dug through the hats and gloves in here."

Frank wasn't surprised. This man's clothes would be useless to him, but Ronnie must've found a hat to fit him.

"Oh, hey—I forgot about something. My son left some clothes up here in this closet. Looks like that's gone too."

"Let me guess—you son's taller and heavier than you."

"Yeah, that's right. What's going on? You know who did this?"

"Haven't you been listening to the news? We have an escaped prisoner on the loose here."

The man's eyes widened. "I drove up from New Jersey, listened to music the whole way."

In the small kitchen, Frank surveyed the evidence of the intruder's presence. Three empty cans of hearty minestrone and two cans of pineapple were stacked on the counter beside a dirty spoon and bowl. A greasy frying pan and a saucepan sat on the stove.

"I had a pound of bacon in the freezer. He ate the whole thing! And look at this." The man opened a kitchen cabinet full of jars and bottles with a few conspicuous openings. "He took my black pepper and chili powder. I just bought those at Costco!"

Jumbo-sized containers of seasonings seemed like an off choice for a man on the lam, but maybe Ronnie hated bland food. Frank produced an evidence bag and put the soup can into it. The lab could dust it for prints. It would probably take days, given how backed up those guys always were. No matter. The test would simply be verification of what Frank was already certain of: Ronnie had been hiding out here, after hiking over the Verona Range. He must've made it here the first night after his escape. The entire time the state troopers and their dogs had been combing the forest in the rain, Ronnie had been relaxing in comfort. But why this house?

"You say you've owned this place for fifteen years? You must know some of the locals, eh?"

"My neighbors along the pond here. And I'm friendly with Marge, who owns the diner. And Rollie over at the hardware store. He always helps me out when something breaks. There's a lot of upkeep with these cottages, you know."

Frank's ears pricked up. "Has Rollie ever recommended any carpenters or handymen when you've needed some work done?"

"Sure. He's tapped into a network of good workers. There was a plumber who installed a new toilet for me and another fella who hung a new back door." The man pointed toward a short hallway. "Now I'm going to have to get him back 'cause that's how the thief got in. Broke the window in the door and reached in to open the lock."

Frank examined the damage. "You remember the name of the guy who did the work?"

"Ron. Ron Somebody. I have his name and number in my desk. I'll get it."

The man handed Frank a Post-It note with Ronnie Gatrell's name and number printed on it.

"How long ago did he work for you?" Frank asked.

"Maybe two years ago. I was going to call him in the spring to rebuild the steps to the back porch. He's the escaped prisoner? He seemed like a great guy to me."

"You're going to need a new handyman. Ronnie's going to be in jail for a long time if I have anything to say about it." Frank put the note in another evidence bag.

"I wonder why Ronnie left the safety of this house when he did. I'm surprised you didn't walk in on him. Did anyone local know you were coming up this weekend?"

"No. Why?" The homeowner's face lit up. "Oh, you're wondering what tipped him off? I bet it was this." He pulled out his cellphone. "I have a remote control on the thermostat. I can turn it on with a phone call. That way, the house is warm when I get here. I had just gotten the system when Ronnie was working here. I showed it to him."

"When did you call?"

"Around six this morning before I took off. I didn't want to forget."

Frank sighed. Ronnie had had six hours to make it to his next hideout.

Frank called the state police to get the dogs over to Mallard Pond. He wondered if it would do much good—how long did a man's scent stay viable in damp weather like this?—but he had to make the effort. Once they arrived, he headed to the hardware store to talk to Rollie Fister. If Rollie was recommending Gatrell's services to people with vacation homes, then Gatrell had a ready-made list of familiar homes where he could crash. If Frank got that list, sooner or later the police would intercept Ronnie Gatrell.

On the way there he considered his strategy. What side of the Ronnie divide would Rollie Fister be on? On one hand, he lived near the covered bridge and wouldn't want a new development of houses spoiling his view. On the other, the new houses would bring new customers for his store.

And Rollie was a local leader of the Republican Party. Would that mean he was anti-government regulation? Or pro-law enforcement?

All these permutations made Frank's head spin.

He strolled into Venable's Hardware as if he wanted nothing more than some new drill bits. Rollie Fister and his team of clerks were all busy with customers. Frank strolled the aisles, perusing the jam-packed shelves and inhaling the pleasant smell of freshly cut wood and turpentine and citronella that enveloped the store regardless of the season. Eventually, Rollie's customer left with two gallons of paint, and Frank waved the store manager over to the electrical aisle.

"How's the remodeling project going?" Rollie asked. "Need something for your new lighting system?"

"Dimmer switch. My contractor has so many lights installed in the kitchen, the CIA could conduct an interrogation in there."

Rollie cackled and plucked a package from the crowded shelf. "Not the cheapest, but the best."

Frank accepted the switch. "Kind of like the contractor you recommended for my project. He's been doing a great job. Tell me, who do you recommend for smaller, cheaper projects?"

"Oh, I have a few boys willing to do handyman type jobs."

"Is Ronnie Gatrell one of them?"

"What are you getting at, Frank?"

"I want a list of the vacation homeowners that you recommended Ronnie Gatrell to. "

Rollie threw up his hands. "I don't keep files of things like that. Someone asks me for advice, I give them some names."

"When Ronnie had a project, he bought his supplies here, right? Who has he worked for recently?"

Rollie cocked his head. "Why did you ask about vacation homeowners? Have you spotted Ronnie in an empty house?"

Frank swore to himself and clamped his mouth shut. Rollie was such a busybody he could ferret out gossip in the most straightforward statement. Frank didn't want to tell the man about the break-in on Mallard Pond. The news would circulate soon enough, but he wanted the investigation to be a few hours ahead of it.

Rollie stuffed his hands in his back pockets and shifted his weight from foot to foot.

Frank waited.

"Aw, geez, Frank. You're puttin' me in an awful bind. I mean, if it was a real criminal you were after, of course I'd help, but ol' Ronnie...well, geez, I hate to rat him out."

Since no one in town except he and Earl seemed to think Ronnie was dangerous, Frank abandoned that line of reasoning. "Look, Rollie. These homeowners are your customers. They're not going to be too happy when Ronnie breaks into their houses and they find out you did nothing to stop him."

"How is it my fault?" Rollie's chin jutted out. "I didn't force anyone to hire Ronnie."

Frank raised an imaginary newspaper. "I can see the headline in the Mountain Herald: 'String of Break-Ins Tied to Hardware Store Recommendations' And what if he breaks into an occupied home? 'Gatrell Terrorizes Customers of Venable's Hardware'."

"Now that's not fair! You wouldn't tell the newspaper a tale like that."

Frank shrugged. "If Greg Faraday calls me to comment on the break-ins, I gotta tell him how I'm investigating and not getting any cooperation. Otherwise, it'll be my ass he fries in the headlines. A man's gotta do what a man's gotta do."

They faced each other in silence.

Rollie pivoted with a harrumph. "Oh, all right. I'll tell you the names I know. But who's to say those are the only houses he'd go to? There could be lots of others. Ronnie does all kinds of handyman jobs just to keep body and soul together. And he knows these woods like the back of his hand. Every hunting cabin, every fishing shack. He could be anywhere."

"He could. But I have to start somewhere. So talk."

CHAPTER 13

FRANK LOOPED BACK OUT TO the cottage Ronnie had broken into to see if the troopers had had any luck with the search dogs. The K-9 van sat in front of the cottage, but Frank heard nothing other than sound of tress rustling in the breeze. Not promising. When the dogs were excited by a scent, you could hear them baying half a mile away.

Meyerson appeared on the porch with a scowl on his face. Another trooper emerged from the house behind him, followed by a bored looking German shepherd.

"No joy?" Frank enquired.

The dog flopped on the porch and licked its front paw.

"The dogs had his scent in the house, but they lost it immediately after he descended the porch steps," the K-9 officer said. "It's like Ronnie vaporized."

"He must be gone even longer than we thought," Meyerson said. Then he squinted at Frank. "Where have you been?"

Frank handed him the list of vacation homes he'd procured. "Ronnie knows the habits of these homeowners. This might be where he'll head next."

Meyerson glanced at the list. "Possibly. Seems more likely he'd try to get out of the High Peaks. Should be looking to steal a vehicle."

Frank had grown used to Meyerson dismissing any idea he presented, so he didn't bother to argue. He'd look into the other vacation homes on his own. If he turned up nothing, Meyerson would be none the wiser. And if he captured Ronnie.... Frank allowed himself a brief fantasy of Meyerson's outrage. The dog handler brought him back to reality.

The officer crouched next to his canine partner. "Something is throwing the dogs off."

The dog at his feet sneezed, then stood up and shook its head from side to side.

"What's the matter, Juno?" The handler stroked the dog's head. "Did you swallow something you don't like?"

Frank contemplated the unhappy dog. "Black pepper? Chili powder? Would that confuse the dogs?"

"Yeah...definitely."

"Ronnie is smarter than we give him credit for." Frank told them about the stolen spices. "He didn't find a gun here, but he still managed to find tools he could use to protect himself. And he's got enough to keep us off his trail when he stops again."

Another trooper emerged from a small utility shed at the edge of the next property. "C'mere and look at this."

Frank and Meyerson trotted down to the shed.

Frank gasped as he gazed into the dim interior. A striped figured slumped in the corner.

Once his eyes adjusted, he understood what occupied the shed. Ronnie had stuffed his jail uniform with peat moss from a ripped open bale and turned a bucket into the dummy's head. Words dribbled out of its markered mouth: "Catch me if you can."

When Frank rounded the last corner before home, his heart swelled with relief. For once, his front yard didn't look like a sales lot for used pick-up trucks. All the workmen had departed for the day. He could enjoy Penny's company in peace and not have to answer a million questions about tile grout and placement of electrical outlets.

But when he entered the house, he could hear Penny talking to someone.

"Penny?"

"Upstairs," she called. Then the low murmur of conversation continued. Why would a guest be in their bedroom? Must be on the phone.

A huge sheet of plastic sealed off the kitchen—they'd been sanding in there today. The fridge had been temporarily relocated to the living room. Frank opened it, searching for a beer and a snack.

Mustard. Black olives. Raspberry jam. Three eggs.

He climbed the stairs, following the sound of Penny's voice.

"Toilet paper...toothpaste...hand lotion...mouthwash..."

He entered the bathroom and found Penny with her phone in front of her mouth. She pressed a button and turned to him. "We have to go to Hannaford's. I'm dictating a shopping list."

Frank leaned against the doorframe. "Not tonight. Can't it wait 'til the weekend?"

"We said that last weekend and never went. Our cupboards are bare."

"So we'll eat at the Trail's End."

Penny shook her head. "No toilet paper, no tissue, no paper towels. That constitutes a crisis. We're driving to Lake Placid. I'm making a comprehensive list so we don't forget anything."

Grocery shopping in the Adirondacks presented a logistical challenge to people who'd spent their younger days in the city and the suburbs. Even after years in the North Country, neither of them had developed the essential stockpiling skills needed for rural life. They persisted in believing they could pop out and get anything they needed, even after so many disappointing forays to The Store and the Stop'N' Buy in fruitless search of guacamole or oregano or soy sauce or contact lens solution.

"Can we eat at the Mexican place next to Hannaford's?" Frank begged.

"After we shop." Penny turned on her dictation app. "Shampoo…dental floss…"

"Beer!" Frank shouted.

For a full big-box store shopping experience—Costco, Walmart, Target, Macy's—you had to drive all the way to Plattsburgh, but Hannaford's, the big supermarket anchoring a strip mall on the far side of Lake Placid, had a wide selection of everyday necessities and a few gourmet treats as well. Frank and Penny pushed two carts through the aisles. The shopping excursion held Frank's interest when they were picking out cheese, and salsa, and cake, and even breakfast cereal, but now that they were in the center of the store, Frank grew restless. "You get the cleaning products. I'll go over to paper goods. We'll finish sooner if we divide and conquer."

"Okay. Don't forget garbage bags. Meet me in Produce when you're done."

Frank stacked the cart with huge bundles of toilet paper and tissue. Unless they both came down with pneumonia and dysentery, they should be supplied for months. He steered his overloaded freighter to the last aisle in the store. Get the fruits and veggies Penny insisted upon and head out for a cold beer and some enchiladas. From a distance he could see his wife pawing through a bin of broccoli—as if the heads weren't all equally distasteful—then she dropped a big green bouquet and approached a man whose back was turned.

Frank stared around the paper towels. Who was that? Penny embraced him, and the man turned in profile.

Edwin!

Frank stopped wheeling the cart. Of all people to run into here. Frank didn't want a repeat performance of the wrenching scene in his office. Could he hide out in Toiletries until Edwin left?

Too late. Penny caught sight of him and waved him forward. Frank steeled himself for the encounter.

Edwin's eyes lit up when he saw Frank approaching. He held his right hand out. "I want to apologize for my outburst the other day."

"Edwin, please...I'm the one who should be apologizing." Relieved, Frank clasped his friend's hand. "I never should have waded into Olivia's foster care situation. I should have let the social workers take care of it. I never wanted you and Lucy to get hurt."

Penny tugged on Frank's sleeve to hush him. "Edwin has good news, dear. Tell him, Edwin."

"Our lawyer thinks we have a good chance of retaining custody because Anita never made any effort to stay in touch with Olivia while she was in prison. That can be considered abandonment." Edwin gripped a bunch of carrots in his hands. "Olivia's future rests on proving abandonment. There's a hearing in Family Court the day after tomorrow.

"Has Olivia ever asked to write Anita a letter or asked to visit her in jail?" Penny asked.

Edwin kneaded the bag of carrots in his hands. "The first year she was with us, she used to ask about her mother. Ask to draw pictures for her. We would help her address the letters. She'd put them in the mail, and then the next day she'd start checking the mailbox for a reply. It never came. Heartbreaking! I ask you, what kind of mother wouldn't answer her own child's letters?" Edwin hurled the carrots into his cart. "So when Olivia would ask if she could visit, we would say the prison didn't allow it. Eventually she stopped asking, stopped writing. We thought that was best. Why dredge up the pain?"

Other shoppers sidled around them, trying to get access to the asparagus or the peppers. The sensible approach would be to finish shopping and find a place to sit down and talk. But Frank wasn't feeling sensible. He wanted to know everything, right here, right now. He shoved his cart in front of the kale—surely no one wanted that—and continued to question Edwin.

"So Olivia reached out to her mother and you and Lucy allowed her to do that—"

"Encouraged her," Edwin corrected.

"And Anita never, ever responded?" Penny said. "That's gotta be a big strike against her. But, did she know where Olivia was? I mean, do they tell prisoners what's going on with their kids?"

"Anita had a court-appointed lawyer and some kind of counselor in prison." Edwin fussed with a potted plant he had placed in the child seat of his cart, pinching off a spent bloom. "They were supposed to keep her informed."

Supposed to. Prisoners had all kinds of rights that were routinely ignored. Frank knew how the criminal justice system worked. Anita might be able to claim information had been withheld from her. Still, Essex County wasn't The Bronx. Kids didn't disappear into the system, never to be seen again. If Anita had really wanted to get in touch, she could have written "Olivia Veech, Trout Run, NY" on an envelope and the letter would've been delivered.

Edwin shredded the petals off the dead flower. "What's killing Lucy and me right now is that we could have petitioned to have Anita's parental rights terminated two years ago and we could've legally adopted Olivia and none of this would be happening."

Frank and Penny exchanged a glance. This was news!

"You decided against it?" Penny asked gently.

"We were afraid to risk it." Edwin grabbed a bag of onions from the bin beside him and tossed them on top of the carrots. "Lucy's whole relationship with Olivia has been a push and pull as Olivia tries to figure out where her loyalties lie. It's been easier for me. Olivia never knew her father. I'm not sure anyone even knew who he was. So when she came to us, it was much easier for her to accept me as a father figure. But Olivia feels guilty about her love for Lucy."

"Weren't you all going to a family therapist for a while?" Penny asked.

Edwin looked pained by the memory. "That was Lucy's idea. We went to the only therapist we could find locally, but none of us liked her. Olivia would clam up and refuse to talk. We all like Trudy better, but she's juggling a lot of cases. She did as much as she could to help, and we just muddled through."

Frank felt paralyzed by the complexity of the situation. How thick-headed he'd been! Olivia had started to improve so quickly after going to live with Edwin and Lucy that he'd never bothered to inquire if the transition had been harder than it looked. He himself couldn't imagine missing Anita; he'd foolishly assumed Olivia didn't miss her either. But a parental bond—even a bad one—wasn't that easy to break.

Edwin backed up to give another shopper a path to the broccoli. "Even though Olivia's always called us Edwin and Lucy, sometimes I overhear her say to her friends, 'Let me ask my parents,' or 'My dad can take us.' But she never refers to Lucy as her mom, not even indirectly like that."

Penny put her hand on Edwin's. "So you were afraid if you started the adoption proceeding, Olivia might resist?"

"Maybe not resist, but...well, it seemed safer not to stir up Olivia's emotions. Trudy told us if we started the proceeding, Anita would have a chance to come to court and challenge us. Olivia would see her mother again after three years apart. It seemed like poking a hornet's nest with a stick. We figured as long as Anita wasn't getting out of jail for another ten years, it was best to just leave our foster parent arrangement as it was." Edwin removed his glasses and rubbed his eyes. "How wrong we were!"

"You made the best decision with the information you had at the time," Frank said. "Let's focus on the present. Tell me about the hearing in Family Court."

Edwin brightened. "Can you two be character witnesses at the hearing? Pastor Bob and Olivia's teachers are also coming."

That would be Edwin and Lucy's strong point. They had all the leading citizens of Trout Run to vouch for what good parents they were, how they'd transformed Olivia from a malnourished pariah to a stellar student with a wholesome circle of friends.

And who would stand for Anita? There was still a lot of prejudice in town against the Veeches. People had long memories when it came to Pap Veech and his threatening signs and vicious dogs and filthy houses.

But testifying for Edwin and Lucy was something he could do to be useful, to stem the terrible sense of powerlessness that had oppressed him since he'd heard the news. "Of course I'll testify for you. I can talk about what Olivia was like when I first encountered her. I was really concerned for her safety, surviving like some third-world orphan in those shacks where the Veeches lived."

Edwin's face registered no reaction. Frank thought he must've made the wrong offer. He tried again. "I could talk about how I recognized from the get-go that Olivia was very bright, and how you and Lucy have helped her do well in school and fit in with the other kids."

"Thank you. You're very kind." Edwin leaned his forearms on his cart handle. "There's no question that Olivia is materially better off with me and Lucy. But that's not what we have to prove, because that's not what the judge is supposed to consider. The question is whether Anita is a fit mother, morally and emotionally fit. The case for abandonment rests on that."

"What has Olivia said about her life before?" Penny asked. "Was there anything—"?

"That we could use against Anita? Believe me, I've thought about it. I know her uncle and grandfather would hit her sometimes, but she's never said that Anita did. I suspect Anita was not at all affectionate, though. Olivia was very unresponsive to being hugged or held for a long time. Then it seemed like a dam broke and she couldn't get enough. She'd sit on our laps and hold our hands and demand to be tucked into bed at night."

"That's something you could use, isn't it?" Penny insisted.

"Maybe if she were still seven or eight. Now that she's a 'tween, she acts like she's too old for that." Edwin bit his lower lip. "But as she's gotten older, Olivia has drawn closer to Lucy. She needs Lucy to help her through all that middle school girl drama. She just got her period. She's not a little kid anymore. This is such a vulnerable time for her."

Penny bit her lip and her head bobbed in agreement. "You tell the judge that. Anita doesn't even know Olivia anymore."

"But Olivia herself is old enough to have some say in where she wants to live. Won't the judge listen to her wishes?"

"Trudy says Olivia will have a Court Appointed Special Advocate—someone who's neutral, who will talk to Olivia in private and represent her best interests. But who is that going to be? How can some stranger just talk to a kid for half an hour and know what's best for her?"

Frank gouged a hole in the plastic binding his paper towel bundle. Could he testify under oath that he knew Anita was unfit? "I don't know what I can say about Anita now, but when I arrested her five years ago, she was certainly unfit."

"That's the problem," Edwin said. "I don't know how we can prove that she's not fit now. In fact, I'm not entirely sure it's a good idea to try."

"Why not?"

"There's a part of me and Lucy that wants to go after Anita tooth and claw. But what if that backfires? We get custody of Olivia and she hates us for it. We could win the battle and lose the war."

CHAPTER 14

THE NEXT DAY STARTED OFF on a positive note. Frank found Lloyd Burlingame in the office talking to Earl when he arrived. They both looked up with smiles on their faces.

"I'm just telling Earl about the plan for you two to take over policing Verona. With Ronnie on the loose and all this nonsense about some people cheering him on, Mayor Abernathy thinks your plan is a good idea. But he wants to do it on a trial basis for three months before they commit to adding so much money to the yearly budget."

"Are you okay with that?" Frank asked Earl. "You don't want to miss out on a sure thing in Saranac or Placid while Abernathy waits to make up his mind."

Earl nodded. "I understand. I was just telling Lloyd, I'm not going to withdraw my applications there. If I get another offer, then we'll have to decide. But I'd rather stay here in Trout Run."

"Very sensible." Lloyd rose and shook Earl's hand, then Frank's. "I'm hopeful this will work out to everyone's benefit. In the meantime, make yourself invaluable to the citizens of Verona."

After Lloyd left, Earl turned to Frank. "Thanks for going to bat for me. How come you didn't mention this before now?"

"Didn't want to get your hopes up." He smiled. "Or mine. Let's try to look brilliant." Frank showed Earl the list of vacation homes that Ronnie might have worked at.

"It's not much, but it's a place to start. Better than searching for a needle in a haystack."

"Won't we get in trouble with Lt. Meyerson if we go out looking for Ronnie?"

"Absolutely. That's why we're doing welfare checks on houses within our jurisdiction instead."

Earl grinned and took the list. "Great. I'll take the first five. Be back after lunch."

Frank blocked his exit. "No, we'll do them all together."

"If we divide it, we can check out all the houses by tomorrow and never leave the office uncovered."

"Too risky. Ronnie is unstable and desperate. I don't want either one of us to encounter Ronnie when we're alone."

"We can't afford to both focus on Ronnie at the same time now that we have Verona to look after. If something happens there while we're both occupied far away, I'll lose my shot at this promotion."

"You can't get promoted if you're dead."

Earl's eyes narrowed. "Frank, I can handle it. What, do you think I'll march right into Ronnie's arms and let him clobber me?"

"That's not—"

"You don't trust me to do the job I was trained for."

Training! As if anything you learned in a police academy classroom truly prepared you to deal with lunatics. Earl had shown skill in the hostage situation, but he'd also been incredibly lucky. They couldn't count on their luck holding. "Ronnie could be armed now. We don't know where he's been or what he's picked up along the way. We need to cover each other. It'll take longer, but it's the best approach."

"We have new responsibilities in Verona. I don't want to screw that up," Earl protested.

Frank turned and headed for the door. "I'm not negotiating. We're doing this together. That's an order."

Earl studied the list as Frank pulled out of the town office parking lot in his own truck. Hardly undercover, but at least it wouldn't announce their arrival like the patrol car. They did not have to discuss who would drive and who would navigate. Frank would have had to sit down with a map and plot out a route of the houses, but Earl could do it in his head.

"The house Ronnie was in yesterday is awfully close to town," Earl said. "His next move might be to head north, away from the most populated areas. This camp on Sunfish Pond is pretty remote. Ronnie could hike there in a day if he kept up a steady pace, but there would be a lot of bushwhacking."

"That's one strategy. On the other hand, he might just want to get inside again as quickly as possible. What's the house closest to the one he just left?"

"There are two about an equal distance, but in different directions. This one on Blue Heron Road is about three miles east of the Mallard Pond house, and the one on Giant View is about the same distance west."

"Let's start by checking those two, then head north."

Earl was subdued. Frank knew if he could get Earl chatting about something else, their little display of power would be forgotten. Earl was never one to hold a grudge.

"Penny and I were supposed to drive down to Westchester to visit Caroline and the kids this week, but now we're not going." Frank made his peace offering.

"Oh?"

"Yeah, Caroline texted me and said something came up at Eric's office and now it's not a good time to visit." Frank sighed. "Just because Eric is busy doesn't mean we couldn't have had fun with her and the boys, but I couldn't say that."

"Why not? Seems reasonable."

"Because Caroline thinks I don't like Eric. When they had that trouble in their marriage last year, I jumped to the conclusion that he was cheating on her or hitting her or something, and ever since then, I think she's held it against me."

"Has she said so?"

"No, but...but I know something's wrong."

"She seemed real happy at your wedding." Despite himself, Earl was taking an interest in the story. Frank knew he loved a good soap opera.

"I don't know. She swore she was happy for Penny and me, but maybe in her heart she can't forgive me for getting married again."

Earl twisted to look at him. "That's crazy. How could anyone not like Penny?"

"I think she does like Penny. It's me she's mad at, but I don't know why. And when I call her, she never picks up. Then she texts me and explains that I called at a bad time. But there's never a good time. I wish texting had never been invented."

Earl smiled. "My mom doesn't have a cell phone. When she's mad at someone in the family, she drives over to their house at yells at 'em face-to-face."

"Good for her. That's why I wanted to go down to Caroline's. Just to see her and look her in the eye and figure out what's going on. But I was disinvited."

"You should go anyway. Get it settled. You'll feel better."

Or maybe worse. "Maybe next week. It's probably best I stick around now with Ronnie on the loose."

"Right at the corner," Earl announced without warning, and they careened onto Blue Heron Road.

Although the first house on their list had a mailbox on Blue Heron, a through-street that people used to get to the lumberyard, it had a long twisting driveway. The house itself was barely visible from the road.

"This looks promising," Frank said as the truck jolted down the drive. But when they got close to the house, they saw a Subaru Outback parked out front, and the main door to the house wide open.

"I sure hope that means the homeowner is up for the week," Frank said.

Before they were even a few steps away from the truck, an older man appeared in the doorway, waving cheerfully. Definitely not a hostage.

"Hi, there! You must be here searching for the escaped prisoner. Rollie at the hardware store told me you might be coming."

Frank took a deep breath. He had specifically told Rollie not to broadcast his vacation home strategy to the whole town. There was a distinct possibility that someone was helping Ronnie stay on the lam. If it got out that the vacation homes were being checked, Ronnie would avoid them.

"Rollie called you to give you a heads-up?"

"Nah. I just happened to be up there this morning. He pulled me aside and told me on the down low. Don't worry, I won't tell a soul. But I'm pretty sure ol' Ronnie won't come to my house."

"Why's that?"

"He knows I've been in and out of here regularly. He's been helping me get it ready for when my wife and I move up here permanently. We just last month sold our house in Schenectady. We're bringing the stuff we need up here one load at a time. Selling all the rest. Finally retired! I'm ready to live the dream."

The guy made sense, so Frank and Earl moved on. The next house was bigger but far more open than the pondside cottage and the house they'd just left. It sat on a hill with a commanding view of the Jay Range. It also sat in full view of the house across the street, which was positioned to take advantage of the same view.

"Ronnie can't hide out here," Earl said. "Right out in the open. And look at those big windows. Let's head north."

"Probably right. But the people across the street are home. Let's talk to them first."

Frank had the sense Earl was tolerating his whims, as one might tolerate Grandma's desire to double-check that she'd turned the iron off. They parked on the road and waved to a woman sweeping her deck.

She pulled herself to attention and set aside the broom. "I bet I know why you're here. You're searching for that escaped convict, aren't you?"

Frank could detect the avid gleam in her eye even at this distance. "Yes, that's right." He didn't bother to correct her impression that Ronnie had been convicted of a crime. "Escaped" and "convict" were words that went together like sugar and cream.

"I think these signs that have been popping up around town are ridiculous," she said, once Frank and Earl were seated on the deck. "If that man shows up here, you better believe I'll be on the phone to you right away."

"Good. Have you noticed any activity at the house across the street?"

"No, but it's been so cold and damp. Today is the first time all week I've been outside." She glanced across at her neighbor's house. "The folks that own that place haven't been up since ski season ended. Then they'll be back in the summer and fall. You should check on their place. I know they'd want you to."

"Do you have their phone number?"

She gazed heavenward. "Hmm. I'm sure I do somewhere. Let me see if I can find it."

Anticipating a long fruitless search, Frank rose. "You let me know if you find it. I think we'll stroll over and take a look around."

Frank and Earl crossed the street. Despite the rain, there were no footprints near the house. But the driveway was paved and the grass thick, so footprints might not be obvious. Nevertheless, they circled around checking all the doors and windows. The house was built on a sloping lot, so the back had a walk-out basement.

"No sign of forcible entry," Earl said.

Frank stood next to the above ground basement door and stared at a plastic box that contained a garden hose reel. "How much you wanna bet I open that up and find a house key hidden inside?"

Earl grinned and flipped up the lid. A shiny brass Schlage key on a plastic Venable's Hardware key chain sat on a ledge inside the box.

Frank shook his head. "No matter how many times I warn people not to do that, there's always someone leaving their house key in the mailbox or under the doormat."

"I wonder if the homeowners told Ronnie where he could find the key if he needed to get in to do work?" Earl said. "You think he could've come and gone?"

Frank picked up the key. "Only one way to find out."

"Isn't this an illegal search?" Earl asked as Frank unlocked the back door.

"Technically, yes. So don't touch anything. If we see any sign that Ronnie's been here, we'll back out and make the neighbor find the number and we'll get permission to enter. If he hasn't been here, we can cross this place off our list and move on. No harm, no foul."

"But really, we shouldn't…"

"Look, Earl, if people don't want strangers to enter their house, they shouldn't leave the key in such a freakin' obvious place. Don't be so squeamish."

Earl pursed his lips, their earlier truce evaporated.

They entered the basement, which was full of fishing and camping gear. A large chest freezer stood in the corner. Frank pulled on a latex glove and opened it up. There were many packages of neatly wrapped and labeled meat. Venison steaks, ground venison, venison roast. "The guy's a hunter. Can't tell if Ronnie helped himself to any of this."

They climbed the stairs to the first floor. The basement door opened into the kitchen. It was immaculate. No signs of cooking, no dirty dishes.

"I guess Ronnie hasn't been here. Let's go." Earl looked over his shoulder as if he expected either the homeowners or a representative of the ACLU to catch them in the act of trespassing.

Frank ignored him and ventured into the dining room. Also very neat, with no signs of recent occupation.

"C'mon Frank. I don't like this."

Frank kept walking. Earl's familiarity with every detail of the New York State criminal code made work increasingly difficult. He entered the great room. One wall lined with windows offered a panoramic view of the mountains. Impossible not to be impressed. "Wow. Nice."

The perpendicular wall held a huge river rock fireplace. "Gee, you could roast a whole deer in there," Frank said.

He turned again. The third wall held a large, finely crafted oak gun cabinet with glass doors and a prominent brass lock. Frank crossed the room and looked at the lock: there were scratches in the shiny finish. He pulled on the door and it swung open.

The lock had been jimmied.

One slot in the rack of rifles did not hold a gun. Instead it contained a yellow Post-It note with a scrawled message: I have now regained my Second Amendment rights.

CHAPTER 15

NOW THE STATE POLICE CHECKED every house on the hardware store list, but none of the others had been entered. When the homeowner on Giant View Road arrived from his primary residence near Albany, he confirmed the theft of a Remington rifle, as well as a one-man tent, hunting knife, sleeping bag, size 12 boots and a weatherproof camo jacket.

The next day Lt. Meyerson called a meeting at the Ray Brook state police barracks. Surprised and pleased that he and Earl had been invited, Frank vowed to sit quietly and soak up as much information as possible

"So what we know now is that Ronnie is armed, he has a backpack, he has boots and a jacket, and he has a tent," Meyerson said as he paced in front of a whiteboard in the cramped conference room. "With his backwoods skills, he really doesn't need to break into homes anymore. He's got what he needs to survive off the grid for a while. That means searching hundreds of square miles of backwoods to find him, and we just don't have that kind of manpower."

"A platoon of troopers crashing through the woods is no match for Ronnie," another trooper said. "He'll hear us coming from five miles off. We need to get the DEC rangers alerted to signs of a lone man camping in wilderness areas."

"He can't live outdoors all year long," a skinny young trooper said.

"That guy in Maine did it. Lasted twenty-seven years as a hermit."

Finally, Frank couldn't stand staying silent any longer. "Even with a rifle, Ronnie can't hunt all the food he needs. Cooking game requires a fire, which could give away his location. And drinking untreated stream and pond water is a great way to get giardiasis. Ronnie knows that. He can't stay out there much longer without help. Have you interviewed his best friends and his extended family?"

Meyerson declined to look at Frank when he spoke. "Gatrell has no extended family. Only child. Parents dead. Some cousins out-of-state. I can't believe staying in the woods is Ronnie's long-term plan. He needs to get out of this area. It's insane to stay where he's easily recognized," Meyerson insisted. "His next move will be to steal a vehicle. How can we head him off?"

"And go where?" Frank asked. "New York City, where he knows no one and has no survival skills whatsoever? There are people here in the Adirondacks willing to help Ronnie. What are you doing to find them?"

The atmosphere in the featureless beige government-furnished room crackled with tension. The other troopers exchanged glances. Frank knew they weren't used to seeing their boss challenged.

"Look, Bennett—I'm under a lot of pressure from upstairs. I don't have a limitless budget. I've got the K-9 team, I've got guys running roadblocks, I've got two men conducting interviews—neighbors, hunting buddies, poker partners. We haven't found anything suspicious. People might be willing to stick up those silly signs, but they're not willing to get arrested for sheltering an escaped prisoner."

"The last house Ronnie broke into had a functioning landline. Have we checked the records to see if he made any calls?" Frank persisted.

"Yes. Nothing."

Frank drained his coffee cup. "Hey, I never heard the final report on the investigation at the county jail regarding Ronnie's escape. Was there any indication he had help from in—"

"None," Meyerson barked. "It was a simple case of the Sheriff's transport team not following procedures to the letter. They've been disciplined. It won't happen again."

"Yes, but did the inquiry include how the fight Ronnie got into—"

Meyerson glared at Frank. "What part of the inquiry is closed don't you understand?"

Frank and Earl rode in silence on the way back to Trout Run. When they passed the golf course, Earl spoke. "You think Meyerson's all wrong about the escape and Ronnie's plans, don't you?"

"Meyerson is friends with the sheriff—they go way back. And the sheriff is up for reelection this year. He can't afford for there to be any hint of corruption in the way he runs the county jail. I think Meyerson is letting him off easy, looking the other way."

"You really think the sheriff is worried? He's been in office for as long as I can remember," Earl said. "It's not like the Democrats stand a chance in hell of winning the election in this county."

"It's not the general election he has to worry about. It's the primary. He's being challenged on the right by another Republican who claims the jail is just a full- employment program for the sheriff's cronies and family members."

"How do you know all this?" Earl asked.

"Trudy told me. She's very involved with the Essex County Democratic party. They think that if the far-right candidate gets the nomination for the Republicans, the Democrats might actually stand a chance in the general election." Frank glanced at Earl as he drove. "Do you know anyone who works at the jail?"

"Sure. My cousin's wife works in the cafeteria. And my mom's best friend's son's brother is a guard."

Frank gave his head a shake. Trying to interpret Earl's family tree required a professional genealogist. "Isn't her son's brother her other son?"

"No. Her first husband got married again, so the kid who works at the jail is her son's half-brother, I guess you'd say. But they're real close."

"Can you get them to meet us at the Mountainside for a beer? I want to ask a few questions about that fight where Ronnie supposedly got injured. I want to know how that went down without letting Meyerson or the sheriff know what I'm up to."

"No problem. They're both at the Mountainside every Friday from the end of work 'til last call."

"I want to talk to him after he's relaxed but before he's shit-faced."

Earl studied his watch. "Come around eight-thirty."

"Someone's helping Ronnie, Earl. That much I'm sure of. We figure out who, we'll find Ronnie."

Earl jumped out of the car in front of his mother's house. "See you at the Mountainside."

Frank glanced at the time: five-thirty. Penny had told him this morning he was on his own for dinner because she had a planning meeting for her big library fundraiser. Why not squeeze in one more welfare check—this one in Verona.

Pam Gatrell.

The order of protection Pam had filed against her husband gave Frank a legitimate reason to pay a call. He wondered, as he knocked at the door, if she'd changed her mind about that. Women sometimes filed for the order following a violent encounter, then reneged and even reached out to their abusers when the heat of the moment had passed. Was Pam one of those?

When Pam opened the door and saw Frank, her face lit up. "You found him? He's back in jail?"

There was no mistaking her eagerness. She hadn't softened on wanting Ronnie back behind bars.

Frank shook his head. "Sorry, he's still out there. Can I come in and talk to you for a minute?"

Pam led the way to the kitchen and poured Frank a mug of strong, hot coffee. Her courage and steadiness during the standoff had already earned Frank's admiration, and the coffee was another point in her favor.

She leaned across the table and spoke in a low, urgent voice. "Haven't you made any progress in tracking Ronnie down? No one at the state police office will tell me anything. I can't sleep at night."

"The state police should be watching this house," Frank said.

"They were, for the first couple days after Ronnie escaped. Then they decided they had better things to do, I guess. But I'm still scared to death he could turn up here. I'm worried about RJ."

"You know Ronnie better than anyone, Pam. What do you think he intends to do now that he's escaped?"

She gazed at the scrubbed pine kitchen table and gouged the soft wood with her thumbnail. A clock on the wall ticked. Two birds squabbled over seed in a feeder outside the window.

Frank waited.

"I don't know him anymore." When Pam spoke, her voice was thick with swallowed tears. "When I met Ronnie in ninth grade, he was the cutest boy in High Peaks High School. Everyone wanted to be his friend. When we got married after graduation, Ronnie was all set for taking over his dad's business. We built this house"—she gestured to her pleasant surroundings. "We had RJ. I had a nice little business going with my daycare."

She paused, stuck in that distant, happy past.

"What changed?" Frank prodded.

"Ronnie's dad keeled over from a heart attack, and his death blindsided Ronnie. He knew how to work on projects, but his dad was the one who brought in the customers, organized everything. I tried to help, but—" Pam shook her head.

"The worse things got with the business, the crazier Ronnie acted. He blamed his problems on everyone else—his customers, his competitors, the bank, the government. Then he started spending more and more time on the Internet, following these crazy conspiracy theory websites and talking all kinds of nonsense."

Frank leaned closer. "Did he ever mention survivalists? You know, those—"

Pam rose and headed for the coffee pot. "Oh, please! He never stopped going on about how we had to be prepared for an invasion. I told him to shut up—he was scaring RJ."

"Invasion by whom?"

Pam threw her hands in the air. "The government, terrorists, space aliens—who the hell knows?"

"So you're saying he was actually mentally ill?"

Pam refilled his cup and plopped back down at the table. "No…I can't explain it right. It's like sometimes Ronnie couldn't separate reality from fantasy. He'd talk to these people on the Internet, or play video games with RJ, and he'd start thinking this global conspiracy stuff was real. Then I'd talk some sense into him and he'd settle down. But then he'd start up again, always looking for someone to blame." Her hands tightened on the coffee mug. "This is why I can't sleep at night. What if now he blames me for everything that's gone wrong?"

"What about real-life friends? Did anyone around here share his…er… interests?"

"Ronnie's got a million friends. He's never met a stranger, and he always went out a lot with the boys. But he's also burned a lot of bridges. Borrowing money. Wheedling favors." Pam stirred her coffee listlessly. "I'm not sure who our friends are anymore. When I go to the Store or Malone's, people avoid me. I see them look away, pretend to be looking for something in their purse or reading the menu so they don't have to talk to me."

"What about these flyers that have sprung up all over town? And Earl says there's something going around on Facebook."

Pam slammed her mug down and coffee sloshed over the top. "I told the people spreading that Facebook crap to lay off, but that picture of Ronnie as Roadrunner kept cropping up every time I logged on. They defend Ronnie online, but then when they see me in person, they look the other way. Well, it doesn't matter now. I can't afford my Internet bill anymore, so I had to shut down my service. Let them post whatever they want."

"But do you know who started it?"

She shook her head. "Who can tell? Seems like everyone in town shared it."

Frank shifted restlessly. "Pam, think. To catch Ronnie, I have to think like Ronnie. What do you think he intends to do? Hole up in the backwoods like some crazy hermit? Or steal a car and get as far away from here as possible?"

Pam shook her head hard enough to make her long hair fly. "Never. Ronnie will never leave the Adirondacks. He'd leave me, but he'll never leave RJ."

Frank glanced at the clock. "Shouldn't RJ be home from school by now?"

"He's been staying after school for baseball practice. He plays first base for the freshman team. Thank God for that. It takes his mind off our problems for a little while."

"I'd like to talk to him. When would be a good time?"

Pam bristled. "The state police already talked to him and it really upset him. I won't have you stirring him up. There's nothing he can tell you."

Frank knew he couldn't talk to RJ without his mother's permission, so he tried to be as consoling as possible. "You know, Pam, sometimes kids open up to a stranger more than to their own parents. He might know something that he's unwilling to tell you....you know, to spare you any more anxiety."

"Huh! As if!" Pam brushed a strand of hair out of her eyes with the back of her hand. "RJ is very worried about his dad. He asks me every day, 'Where do you think Dad is now? 'Do you think he's hungry?' 'Will the cops shoot him if they find him?' It's heartbreaking."

Pam rose and started walking toward the front door. Frank had no choice but to follow. In the foyer, she faced him. "Please, find Ronnie and lock him up right this time. At least then RJ will know where his dad is. We can't take this uncertainty."

CHAPTER 16

THE MOUNTAINSIDE TAVERN WAS TROUT Run's premier workingman's (and woman's) watering hole. Any tree-hugging hikers and foliage-admiring tourists who stumbled in unaware were given the collective cold shoulder. Let them eat and drink at the Trail's End if they wanted Adirondack atmosphere with antique snowshoes and wooden skis mounted on the wall. The Mountainside was local local. Its only nod to décor was a flickering neon Budweiser sign and a crudely defaced Heimlich maneuver poster that impugned the masculinity of both choker and rescuer.

Frank tripped over a chair as he made his way toward the bar. A fifty-year-old like him had no business in a place this dark. Perching on the one empty stool, he ordered a beer and squinted, trying to locate Earl among the dancing couples and the pool players. Finally, he spotted him at the dartboard.

Earl held the dart with the tips of his fingers and sent it sailing with a deft flick of his wrist. It must've struck the bull's eye because Frank heard a roar of admiration go up from the other players. With his eyes more adjusted to the low light, he sauntered across the room.

Earl hit the center of the board again. All that target practice at the Academy must've really improved his darts game. He caught sight of Frank and grinned. Then he threw the next dart and hit single five. The intentional miss allowed one of Earl's companions to take his place before the dartboard.

Two men who resembled each other—brown wavy hair and barrel-shaped torsos—one a little older than Earl, the other a little younger, took their turns as Frank watched. Neither one could hit the target like Earl could. The game ended with good-natured laughter and some slaps on the back.

Then Earl waved to Frank and invited him to join the next round. "Brett, Devin—this is my boss, Frank Bennett."

The brothers nodded distinctly unenthusiastic greetings. Who could blame them? The arrival of a police chief twice their age was hardly call for celebration.

Frank set about dispelling the wet blanket he'd thrown on the group. He offered to buy beers for everyone if Earl could beat him in a game of Round the Clock. Although he put up a good fight, Frank eventually went down in flames and the waitress brought four bottles of Bud.

After that, they played on teams: Earl and Frank versus the brothers. Then Earl suggested switching up, so Frank found himself partnered with Devin, the brother who was a guard at the jail. Frank kept it light: they chatted about baseball and fishing and cars between turns. When a girl in tight jeans and too much makeup who had been cheering for Brett succeeded in persuading him to dance, Frank saw his opening.

"Let's take a break. I'm ready for a snack. How about you, partner?"

Frank spied an empty table and guided Devin, who staggered slightly, into a chair. He ordered a basket of fries from a passing waitress and when the snack arrived, Devin fell on it with gratitude.

"Thanks, man. I didn't hardly have dinner. Work was crazy today and I only had time for a ham sandwich."

"I guess things must be kinda tense over at the jail since Ronnie escaped, huh?" Frank held his beer bottle but had stopped drinking from it a while ago.

Devin gestured with a ketchup-drenched fry. "You better believe it. Cell checks five times a day, isolation for any infractions. Everyone's as jumpy as a cat."

"I hear the transport team got disciplined for letting Ronnie escape."

Devin leaned across the sticky Formica table. "Those guys got a raw deal. They took all the heat, but it wasn't their fault Ronnie wasn't wearing shackles." Devin took a breath as if to say more, then thought better of it.

Frank waved a beer bottle and held up two fingers to the waitress just as Earl joined them at the table. "Devin was just telling me about how the transport team couldn't get shackles on Ronnie."

This was what he wished Devin had been telling him, but luckily Devin was just buzzed enough to rise to the bait.

"The damn nurse had him all wrapped in Ace bandages and shit 'cause she believed him when he said his ankle got twisted in that fight."

"Did you see the fight? How did it start?" Earl asked.

"Happened on my watch. Some punk called Ronnie a pussy. Said a real man woulda taken hostages at the bank, not at home. So Ronnie pushed him up against the wall. I mean, you can't let another inmate disrespect you like that."

Devin took a long pull from one of the bottles the waitress had dropped off. "Then one of the other guy's friends pulled Ronnie off and all hell broke loose. They went down in a pile, and the next thing you know, Ronnie's hand is bleeding and he says his ankle's broke. He's limping and dragging his right foot. We take him down to the infirmary and the nurse bandaged his hand and said his ankle was just sprained, so she taped it up."

"But he must've faked it," Earl said. "When he got the chance, he took off running like he used to on the track team."

Devin waggled his Budweiser in Earl's face and his voice rose. "He really was cut pretty bad. I saw the blood. We found a shank made from a ballpoint pen later. Course, nobody would say whose it was. The ankle, I dunno. Ronnie was at the bottom of a pile of guys, and his leg was twisted under him. It seemed like he coulda twisted it. But people said he took off like a jackrabbit, so I guess that sprain musta been fake."

"Who was the inmate who started the fight?"

"Dude named Wade Cochran. Real pain in the ass."

"He from around here?"

"Nah. Lives clear on the other side of the county. When he's not in jail, that is."

"Still there now?"

"Just got released. He was only serving thirty days for drunk and disorderly. But he'll be back. He's a frequent flyer."

At that moment, Brett returned from his sojourn on the dance floor. The conversation turned to other things and the beer flowed even faster than before. Frank could see he'd reached his limit pumping Devin. He waved to Earl and took off, shouldering through the knot of smokers standing just outside the door.

At home, the house was silent. He slipped into bed next to Penny and she reached out to him groggily.

Then she recoiled. "Where have you been? You smell awful."

"Conducting an interrogation. At the Mountainside."

Penny scooted over to her side of the bed. "You're lucky I'm not the suspicious type."

CHAPTER 17

THE NEXT DAY FRANK RAN a background check on Wade Cochran and found seventeen years of steady but minor trouble with the law: vandalism, shoplifting, possession of stolen goods, DUI, possession of marijuana, drunk and disorderly. One conviction for breaking and entering that got him a year in Dannemora, but all his other time had been served at the county jail.

For every arrest on his record, Cochran had probably committed ten other crimes that he'd gotten away with. He looked like a full-time low-life who earned enough money to keep himself intoxicated by stealing, fencing, and dealing. But there was no violence in his record—no assault, no domestic abuse, no weapons. For every crime, he'd done his time and been released.

Cochran lived in a little hamlet west of Newcomb, which was about as far away from Trout Run as you could get and still be in Essex County. He didn't seem to have much in common with Ronnie Gatrell, who before his recent spectacular crime spree, had been a law-abiding, more-or-less gainfully employed member of society. Could they have known each other before meeting up in jail?

A mug shot in the file showed a gaunt, weasely face framed by stringy dark hair. Stats: 5'9", 150 pounds. Why would a scrawny punk like Cochran pick a fight with a man who had six inches and sixty pounds on him? Frank had known brawlers who couldn't seem to stop themselves from fighting even when the deck was clearly stacked against them, but Cochran had no record of violence. The fight at the jail looked more and more suspicious.

Frank finished the morning patrol and set off on the long drive to Newcomb, taking the Northway south, then driving west on county roads. The landscape here was less mountainous than in Trout Run and the road ran past a network of pretty lakes. But it was still too chilly for lakeside vacationers, and the four or five modest motels looked empty.

Small wonder that Cochran was a hustler. The region didn't offer much in the way of gainful employment.

Wade Cochran lived in an apartment above a convenience store on the main street in town. There was no doorbell and no name over the rusty mailbox, but the clerk in the store had confirmed that Cochran lived here. Frank looked up at the windows before he walked up the rickety wood staircase that led to the second floor. One had a crooked, torn blind pulled halfway down; the other had a faded, pink-flowered sheet tacked over it. A shiny purple Harley Superlow that still had dealer tags was parked on a small patch of gravel by the back door. Cochran's? Or did he have a visitor?

Frank climbed the stairs and knocked. He heard rustling inside, but no one opened the door. He pounded louder and raised his voice, "Wade Cochran, open up. This is the Trout Run police. I need to talk to you."

"Go away. I ain't done nothin'."

"That motorcycle parked out here was reported stolen."

The door flew open. "That bike ain't stolen. I bought it fair and square. I got the papers to prove it."

A disheveled and weed-reeking Cochran stood in the doorway, attempting to zip his jeans over a pair of tighty-whities that looked to have been washed in the same load as his Red Sox t-shirt. He was even scrawnier in person than in his mug shot. If he weighed one-fifty, Frank was Mr. Universe.

"I'd like to see those papers."

"You got no right..." Cochran's voice trailed off, too stoned to recall exactly what Frank had no right to do.

Frank stepped past Cochran into the putrid interior of the one-room apartment. Honestly, some days his job was so easy it wasn't even fun.

"I hear you're some fighter, Wade. Put a man twice your size in the jail infirmary. That's quite an accomplishment."

"Yeah, well...he shoudn'ta messed with me."

"I hear you started it. What made you do that?"

Wade backed away and stumbled into a lawn chair that made up one-third of the apartment's furniture. A TV and a mattress on the floor completed the décor. He raked his fingers through his greasy hair and left his hands on the side of his head. Maybe he was afraid his brains would leak out. "Wait...why you askin' me about that fight? I thought you were here about my bike."

Frank took a shot in the dark. "I'm thinking they're related. Where did you get the money for a Harley? You just get hired on at Google?"

The wisecrack sailed over Wade's head. "I…uh…I won some money."

"In the Lottery?"

Wade grabbed the lifeline thrown to him. "Yeah. Yeah. Bought a winning Lotto. Finally hit."

"You know Lottery winners are a matter of public record. Easy enough to check." Frank pulled out his phone.

"I mean a poker game. I won at poker. Yeah."

"High-stakes poker is illegal here in New York. You haven't been to Vegas lately, have you?"

Wade plopped into the lawn chair and rocked. "Leave me alone. That bike is mine." A wracking cough convulsed him and he spit into an empty Red Bull can on the floor.

Frank almost felt sorry for the guy. Clearly, he had so little. "What did you have to do to get that bike, Wade? Pick a little fight with Ronnie Gatrell? Get your buddies to pile on? Scratch Ronnie up some?"

"I dunno what you're talkin' about."

"Someone offered you money to do that, didn't they?"

Wade shook his head. His forehead creased with the effort of thinking of a response. Then he brightened. Cue the lightening bolt of inspiration. "Ain't nobody in jail has any money." He leaned back, satisfied that he'd bowled Frank over with his logic.

"Ronnie Gatrell himself offered you money to start the fight, didn't he? How did you know him?"

Wade snorted. "That's crazy. Why would he want to get himself beat up?"

The combination of low IQ and high intoxication had rendered Wade incapable of deception. He probably hadn't made the connection that the fight had been a necessary precursor to Ronnie's escape. But if Ronnie hadn't approached Wade himself, who had made the offer?"

Frank had memorized the names of the guards on duty with Devin during the fight. He rattled them off to Wade. "Which one of them paid you?"

Wade looked like the kid in the back row called out by the algebra teacher, so Frank knew he'd taken a wrong turn in the questioning. He backed up. Who else could have made the offer?

Then the lightening bolt hit him.

"You've been in the county jail a lot, haven't you, Wade?"

"Yeah. Shit happens."

"Sometimes, when the weather's cold and you're hungry and sick, you probably look forward to jail. Maybe you go over to Lake Placid and sit on a bench in front of the police station and light up a joint. That's probably good for a couple weeks of steady meals and a warm bed."

"Whatever. My cousin kicked me outta his house. You try livin' on the street in February." Wade coughed again and wiped his nose with the hem of his shirt.

"Sounds like you might have had a touch of bronchitis this winter. Did the nurse in the infirmary fix you up?"

"Yeah, she gave me some shit to take. She—" Wade glanced at Frank, then quickly averted his eyes.

"The nurse is your friend, isn't she, Wade?" Frank spoke softly. "She looks out for you. So naturally, you look out for her. She asked you to do her a favor. It wasn't hard. So you did it, right? And then when you were released, this nice bike was waiting for you."

"I don't have to talk to you. You didn't read me my rights or nuthin.'"

"That's because I haven't arrested you." Maybe with a little more rope, Wade would hang himself and Nancy Tomlinson too. Frank clapped Wade on the shoulder. "You take care of yourself, Wade. You wouldn't want to have an accident on that bike."

Wade breathed unsteadily through his mouth until Frank was out the door. From the corner of his eye, Frank caught the twitch of the sheet over the window as he descended the stairs. He got into the patrol car and drove off. Once he was out of sight of the apartment, Frank turned into the parking lot of a closed motel and parked behind the building. A few minutes later he heard the roar of a Harley racing down the street. He counted to twenty, then looped back to the convenience store on the ground floor of Wade's building.

Another set of eyes would be useful.

CHAPTER 18

ANYONE MIGHT THINK THAT LEW Meyerson would be grateful for the lead that Frank uncovered in the investigation of Ronnie Gatrell's escape. But gratitude was one emotion distinctly absent from the room.

"What were you doing clear over in Newcomb talking to someone who hasn't committed a crime in your jurisdiction?" Meyerson demanded.

"I received some information from local contacts and followed up on it." Frank had anticipated Meyerson's bluster and vowed not to let himself get testy in return.

"Received how?"

"By keeping my ears open. By talking to people who know other people who know Wade Cochran."

Meyerson swiveled his desk chair and jabbed an index finger in Frank's direction. "You interfered in an ongoing investigation being managed by the state police and the sheriff's department. You charged in and upset a delicate process."

"Delicate, my ass! You and the sheriff didn't have a clue as to what was going on at that jail. I'm telling you, you need to bring in that nurse for interrogation. She's the inside contact who facilitated Gatrell's escape."

"Nancy Tomlinson has been a solid, reliable employee of the county jail for nearly twenty years. I'm not ruining a woman's career based on your fantasies and dubious information you coerced out of a scumbag like Wade Cochran."

Frank chose to let the "fantasies" insult pass. He knew Meyerson well enough to see he was lashing out to defend himself. "I didn't have to coerce Cochran. I just interviewed him. If you and the sheriff had done it, maybe you would have learned what I did."

"We talked to him at the time of the escape. He didn't say anything about Nurse Tomlinson or any payments he received to attack Gatrell."

Frank clenched the arms of his chair. "Of course he didn't announce it.

Doesn't it strike you as suspicious that the guy who picked the fight with Gatrell, a guy who was practically homeless, suddenly has nine thousand dollars in cash to buy a new motorcycle?"

Meyerson snorted. "I'll grant you Cochran didn't save up his pennies to buy the bike, but I can't concern myself with how punks like him survive. He got lucky for once and came out ahead in one of his deals. Give him a few months and he'll lose the bike to the next meth cooker he deals with."

"So you're not going to talk to Cochran again? The guy's dumber than dirt. You don't need Dick Cheney to make him crack."

"He's a scumbag drug addict. I could get him to say that space aliens persuaded him to attack Gatrell. Any information he provides is worthless."

"Granted Cochran wouldn't be a stellar witness in court. But you can use his information to put some pressure on Nancy Tomlinson. C'mon—talk to the woman!"

"Don't insult my intelligence, Bennett. Do you honestly think we never questioned the nurse whose bandages made it impossible to put cuffs and shackles on Gatrell? We talked to her within an hour of the escape. She was totally calm and professional. She showed us other inmate files that indicated the measures she took were standard procedure for treating the kind of injuries Gatrell sustained."

"You mean the kind of injuries she told Cochran to inflict. She ordered up those injuries so she could deliver those particular treatments."

Meyerson threw his hands in the air. "Oh, the vast conspiracy! Why would she risk a well-paying job with benefits to help an inmate she didn't even know?"

"What makes you so sure she didn't know Ronnie? They both live in Verona. She's divorced, he's a good-looking guy. You simply asked her and took her word when she said no?"

Meyerson untwisted a paper clip until it snapped in his hands. "She works in Lewis; he works in Trout Run and Verona. She sent her son to Catholic school; the Gatrells' son is older and goes to public school. The Gatrells are into hunting, fishing, camping; Nurse Tomlinson does scrapbooking in her spare time. She told us she recognized Ronnie's face. She knew where the daycare center was because she'd passed the sign many times. But she wasn't acquainted with either of the Gatrells. Their paths simply didn't cross. And Pam Gatrell herself verified that."

"So that's it? You're not willing to dig any deeper?" Frank shed his vow to remain calm like a too-heavy sweater. Why were cops everywhere so territorial? The NYPD vs. the NYFD, the FBI vs. the CIA—big fish or small, no one was ever willing to share information, yield control, accept advice.

"We've questioned her. We're satisfied."

"Are you telling me in all your years as a cop you've never gone back and re-interviewed someone based on new information?"

"New valid information." Meyerson rose from his desk. "The state police will handle this investigation. I would think you and Earl have more than enough to keep you busy now that you're responsible for both Trout Run and Verona."

Frank knew when he'd been dismissed. But he wasn't done with Gatrell's escape. Not by a long shot.

As he was about to leave the office, Meyerson's voice called him back. "And I better not hear that you're hassling Nancy Tomlinson. Or there will be trouble."

CHAPTER 19

WADE COCHRAN AND RONNIE GATRELL were soon pushed out of Frank's mind by matters closer to home.

Penny clutched Frank's arm as they entered the Family Court hearing room in the Essex County courthouse. She was almost unrecognizable as the wife he loved. Her usual colorful scarves and clattering bracelets and sparkly earrings had been left at home. She wore a shapeless navy blue suit Frank hadn't even known she possessed. A sedate clip held her dark hair back from her pale, worried face. He would have told her she looked like a banker at a funeral to make her laugh, but he was pretty sure she'd cry.

Family Court was a grand title for a place no more imposing than a corporate office park meeting room. Anita and her court-appointed lawyer sat in chairs on the left side of the room, while Edwin, Lucy, their well-paid lawyer and all their character witnesses—Pastor Bob, two of Olivia's teachers, and a neighbor—clustered on the right.

No Olivia.

After a few preliminaries, the hearing got underway. The character witnesses came forward and testified to Edwin and Lucy's skills as parents: their involvement in the PTA, their commitment to the church youth group and the library reading club, their dedication to improving Olivia's education, health and nutrition. Others testified to the material benefits Olivia enjoyed: her own bedroom with an extra bed for sleep-over guests, a piano, shelves of books, swimming lessons in summer, ice-skating lessons in winter.

Frank stole a glance at Anita. She stared blankly at the New York State seal above the judge's head as the witnesses described all the benefits she would never be able to offer her daughter. These things weren't supposed to matter, but Frank felt sure they must. The judge was human; he couldn't help recognizing the quality of life Edwin and Lucy had provided for their foster child. Frank began to feel more confident that Lucy and Edwin would prevail, but at the same time, he couldn't help but feel a little sorry for Anita. How might her life have turned out if she'd had guardian angels like Edwin and Lucy to rescue her?

When the character witnesses finished their testimony, Edwin's lawyer outlined the true crux of their case: Anita had never tried to contact her daughter in the five years she'd been imprisoned, and that was grounds for abandonment.

The judge turned to Anita. "Can you answer that, Ms. Veech?"

Anita had been sitting with her head bowed throughout this part of the proceedings. Now she lifted it and gazed around the courtroom, taking the time to make eye contact with Edwin, Frank, Trudy, and finally, the judge.

"When I first got to Albion, I was getting hassled by some of the other prisoners, you know, 'cause of my weight…and my teeth. The guards kept moving me around to different cellblocks. I never got those first letters and drawings Olivia sent to me." She attempted a smile that was more like a grimace. "Mail at the prison doesn't come with a tracking code. Sometimes you get it, sometimes you don't. And it's not like I expected anyone to be sending me anything."

"But that didn't stop you from writing to her," the judge said.

Anita nodded. "I should have. But I was ashamed. And scared. I thought Olivia probably blamed me for what happened. If I wrote to her first, and she wrote back telling me she didn't want to hear from me, well, that would mean I had nothing to look forward to when I got out. So I figured, no news is good news, ya know? And nobody told me it was important to stay in touch if I wanted to get her back."

"Not your counselor?"

Anita waved a dismissive hand. "Which one? I had four, and none of 'em could remember my name. Probably each one thought the other one had told me."

Frank scowled. Excuses. Nothing but whining excuses. Surely the judge would see right through this.

Anita straightened her shoulders and smiled, this time more sincerely. "That's why when I started getting letters from Olivia last year, and they were all so nice, I got really excited."

A shocked murmur passed through the courtroom. Penny grabbed Frank's arm and Edwin and Lucy looked at each other in confusion.

The judge leaned forward. "You got letters from Olivia recently?"

Anita reached into the frayed cloth tote bag on her lap and produced a bundle of envelopes—mostly white, some colored. "Yes, Olivia started writing to me last year and I answered every one of her letters. She sent me twelve. I sent her thirteen."

The judge turned to Edwin and Lucy. "You were unaware of this?"

"Yes!" Edwin's outraged voice was louder than necessary. "There were no letters from Albion State Prison delivered to the inn. I go out to the mailbox every day around noon. I would know if anything came for Olivia."

The judge extended his hand for the letters and Anita rose and handed them over. He held up a letter written in a teenage girl's round, awkward script. "Is this Olivia's handwriting?"

Lucy's face had the gray, unbelieving expression of a parent called to identify the dead body of a child. She nodded.

"The return address on the envelope is P.O. Box 492, Trout Run," the judge said.

"We don't have a P.O. Box!" Edwin protested. "We get all our mail delivered to the inn's mailbox." Edwin raised an accusing finger. "She sneaked those letters to Olivia behind our back, without our knowledge. Without Trudy's knowledge. Encouraging a child to be deceptive isn't good parenting."

"Calm down, Mr. Bates," the judge warned. "Ms. Veech?"

Anita raised her hands, palms up. "How would I know where they get their mail? Lots of people in Trout Run have post office boxes. My father always did. P.O. Box 492 is the address Olivia gave me, so that's the address I sent my letters to."

Anita leaned forward in her seat and fixed her gaze on the judge. "I didn't abandon my daughter. I've been writing to her regularly this whole year. I know what classes she's taking in school. She likes history and algebra and likes the books they read in English but doesn't like the teacher so much. She thinks Earth science is boring—"

"That's all true," Penny whispered in Frank's ear.

"She says Edwin and Lucy are nice to her. But she misses me. I'm her mother. And I want to raise my daughter."

The judge rose. "I'll need to read these letters and talk to Olivia and her advocate. We'll find out whose P.O. box that is. I'll have a decision on Monday."

Frank braced himself for tears all around but they never came. Lucy looked numb, like the sole survivor of a massacre. Edwin clasped her arm as they pushed out of the courtroom.

Penny rubbed Edwin's back as they huddled on the sidewalk outside the courthouse. "Let her explore this reunion with her mother, let her resolve her feelings for Anita, and once she does, she'll come back to you. I'm sure of it."

"You don't get it, Penny. This is not, 'I'm dropping out of college to tour with my rock band.' And when it falls apart, she goes back to college older but wiser. This is dangerous. She's twelve." Edwin pounded the wall with his clenched fist. "Twelve. She doesn't know how to protect herself. She can get hurt, more than emotionally—physically. She can lose every opportunity she has for an education and a healthy, prosperous life. Am I supposed to stand by and watch that happen?"

CHAPTER 20

A COLD, DRIVING RAIN PELTED THE windows of Frank and Penny's house. They had been planning to go out for a joyous celebration after the hearing, and with those plans in ruins, they found themselves at home contemplating the grim assortment of TV dinners in the freezer.

"When will the workmen be done with our kitchen?" Penny wailed. "Every time I ask, they say 'a few more days'. We've gone a month with no stove. Once that kitchen is done, I'm never going to microwave anything again as long as I live."

"Mac and cheese or chicken pot pie?" Frank held out two frozen bricks to let his wife have first choice.

"That mac and cheese has seven hundred calories. You eat it." Penny poured them each a large glass of red wine. "What's going on with the search for Ronnie Gatrell?"

She spoke with the feigned interest of a mother inquiring about a geography class assignment. On the ride back from Elizabethtown, they'd both been too stunned to talk about Olivia, Edwin, and Lucy. Frank knew his wife's mind was fully focused on them, but that she still wasn't ready discuss what had happened at the hearing. He played along by answering her question. "Meyerson has warned me off the investigation. He absolutely refuses to consider the possibility that Nancy Tomlinson conspired to help Ronnie escape."

Penny got interested despite herself. "So what are you going to do?"

"If I were smart, I'd leave Ronnie to the state police." Frank took a big gulp of wine. "But I can't rest easy knowing Ronnie is out there. I can't shake the feeling that someone else is going to get hurt."

Penny stroked the back of his hand. "Does that mean you're going to keep looking for him?"

"That means I'm going to keep my ears open. Meyerson can't stop me from doing that, right?"

"In my experience, no one can stop you from doing anything you've set your mind on."

Frank drew his hand away from his wife's. Penny had meant the remark as a compliment, but it had struck him wrong. He thought of the morality tales he read to his grandkids. Was he the determined Little Engine Who Could? Or the controlling, know-it-all Bossy Bear? "I set my mind on placing Olivia with Edwin and Lucy. That didn't turn out so well."

"Oh, Frank!" Penny busied herself with wiping the fine film of plaster dust off the table and setting out the plates. "You did what you thought was best at the time. I can't believe Olivia has been writing to Anita for a year behind Edwin and Lucy's back." Now Penny's dismay gushed out. "Why didn't she just tell them she wanted to try again to get in touch with her mother?"

"She must feel guilty, torn between Edwin and Lucy and Anita. And kids that age are always testing the limits of what they can do for themselves. When Caroline was twelve, she rode her bike seven miles on the shoulder of a busy four lane road to get to the shopping mall to buy a hat for a school play costume. Apparently, she'd asked her mom to take her and when Estelle said 'later,' Caroline took off on her own. When she didn't show up for dinner, I went out looking for her and found her pedaling along in the dark."

The mention of Caroline darkened their mood even further. The microwave dinged and Frank prodded the still-solid center of his dinner.

"And who did Olivia get to help her?" Penny asked. "What kind of adult would help a child secretly correspond with a prisoner?"

"I don't know, but you'd better believe I'm going to be first in line at the post office tomorrow morning to find out."

If it was unethical to report who owned a particular post office box, Roxanne, the clerk at the Trout Run post office, was unconcerned. She cheerfully told Frank that box 492 belonged to the Kellum family.

"Kellum? Isn't that the woman who uses a wheelchair?"

"Yes, poor Denise has multiple sclerosis, but she can still drive her special van. Her daughter always comes in to pick up the mail so Denise doesn't have to struggle up the ramp."

Frank could see where this was leading. "How old is her daughter?"

"Jenny? Oh, twelve, thirteen, I guess. Why?"

But Frank was already out the door.

He had Edwin on the phone before he even made it back to the town office. "I know who was helping Olivia send the letters to Anita."

"Yeah, Jenny Kellum. Olivia told us last night." Edwin's voice, usually so animated, sounded flat and exhausted.

"Did she say why she suddenly started writing to her—, to Anita?"

"Olivia just said she'd been thinking about her mother and wanted to know how she was doing."

"But why did she hide—"

"Why? Because she's twelve." Edwin's voice got louder. "Because she'll never fully recover from seven years of neglect. Maybe because her grandfather was a paranoid lunatic and she's got some of his DNA. I'm surprised you don't have the answer. You were so full of insights when you persuaded Lucy and me to foster Olivia."

How was he supposed to respond? "Edwin, believe me, if I had known this was even remotely possible, I would never have—"

"Forget it." Frank could hear the clatter of meal preparation over the phone line. "I'm sorry I lashed out, Frank. I know there are no guarantees with kids. If we'd have had a biological child, she might've gotten a brain tumor, or been paralyzed in a car accident, or gotten snatched by an alligator like that poor kid in Florida. Terrible things happen."

Frank felt like a sock had been stuffed in his mouth. Terrible things did happen to kids sometimes. The only way to survive parenthood without losing your mind was to convince yourself the terrible thing would never happen to your child.

And now it had.

"Don't feel guilty." Frank strained to hear Edwin's final words. "I wouldn't have traded our time with Olivia. Not even to avoid this pain."

When Frank walked into the library with lunchtime sandwiches the next day, he saw a man sitting beside Penny at the Circulation desk computer. His black glasses slipped down his nose as he stared at the screen and bit his lower lip. Then his fingers burst into furious typing. Then more staring and lip-biting. Penny watched as if he were blowing molten glass.

"Lunch delivery." Frank plonked the bag from the Stop 'N' Buy down on the desk, making them both jump.

"Hi, honey! Guess what? Gage is helping me fix my problem with the catalog. Or I should say, Gage is fixing it and I'm just watching in awe and wonder."

The guy bobbed his head without tearing his gaze away from the computer screen. Another flurry of keyboarding ensued. Penny had been complaining about the endless hours she spent on the phone with a tech support person in Bangalore trying to get the bugs out of the library catalog system. Now it seemed someone had come to fix it in person.

"Your vendor sent a technician clear out to Trout Run?"

Penny's peal of laughter disturbed an old lady reading in the corner armchair, who scowled over the top of her bodice-ripper. "No, he doesn't work for the software company. This is Gage Shelby, Leon's son. He's doing me a favor because he's so smart."

With a final rat-a-tat of the keys, Gage leaned back in his chair, revealing a t-shirt that read, unaccountably, Trampled by Turtles. "That should do it." He was lean, and despite the glasses, looked fit. He rose with a smile and extended his hand to Frank. "I hear my dad couldn't manage to sell you a house."

"He could have sold Penny a house. And he could have sold me a house. He just couldn't sell us both the same house."

Gage laughed, but Frank didn't think he sounded all that amused. "That's the problem with the real estate business in the High Peaks. The great properties never seem to be on the market at the time qualified buyers want them."

"Dilapidated money pits are certainly in good supply," Frank offered.

"It takes a lot of marketing skill to sell those. And hand-holding." Gage sat back down next to Penny and arched his back, stretching the t-shirt across his chest. "I learned the hard way that while I had plenty of ideas about marketing, I wasn't very interested—or good at—hand-holding. Not like the old man."

Frank wondered if Gage was still working or intending to join them for lunch. Did Penny know what Trampled by Turtles meant? Frank worried that she did.

"Gage has been telling me that his original life plan was to come back to Trout Run after college and partner with his dad in the real estate business," Penny said.

"But that didn't work out?" Frank pulled up a chair. He didn't have much time for lunch, but despite his impatience to dig into his meal, he was curious about this man who'd given Anita Veech a job.

"Nope." Gage tapped a pencil on his knee. "Dad told me the business wasn't big enough to support us both, but I was sure the old man was just doing it all wrong." He poked his heart with the pencil. "I'd be able to grow the business. I soon learned that my undergrad courses in marketing didn't really apply in a rural economy where there's too much supply and not enough demand. Dad was right, as always."

"So you switched to computers?" Frank asked.

"Not really. I moved back to Boston where I still had college friends and got hired by a high-tech start-up to do their marketing. Then I became marketing VP at another high-tech firm. I still consider myself a marketer first and foremost, but I've picked up some programming skills along the way." He smiled at Penny. "Enough to fix a glitchy database, at least."

"VP of marketing in Boston sounds like a nice life for a young guy," Frank said. "What made you come back here?"

Gage directed a dreamy gaze to the big window at the rear of the reading room, which offered a panoramic view of the Jay Range. "My heart is in the mountains. Always has been. I was born and raised in Trout Run and my time in Boston just served to confirm that this is where I want to make my life."

Gage seemed lost in thought contemplating the view. The birch and maple on at the lower elevations were flushed with a light, bright green that contrasted with the darker green of the conifers above them on the slopes. A lovely scene, true, but Frank still didn't understand how Gage had been able to return to his hometown. He prodded for answers. "So you packed in your big job in the city to open a business here?"

Gage swiveled around. "I got lucky. Some shares I was holding skyrocketed in value just at the time when I got the idea for my new app. I cashed out and moved. I can do the work from anywhere, so I might as well start living the dream." He stood up. "I'm keeping you from your lunch." He picked up a stack of books on the desk and turned to leave. "Thanks for your help with the research, Penny. Nice meeting you, Frank."

Gage loped out of the library, hugging the books to his chest.

Frank handed over the bag of sandwiches. "I'm starving. I thought he'd never leave."

Penny unwrapped hers and examined it with a frown.

"Did I forget something?" Frank asked.

"No, it's okay. I just don't care for yellow mustard, remember?"

Estelle had loved yellow mustard. Penny liked brown. My God, would he never keep it straight? "I'm sorry. Do you want to trade?"

"No, it's fine." She used a plastic knife to scrape mustard off her bread as she continued talking. "Gage is such a great guy—smart and accomplished. He's just the kind of person Edwin and Lucy would normally love to meet. But that's out of question given the Anita issue."

Frank told Penny about Jenny Kellum and his conversation with Edwin. "So many situations broke against Edwin. If Olivia hadn't befriended a girl whose mother couldn't collect her own mail...if Anita hadn't taken that coding class...if Gage hadn't hired her..." Frank shook his head. "I still don't understand—what exactly is his business and why did he hire Anita, of all people?"

"He came up with this idea for an app that helps hikers and bikers calculate exactly how much food and water they need to pack for a trip depending on the heat and their weight and the speed they're traveling." Penny ate a bite of her sandwich. "And he got some angel investors to back him. So now all he needs to do is finish the programming and the marketing and those are things he can do from right here in Trout Run."

"You seem to know quite a bit about him. He told you all that while he was checking out his books?" Frank tried to keep his tone light. He didn't want to sound like a jealous old fool, but he hadn't cared for the way Gage Shelby looked at Penny.

"Oh, this isn't the first time he's been in."

Penny chewed a mouthful of turkey and cheese, keeping Frank in suspense. Was the library Gage Shelby's home away from home?

"I've been helping him with some research."

Frank glanced at the stacks, filled largely with romance and mystery novels, local history, and nature guides. "Research? The closest thing you have to a high-tech book here is Excel for Dummies."

Penny clapped her hands in amusement. "Not research for his business. Genealogical research. Gage's family has lived in Trout Run since 1832. He's fascinated by all the economic forces that have shaped the area. The rise and fall of the logging industry. The failure of subsistence farming. The influence of tourism. And in the process of researching that, he's told me about himself, and how he's working to create some new economic opportunities in town. Pretty neat, huh?"

Frank scrutinized the carrot sticks Penny had produced from her tote bag and placed before him. Healthy supplements and hipster doofuses were ruining his lunch hour. "Yeah. Fantastic." Frank gnawed on a tasteless orange twig. "So what does Anita do for him?"

"Coding. Gage says his app is very code-intensive, whatever that means, and he needs someone who's willing to do a lot of tedious de-bugging. It's not creative, fun stuff. He had two kids who'd just graduated from college and they both got bored and quit. But apparently Anita is willing to chip away at it. Gage seems very satisfied with her work."

"How did he connect with her?"

"Some organization that teaches coding to prisoners and ex-cons and gang members and then places them in jobs. Isn't that great?"

Frank scowled. "How would Mr. Collegiate Granola connect with a group like that?"

"Who knows? LinkedIn? Social media?" Penny collected their garbage, sealed it in a plastic bag, and spritzed her desk with cleaner. She wasn't much of a housekeeper at home, but she lived in fear of insect or rodent attacks on the library's collection.

"So there's no chance he's going to fire Anita?"

Penny nudged him with the tip of her stylish boot, a gesture meant to be scolding but that Frank found distractingly sexy. "I feel so conflicted. Anita's job with Gage is a wonderful success story. It's tragic that her good fortune guarantees Edwin and Lucy's unhappiness."

"Just because she's managing to hold down a job doesn't mean she's going to be a good parent. I'll be keeping an eye on her."

"Frank! You can't use your position to interfere. It's up to Trudy to monitor Anita's parenting."

"I'm not interfering. It's my job to keep Olivia safe. I'll never abdicate that, no matter who has custody."

CHAPTER 21

AS SOON AS FRANK RETURNED to the office after lunch, he got a call on his cellphone from an unfamiliar number.

"Hey, it's Jimmy from the market," a gruff voice said.

Frank's mind was blank. What market?

"You told me to call if Wade got any visitors."

Oh, that market, the market beneath Wade Cochran's apartment. "Yeah, thanks for calling." Frank pulled out a notepad. "What do you have for me?"

"Some broad was in here late yesterday afternoon asking for Wade. I got busy and forgot to call until now."

Frank had given the guy in the market twenty bucks to report on Wade's visitors. The store clerk hadn't required much persuading—it seemed no one liked Wade much. Now, Frank kept his voice disinterested, so the clerk wouldn't embellish his story for a bigger reward.

"Uh-huh. Can you describe her?"

"Hmmm. Nuthin' special. Light brown hair. In her thirties, I guess."

That could be Nancy Tomlinson, but hundreds of other women too. Maybe even Pam Gatrell. "Tall, short, thin, fat?" Frank prompted.

"Uhm, kinda in the middle. Not skinny, or, ya know, sexy or anything. But not fat." He rambled on trying to say something usefully descriptive, but failing.

Frank took a deep breath. No wonder prosecutors hated eyewitness testimony. "Glasses, scars, birthmarks, tattoos?"

"No glasses. I only saw her face and hands. She was wearing a raincoat. She asked if I knew where Wade was. I said he comes and goes. She bought a coffee and sat at one of our tables and read a book for a while. She kept checking her phone for the time, looking annoyed. Then finally, Wade pulled up on his bike. She went out and said a few words to him and pulled something out of her purse and gave it to him. Then she walked away."

"What she handed him—what did that look like?"

"An envelope, I think. Probably drugs. Wade is always high on something."

"Did he give her something back?"

"No…maybe he paid in advance." The clerk snorted.

It could be drugs, of course. That's what Meyerson would assume. But surely if this woman were Wade's regular dealer, they wouldn't be doing their transaction in broad daylight right in front of the market. Wasn't it more likely that this was another payment? Where was the money coming from?

"Did you see what kind of car she was driving?"

"No. She was parked off to the side. And then it got busy and I couldn't be lookin' out the window all day, ya know."

"Okay, Jimmy—thanks. Call me if she shows up again."

"Will there be…?"

"Yeah. Another twenty. If you notice some more details."

Frank hung up. He was probably throwing money down a rat hole, but if the woman returned, he would get the clerk in to look at a photo array with Nancy Tomlinson's picture included.

Common wisdom held that everyone knew everyone else in a small town. But the truth of small town relationships was more subtle. Sure, people waved to every passing car, greeted anyone they encountered while shopping or dining or getting something repaired. But combined, Trout Run and Verona had nearly four thousand residents. Everyone didn't literally know everyone else.

However, that expression that there were only six degrees of separation between any two people was really true here. In fact, there were probably only three degrees of separation between any two people in the High Peaks, as Earl managed to prove on a daily basis. So the trick was to uncover the degrees of separation between Nancy and Ronnie.

Nancy had eliminated the obvious choices: work, neighborhood, church, hobbies. Pam herself verified that she didn't know Nancy. So what could have brought Nancy and Ronnie together? Frank thought about the network of friends and acquaintances he and Estelle had shared back in Kansas City. It seemed like Caroline was the common denominator in most of them. He still got a Christmas card from a couple they'd befriended during pre-natal exercise class.

Nancy's son Max was two years younger than RJ Gatrell, and they hadn't gone to the same school. Could the boys have been friends though some activity?

Frank jumped as Earl walked into the office.

"Why are you staring into space like that," Earl asked.

"What are some activities that boys of different ages do together?"

Earl was used to Frank's tendency to answer a question with another unrelated question. "Uhmm…Boy Scouts, 4H, Little League. Why?"

"I want to know if RJ Gatrell and Max Tomlinson know each other. Who runs those organizations?"

The question was barely out of Frank's mouth before Earl was on the phone with leaders and coaches. In fifteen minutes, he had an answer. "RJ is in Boy Scouts, but not Max. Max is in 4H, but not RJ. They were both in Little League last year, but now RJ is too old for Little League, so this year only Max plays."

"When are the games?"

"Tuesday and Thursday afternoon practice, Saturday morning games. The season just started."

Frank looked at his assistant, imagining him as an energetic child. "Did you do all that when you were a kid?"

"Boy Scouts and 4H. I loved 4H—won a prize for my rabbits. Little League, not so much. I dropped out by fourth grade. I was okay in the field, but I wasn't much of a hitter. Too skinny."

"Did your parents go to your games?"

"If they weren't working. My cousins were on the team too, so my aunts and uncles and parents took turns coming and cheering for us."

"But the team parents all knew each other?"

"Oh, definitely."

When Frank completed the afternoon patrol, he headed to Pam Gatrell's house. The landscape was as bleak as his thoughts. Mud, mud everywhere, with no end in sight to the relentless rain. Had Ronnie found an empty house to offer him a dry bed, or did he have nothing but a damp tent over his head? It seemed to Frank that a few days out in this weather would make a man surrender.

Or drive him to take crazy risks.

The Little League connection had unleashed conflicting theories in Frank's mind. Pam and Ronnie were devoted parents, so if both of them had attended RJ's games, why had Pam denied knowing Nancy? Could the women actually be close friends? Had Pam convinced Nancy to help her husband escape? Pam's anguish over her collapsing way of life was real, but maybe her desire to have Ronnie back behind bars had been a carefully performed act.

Frank didn't want to believe Pam had been involved in Ronnie's escape, but he couldn't ignore the possibility. On the other hand, maybe Pam really didn't know Nancy, but Ronnie did. Maybe Ronnie and Nancy had been carrying on behind Pam's back.

Through the gray drizzle, Frank spotted the bright colors of the Happy Camper sign and made the turn. Late afternoon would normally have been a busy time at Happy Camper Daycare when parents came and went picking up their kids. But today rain fell on an empty driveway. The house stood quiet and dim, with only one light glowing in a side window. Frank could see movement behind the curtains and guessed Pam was in the kitchen. He pulled up as close as possible to the back door and dashed through the downpour.

Pam answered his knock promptly, but she seemed less eager to see him this time. Maybe she could tell from the expression on his face that he hadn't come bearing good news. He followed her into the kitchen and sat at the table. She didn't offer coffee.

Frank dove right in. "Last year, RJ was on the Little League team, correct?"

"Yeah—what about it?"

"Did you and Ronnie go to all his games?"

Pam shook her head. "Ronnie took RJ to practice and went to most of the games, but I couldn't go on Saturday mornings last season. I had two customers who needed me to babysit on Saturdays. With money being so tight, I couldn't afford to say no."

"Did Ronnie talk about the parents of the other players?"

She shrugged. "Sometimes they'd take the kids out for pizza. I think he liked them all. Well, he thought one dad coached from the bleachers, but I told him that was the pot calling the kettle black."

"He ever mention the mothers?"

Pam narrowed her eyes. "What are you getting at?"

"I have to ask you this. Is there a possibility Ronnie had a girlfriend?"

Pam's eyes widened and her lip trembled. She let her head drop onto her folded arms on the kitchen table. Her shoulders shook, but her sobs made no sound. Frank let her have the time she needed. He wouldn't have thought Ronnie had the capacity to hurt her any further, but apparently he did.

Finally, Pam lifted her head and stared at him through swollen eyes. "What do you know?"

Frank shook his head. He wasn't going to plant any possibilities in her head. "Money…revenge…sex—those are what motivate people to take crazy risks. And helping Ronnie stay on the lam is a crazy risk."

"A year ago I would have said no way. Ronnie was the love of my life. But now I'm not sure. I don't know. He's capable of anything."

"But before the stand-off, did he show any signs of seeing someone else? Phone calls that he wouldn't answer in front of you? Sneaking out at night? That sort of thing."

Pam squinted up at the ceiling. "Ronnie was always getting calls from the bank and from lawyers. He'd go out on the porch to talk to them because he knew it upset me to hear the arguments. Who knows—maybe some of those calls came from a woman." Pam leaned across the table as determined to pry information from him as he was to get it from her. "You suspect someone from the team? You mean to tell me when I was working my ass off, he was at the games picking up other women?"

Pam snatched up one flyer among many pinned to the fridge with magnets. Frank saw the Little League logo at the top of the page and watched Pam scan what was obviously a team roster. Her brow knit in concentration as she considered each woman on the list. Then Frank saw her eyes widen. The list fluttered onto the floor. "Nancy Tomlinson. She's the nurse at the jail that the state police asked me about. You think she helped him escape, don't you?"

"There's no solid proof, but Nancy told the state police she didn't know Ronnie. Said she recognized his face because she might have seen him around town, but nothing more."

"Liar! Ronnie knew all the kids on the team, knew their strengths and weaknesses." Pam studied the roster again. "Max. Max is her son. Ronnie used to talk about how Max needed extra help with batting. He said the kid's father wasn't in the picture, and he had no one to practice with him"

Pam twisted her fingers together. Her eyes were glassy with a second batch of tears. "Once, he and RJ were really late getting home from a game. When I asked about it, Ronnie said the game went into extra innings. But RJ was really quiet and acting funny. He went to his room and said he wasn't hungry for dinner. Ronnie claimed RJ had struck out and felt bad. He told me not to say anything about it, and the next day RJ seemed fine, so I let it drop. Now I wonder…maybe Ronnie drove somewhere with Nancy and her son. Maybe RJ knew there was something fishy with that. Kids can tell."

"Is RJ home now?"

Pam shook her head. "He's at his friend's house playing video games. Normally, I limit his screen time, but honestly, those games are the only thing that lets him get away from what's going on in his life. And thank God Denny hasn't abandoned him like some of the other kids." She waved a weary hand. "Let him play."

"I'd really like to talk to him. How's tomorrow?"

Pam stiffened. "I don't want RJ upset. He's suffered enough. I'll talk to him and let you know what he says."

"It would be better—"

Pam stood, looming over him. "I don't want you putting ideas in RJ's head about his dad having sex with some—" Her voice cracked. "I know what's best for my son. I'll talk to him."

At that moment, the phone on the kitchen wall began to ring. Pam glanced at the caller ID. "I have to answer this."

He was dismissed.

"Okay, Pam. Call me if you learn anything, either about Nancy Tomlinson or anyone else."

Pam nodded as she kept talking to whoever was on the phone and walked Frank to the back door.

In the cluttered mudroom, Frank had to squeeze past a tower of stacked cardboard boxes. He caught his boot on the bottom box, which jutted out further than the others.

Pam gave the box a vicious kick, and it rattled. "Another one of Ronnie's stupid projects," she muttered under her breath while listening to her caller.

"Talk to RJ and let me know what you find out," Frank said.

She nodded and held the door for him.

Once Frank was back in his car, he wrote one word in his notebook.

Denny.

"You know what I'm in the mood for?" Frank had peeled off his wet socks when he got home, grateful for a warm, dry house, even if it was full of construction dust.

Penny eyed him as she shook some bagged lettuce into a bowl and prepared to squirt it with Wishbone. "A gourmet meal prepared by a wife who can cook?"

"Nah. A baseball game."

"The Red Sox are playing the Yankees tomorrow." Penny was a devoted Yankees fan, while Frank still rooted for Kansas City. "We could watch it at that bar in Lake Placid that serves the amber ale you like."

"The last time Boston played New York, I got called to the Mountainside twice to break up fights. I'd better stick closer to home…like Stevenson's Lumberyard vs. Al's Sunoco tomorrow at nine. I think you could recruit some boys for your summer book club if you showed an interest in their Little League games."

Penny handed him a jar of spaghetti sauce to open and watched with her hands on her hips. "You're up to something."

Frank attempted to open the jar with one twist, but the manufacturer of the marinara with basil and garlic wasn't about to let him look heroic to his wife. "I thought we could help each other," he said through gritted teeth.

Penny took the jar away and ran it under hot water. "Why do I suspect that I'm the one who will be doing all the work?"

"Not work. Just do what you do best—be friendly with the other parents, chat with them about their kids, and let me observe."

"Observe what?"

"The jail nurse who might have helped Ronnie Gatrell escape. Meyerson has explicitly forbidden me to talk to her. But he hasn't said a word about you."

"Oooo! Is this a sting operation? You want me to entrap her?"

"You've been reading too many mystery novels. I just want to get a sense of what kind of person she is. You chat; I'll listen."

"Chat about what?"

"You'll think of something." He accepted the warm jar back and popped it open. "You're the brains of this operation."

CHAPTER 22

ON THE WAY TO THE baseball game, Penny stared out the window at the beaten down grass in the front yards of the houses in town. Occasionally, a few daffodils would lift their brave yellow heads toward the watery sun that had finally emerged. As they drove further away from the center of Trout Run, the mist hanging over the meadows refused to burn away unless the sun cranked out a little more wattage.

"Oh, no! Look at that!" Penny shouted.

Instinctively, Frank slammed on the brakes.

He swerved onto the shoulder. "What?" There was no sign of an animal, alive or dead, on the road.

"I'm sorry." Penny pointed to one of Leon Shelby's Mountain Realty signs pounded into the muddy grass in front of a boarded-up building. "The Honeycomb Bakery is out of business? I'm shocked."

Frank peered out the window. The cheery yellow paint made the deserted little store seem even sadder. "They only lasted six months."

"I thought they were doing okay," Penny protested. "That cake you bought for my birthday was delicious."

"Yeah, but we haven't been back since. The place is so out-of-the way. For a special occasion, customers might drive over here, but you're not going to go ten miles to get a coffee cake on Saturday morning." Frank pulled out onto the road again. "And they were pricey for Trout Run."

"I know. For years, Marilee and her daughter made stuff special order at home and everyone told them they should open a shop. And then they did, and they failed in short order."

"That's the problem with trying to make money from a retail establishment around here. To be successful, you've got to appeal to more than just the locals. Tourists wouldn't ever stumble upon that place."

Penny looked over her shoulder at the receding bakery. "Marilee and her daughter are so sweet. They were so full of high hopes for their business. I hope they didn't lose their shirts."

"They were naïve. They thought they could just bake the stuff and customers would come. They could've used some marketing advice from your buddy, Gage."

Penny squeezed Frank's knee. "How come you don't like him?"

Frank kept his eyes on the road. "I like him fine. I barely know him."

"Well, happy news—you're going to get to know him better."

Good lord, he hoped Penny hadn't invited that twit over for dinner. "Oh?"

"This weekend we're going to go to the Abolitionist Reenactment at the John Brown Farm historical site. Gage is involved in the Essex County Historical Society and he asked me for my help."

"Whoa, back up. Gage Shelby is one of those people who gets dressed up in moldy old civil war uniforms and shoots a musket?"

"I believe muskets were used in the Revolutionary War, dear. They used breech loaders in the Civil War."

"You scare me when you know things like that."

Penny tapped her head. "Librarians have a vast storage capacity for arcane information. And, no, Gage isn't getting dressed up, but he is very involved in the Historical Society. He's worried that he's the youngest member. See, they've been doing the reenactment at the John Brown site exactly the same since Gage was a kid. He thinks we need to make it more relevant. He thinks the Historical Society will die out if we can't get younger people engaged in local history.

What was this we business? "By doing what? Setting the old Civil War camp songs to a hip-hop beat?"

Penny laughed. "That's not such a bad idea. It worked for Hamilton. No, Gage wants to shoot a short video with John Brown's Farm as a backdrop, and share it on social media. On one hand, John Brown could be seen as a warrior fighting for racial equality. On the other hand, his raid at Harper's Ferry was an act of violent extremism. So, hero or terrorist—it all depends on how you look at it. That's the question Gage wants to explore in his video, and tie it in to what's going on in the world today. He wants me to narrate it. Apparently, several of the old people in the Historical Society wanted to do it, but Gage wants someone chatty and friendly."

"That's certainly you."

"Thanks, dear. So you'll come with me?"

Damn straight he would come if Gage Shelby had plans to collaborate with his wife. "Sure. How could I miss a star being born?"

By the time Frank and Penny arrived at the baseball diamond, the game was in the second inning. About twenty parents sat in the bleachers, fans for both teams intermingled. He didn't know Nancy Tomlinson, but he'd looked up her driver's license after his conversation with Jimmy the clerk. Five foot six, one hundred sixty pounds, brown hair, brown eyes, thirty-five years old. There were other women in the stands who could answer to that description, but only one wasn't with a husband.

"Sit in the third row," Frank murmured to Penny, urging her forward. He sat a couple of rows behind Penny where he could observe without being noticed by Nancy. Maybe Nancy would recognize Penny as the Trout Run librarian, maybe not. But she'd surely recognize Frank. He nodded to a few of the other parents. If they thought it odd he wasn't sitting with his wife, they didn't comment. They were all too absorbed in the game, which was tied two-two.

Just as they sat down, the stocky kid at bat for Al's Sunoco belted one to the outfield and the crowd roared. The hit would have been a double, but the right-fielder flubbed the throw to second, and the runner continued to third.

"Way to hit, Joey," a dad yelled. The Stevenson's parents groaned. The woman Frank had pegged as Nancy Tomlinson chewed her thumbnail.

Penny slid down the bleacher to take a seat behind the woman, but slightly to her right. Nancy was not what he'd expected. Not a flirtatious divorcee, but a plain, solid, dependable mom.

And a worried one.

The next batter hit a high fly to right, and the same kid who'd bungled the throw to third got under it. Nancy brought her shoulders up to her ears and squeezed her eyes shut.

The ball dropped into the kid's mitt, and the Stevenson's parents cheered.

"He got it that time, Nancy," one of the fathers said.

Nancy opened her eyes and clapped when she saw the Stevenson's team heading in as the inning changed.

Penny leaned forward. "That was a good catch."

Nancy turned toward her with a grateful smile. "I get so nervous when Max plays. Sometimes I can hardly bear to watch."

"My aunt used to pray the rosary whenever her son pitched," Penny said.

Frank kept his eyes focused on the game and repressed a smile. This rosary-toting aunt had sprung to life on the spot. Penny had no close relatives and she hadn't been raised Catholic.

Nancy sighed. "It's not fair that they put so much pressure on the kids. Max gets so upset every time he makes a mistake. How about your son? Which one is he?"

At that moment one of the boys caught sight of her and waved. "Hi, Miss Penny!"

"I'm the librarian in Trout Run. I came by to cheer for the kids in my summer book club…and maybe recruit a few more. Would Max be interested?"

From then on, Nancy and Penny chatted like old friends. Frank watched the game and listened. Sports…school…junk food…appropriate reading…inappropriate TV—one thread ran through the entire conversation: anxiety. Nancy Tomlinson seemed to be a real worrywart. Could someone like that take the colossal risk of helping a man to break out of jail?

After the fifth inning, Nancy got up to use the restroom on the far side of the field. Frank watched her walk—she was broad in the beam and had the kind of haircut mothers got when they couldn't be bothered with blow dryers and curling irons. Pam was more attractive by a long shot. Still, that didn't always matter. In Frank's experience, men who strayed were more interested in variety than an upgrade.

"What do you think?" Penny asked, slipping back to sit with him.

"What do you think?"

"She seems nice enough…anxious…a little whiny…very concerned about her son. Honestly, she doesn't strike me as the type to run off with a prisoner."

"I was thinking the same thing. But what were we expecting? We knew she was a nurse and a mother, not a gang member. When she comes back, see if you can steer the conversation toward her job."

When Nancy sat back down in the bleachers, Penny began a long soliloquy on her own job: the rewards of running the library versus the challenges of finding enough money to keep the doors open. Finally, she ended with, "Looks like you're a nurse. Do you work at the Cascade Clinic?"

"Ha! I wish. The clinic would be a nice place to work, but I couldn't live on what they pay. No, I work at the jail. Instead of stitching up kids who fall off their bikes, I stitch up inmates who get in fights." Nancy gazed into the outfield. "Not what I imagined when I enrolled in nursing school. Thought I might be an OR nurse at the medical center in Albany. But they don't give jobs like that to nurses who don't have a degree from a big-name school."

"Really?"

"Yeah, you have to know someone to get hired there. It's all an inside game. Just like with this Little League. The coaches' kids get to play all the best positions. Max would like to play first base, but they always put him in the outfield. Or on the bench, like now."

Frank's ears perked up. Nancy's tone had shifted from anxious to aggrieved. That sense that life was unfair and she'd gotten the short end of the stick might lead her to do something reckless.

"That's a shame." Penny's voice was noncommittal, but Frank could sense his wife's natural sympathy ebbing. Anyone paying attention could see that each of the players had been rotated out of the game for one inning. And a couple different kids had played first, even if Max hadn't.

Eventually, the game ended with a base-clearing walk-off homer from the Al's Sunoco power hitter. The Stevenson's team trudged off the field and Nancy Tomlinson rose to meet her son. "Bye," she said to Penny. "Nice—" For the first time she noticed Frank and blinked rapidly. "Uhm, nice talking to you."

She hurried away.

"I didn't think the coaches were playing favorites, did you?" Penny asked.

"Prisons are full of people who blame others for their predicaments. Maybe some of that rubbed off on Nancy."

CHAPTER 23

SUNDAY DAWNED CLEAR AND BRIGHT.

Perfect weather for the historical reenactment at John Brown's Farm.

Frank had secretly been praying for more rain, but now that he and Penny had arrived at the little cabin outside of Lake Placid, he found himself taking an interest in the proceedings despite his wariness of Gage Shelby.

Ten men and two women dressed in 19th Century farmers clothing milled around. Gage was there, discussing something intently with one of the costumed men. They gestured toward the green but muddy field surrounding the farmhouse. Gage walked him to a certain spot, and placed another re-enactor a few feet away.

"What are they going to re-enact?" Frank asked Penny.

"Well, John Brown came here in 1848 with the idea that he would train freed slaves in the techniques of farming. Unfortunately, we've only got one black re-enactor to play the part of the slaves. Gage must be trying to figure out how to frame the shot."

"I'm surprised you have even one, given that Essex County is about ninety-nine percent white."

"I think he drove up from Albany," Penny admitted.

Finally, Gage finished his conversation and glanced around. His face lit up when he saw Penny, and he trotted toward them.

"Great! You're here." Gage nodded briefly to Frank, then pulled Penny aside. "We'll shoot your intro and conclusion first, then I'll shoot the re-enactment and I'll edit it later."

He posed Penny in front of the farmhouse and aimed a video camera on a tripod. "Look straight into the camera. Three…two…one, roll."

Frank watched with pride as Penny started chatting about the life of John Brown, his two wives and twenty children, his fervent abolitionist beliefs, his violent methods, and the assessment of historians that he had been mentally ill. She talked to the camera as if she were talking to one of her book clubs at the library, and John Brown soon came alive as a real person.

"Fantastic!" Gage shouted. "You're a natural."

Frank had to agree.

"Now let's do the conclusion." Frowning, Gage fiddled with something on his video camera. "Anita!" he called.

To Frank's surprise, Anita Veech emerged from the crowd of onlookers and approached Gage. He spoke to her, using his hands to describe something. She nodded and walked over to an SUV, got something out of it, and brought it to her boss. Apparently, Anita was Gage's assistant in more than just his app development venture. Frank wondered if she minded working on weekends.

Penny took a drink of water and continued. This time she was more somber as she told the tale of Brown's conviction for murder, conspiracy to incite a slave rebellion, and treason; his execution by hanging; and the return of his body here to the farmhouse. When she finished, Gage hugged her, an outpouring of enthusiasm that Frank couldn't begrudge the younger man. Penny really was terrific.

"How did I do?" she asked Frank.

"You knocked it out of the park. Everyone will want to join the Historical Society with you as the spokeswoman." Frank guided Penny to a seating area where they could watch the recording of rest of the proceedings. A small crowd filled the other chairs.

"I think that tall guy in the blue shirt is going to play John Brown," Penny said.

Gage cued him to begin and the man started reciting John Brown's most fiery speech. "Here, before God, in the presence of these witnesses, from this time, I con—, conse—"

"Cut. That's okay. Try again."

The re-enactor took a deep breath and looked up at the sky. "Here, before God, in the presence of these witnesses, from this time, I consecrate my life to the destruction of slavery!"

"Better," Gage said, "Remember to look into the camera. Try again."

The man stumbled again. Finally, on the fourth try, he made it through but he sounded like a nervous kid in the class play.

"He's not very good," Penny whispered.

A man seated behind them was less discreet with his opinion. "That sucked. Too bad Gatrell's not here. Ol' Ronnie made a crackerjack John Brown."

"That's because Ronnie is every bit as crazy as John Brown was," another spectator said.

"Ronnie Gatrell is a member of the Historical Society?" Frank asked Penny under his breath.

She shrugged. "His family has lived in the area for generations. I guess it makes sense."

The re-enactor was back on camera, muddling through one more John Brown speech. "Now if it is deemed necessary that I should forfeit my life for the furtherance of the ends of justice, and mingle my blood further with the blood of my children and with the blood of millions in this slave country whose rights are disregarded by wicked, cruel, and unjust enactments, I say let it be done!"

"Ronnie did that one real good last year," the theater critic behind Frank said. "I bet he was thinking about the APA and banks that took his land when he said it."

Before Frank could comment, six men appeared carrying a wooden coffin. They set it down next to John Brown's tombstone, and a woman in a long gray dress and white apron dropped to her knees and draped herself over it, sobbing.

"That's John's wife, Mary Anne," Penny said. "John managed to get three of his sons killed in his attacks on slaveholders, one in Kansas and two at Harper's Ferry. I'm not sure if they were Mary Anne's sons or the sons of his first wife, Dianthe."

Frank watched the little tableau of tragedy. "I bet Mary Anne would have a lot to say to Pam Gatrell. It's not easy being married to a zealot."

CHAPTER 24

MONDAY GOT OFF TO AN auspicious start. Earl quickly determined the only Denny in the eighth grade class at High Peaks Middle School. "Denny Webber. His Dad's name is also Dennis. They live on the Trout Run-Verona border, pretty near the Gatrells. In fact, I bet their property backs up to the Gatrells'."

"So Denny and RJ have probably been playmates for a long time," Frank said. "Do you know the parents? Are they part of the 'Run Ronnie Run' coalition?"

"Nah," Earl said. "Mr. Webber is kinda serious—a real straight arrow. He drives a forklift at Stevenson's Lumberyard."

"I think I'll drop by and see him there. If I can get permission to talk to Denny now, I can see the kid right after school."

Stevenson's Lumberyard bustled with activity. Frank maneuvered around a flatbed sixteen-wheeler waiting to drop off a load of logs and found a place to park near the warehouse. He asked a passing worker where he could find Dennis Webber and soon found the man ferrying pallets of two-by-fours with a small forklift.

Webber parked the vehicle and jumped down with a worried face. "What's wrong? Please don't say my wife had an accident driving to Placid."

Frank patted his shoulder. "No, nothing's wrong. I just wanted to ask your help with something."

The crease of worry in Webber's forehead relaxed a little, but didn't disappear.

"I understand your son Denny is friends with RJ Gatrell." Frank said.

"What did they do? If Denny drove his ATV on the road, I'll kill him!"

Geez, Earl was right when he said Webber was a straight arrow. The man immediately jumped to the worst conclusion. "Believe me, Denny has done nothing wrong. I'm, uh, assisting, in the investigation of Ronnie Gatrell's escape. I'd like your permission to talk to Denny this afternoon.

I'd just like to explore whether RJ may have told him anything that might be useful to us."

Dennis Webber's earnest gray eyes searched Frank's face. Then he glanced over his shoulder, and seeing the nearest warehouse aisle empty, gestured for Frank to follow him. They ducked into a small break room, where stale coffee scorched on a burner. Webber started talking before they had even sat down at the scuffed Formica table. "I told my wife we should contact the police, but she said we didn't know anything for certain and if the cops wanted us, they'd call. So I guess you have."

Frank felt a flicker of excitement. His hunch had paid off. He was about to learn something the state police didn't know. But he could see that Webber was conflicted about talking to him. "You've been good neighbors to the Gatrells for a long time, haven't you?"

"Fifteen years. The boys have been playing together since they could walk." He paused. "He's a good kid...it's not his fault his dad is, well—"

"You're not a great friend of Ronnie's?"

Webber shrugged. "My wife and I are homebodies. Ronnie is more of a partier. But RJ is a good friend of Denny's. The boys could play together for hours—building forts in the woods, fishing, and now that they're older, riding their ATVs. But recently...." Again Webber glanced around as if he suspected the break room was bugged.

"Something changed between them?"

"In October, Denny asked for a video game system for his birthday. I was against it—kids should play outside—but my wife said that the boys were spending too much time at RJ's house playing video games there. Denny would come home and tell his mom about Pam and Ronnie arguing. My wife said if we got Denny the game system, then we could keep an eye on them both at our house, so we got it."

Frank wasn't sure where this was headed, but he vowed to be patient. Webber took a deep breath and continued.

"I would pop into the family room and watch the boys play, and the games all seemed the same to me: shooting aliens, shooting zombies, shooting dragons. Silly, but they got a kick out of it, and they could play with other kids from school over the Internet. But then, after Christmas, RJ brought over a new game called Resist or Die."

Webber looked down at his clenched hands on the table. Frank wondered how bad the new game could have been. Was it gruesomely violent?

"RJ wanted to play this new game every day, and at first I overheard them arguing because Denny said it was boring. This game didn't have any loud explosions or shooting –all I could see on the screen was a guy in a forest. Pretty soon Denny seemed to change his mind about the game, and I could hear them talking very intensely about their strategy with the other players on the Internet."

He looked up at Frank. "This is where it gets weird. One day my wife was going to the supermarket, and Denny said he wanted to come along. Now, he hasn't gone grocery shopping since he was a little boy, too young to stay home alone. So he goes, and the entire time they're in the store Denny keeps trying to put more canned goods in the cart. And he says we need stuff we never buy—powdered milk and protein bars. And Denny's getting agitated when my wife says no to all this crap. Then later that week he starts in on me. Says we need more ammunition! I only have one gun—a twenty-two I keep around to shoot groundhogs in my garden. One box of shells lasts me a couple of years. When I said we didn't need more, I thought Denny was actually going to cry."

Frank thought he could see where this was headed. "The game was putting ideas in his head?"

Webber nodded. "It took me a while to get it out of Denny, but when he finally told me, he was so relieved to get his worries off his chest. Seems that RJ had convinced him that everyone has to be prepared for the day when the government comes and tries to take away our property and enslave us. The game is a way to practice. RJ told Denny that Ronnie said lots of people don't believe this will happen, and if you don't like those people, then you just let them be enslaved. But if you do like them, like if they're your parents, then you have to find a way to prepare them without them knowing about it."

Frank nodded. "Pam told me that Ronnie spent a lot of time on the Internet on conspiracy theory websites. She thought it was crazy."

"RJ said his mom wasn't a believer—that's what they call themselves—but that Ronnie and RJ would protect her anyway. And Denny should protect us without telling us about the coming invasion. Can you believe this shit?"

"So what did you do?"

"I went over and found Ronnie out in his garage. You can't believe what he's got out there—floor-to-ceiling supplies, enough to feed an army. I told him to lay off—he was scaring the kids." Webber kneaded his temples. "He went ballistic. Told me I was a sheep who deserved to be enslaved. There was no reasoning with him. I came back home and laid down the law: the boys could only be together at our house and no more

Resist or Die. They could play the other games or do stuff outside."

"How did Denny react?"

"He was glad. It was like we deprogrammed him and he came to his senses."

"What about RJ?"

"We didn't see RJ for a while, and my wife and I thought that was for the best. Then Ronnie pulled that hostage stunt and escaped from jail, and Denny said RJ was really upset. The other kids at school couldn't stop talking about it. Some of them said Ronnie was an escaped convict who deserved to be shot on sight. But some called him this freedom-fighter hero. They're kids—they're just repeating what they hear at home." Webber lowered his voice. "That's what it's been like here at work. People have gotten into fights over Ronnie."

Frank kept his voice casual. "Really? Who defends him?"

Webber wasn't that easy to con. He shook his head. "I walk away when that nonsense starts. I'm here to do a job, that's all."

Frank let it go for now. There was more to learn. "What about Denny and RJ—Pam said they still hang out together."

Webber sighed. "We felt bad for the kid. This is too much for any kid to deal with. So we told Denny to invite RJ over."

"And did RJ abide by your rules?"

Webber nodded. "He's always been a polite, helpful kid. Denny said RJ never mentioned the survivalist nonsense again. And now that it's spring, they've been spending more time fishing and riding their ATVs. When it rains, they play that shoot-the-dragons game. Sometimes we feed RJ dinner because Pam just started a job clear up in Plattsburgh. Honestly, the kid seems relieved to be around normal people."

"This has been really helpful, Dennis."

"I'm sorry I didn't call you sooner," Webber said. "It's just...well, we feel bad for Pam and RJ. We didn't want to make things even worse for them."

"I understand. But I'd still like to talk to Denny. And I'd like to bring along my assistant, Earl Davis. He's the one who understands how these Internet video games work."

"Okay, but not tonight, please. My wife won't be home, and I told Denny I'd help him study for his algebra test."

Frank rose and extended his hand to shake Webber's. "Talk it over with your wife and we'll set up a time. I'll be in touch."

On Monday evening, Frank opened the door from the garage into the back hall and heard a sound he'd never heard in this house: hysterical crying.

"Penny? Penny, what's wrong?" He followed the sound into the kitchen, where he saw two heads—one light, one dark—huddled together.

Penny looked up. Her face was dry. "Lucy's a little upset."

Frank knew he was often clueless when it came to interpreting the emotions of women, but even he could've figured that out. "Has something happened with Olivia?"

Penny's big dark eyes met his. "The judge has awarded custody to Anita."

Her words set off a more intense fit of crying from Lucy.

Frank sat down at the table but remained silent. What was there to say? He'd been hoping for the best but in his heart, he'd been uneasily sure it would end this way. Anita had found a job, a surprisingly well-paying job for Trout Run. She'd found a place to live: an apartment on the second floor of a house with two bedrooms, a separate entrance, a back porch and access to the yard. It was less than a mile from the Green, which meant Olivia could walk to the store or the diner to meet her friends. In some ways, it was a better location than the inn for a teen not old enough to drive. And she hadn't abandoned Olivia, according to the story she told at the hearing, a story that was almost impossible to disprove.

Lucy's sobs eventually abated. She blew her nose in the proffered tissues and accepted a cup of tea.

"What about this advocate who's supposed to represent Olivia's best interests. Wasn't she on your side?" Frank asked.

"Olivia met with her this week, but she wouldn't tell me what they talked about. If I pry, she clams up and goes off to sulk in her room. Lately, Olivia and I have been struggling." Lucy's eyes were bloodshot. She had no tears left, but her voice trembled. "I was worried Olivia has told the advocate she wants to leave us, and I guess I was right."

Penny squeezed her friend's hand. "I think you're reading too much into Olivia's moodiness. She loves you and Edwin—anyone can see that. She just doesn't know how to express all her conflicting emotions."

"It's more than that," Lucy insisted. "Olivia knows she'll have more freedom with Anita. Edwin and I won't let her get her ears pierced yet, or wear eye shadow or buy sexy-looking clothes. Olivia accuses me of wanting her to dress like an Amish farm girl when all I'm doing is keeping her from looking like a hooker working the streets near the Lincoln Tunnel. I'm sure she thinks Anita will let her get a tattoo and wear belly shirts to school. At twelve, she thinks those things are important. She doesn't realize..."

Lucy took a deep breath. "She doesn't realize what she's letting herself in for. It took years for some people in this town to forgive Olivia her gene pool and think of her as a nice girl from a good family. Now that she's living with her mother, will the town turn on her again? Will her friends be allowed to associate with her? I'm not sure she recalls how she was bullied and ostracized back in first grade. Who's to say those kids won't start up again now that Olivia is Anita Veech's daughter again?"

CHAPTER 25

ON TUESDAY AFTERNOON, EARL WENT to Denny Webber's house to talk to the kid about the video games he played with RJ Gatrell. While Earl was occupied, a park ranger that Frank knew at the Adirondack Loj called. Some backpackers reported finding a campsite that hadn't been properly cleaned up. They'd picked up some empty cans and packed them out, but they were concerned there was still food waste there that might attract bears.

"These backpackers were pretty outraged by what they'd found," the ranger said. "They attributed it to rudeness and laziness, but I'm wondering…"

"…if they surprised Ronnie Gatrell. Are the hikers still there?"

"Yeah, they're relaxing on the porch before they hike back to their cars. Should I call the state police?"

"Yeah, report it. But I can be there in fifteen. Don't let the hikers leave."

When Frank arrived at the Loj, he found three scruffy but very fit young men sprawled in Adirondack chairs with a large black Lab at their feet. One had a grubby bandana tied around his head. One had matted strawberry blond dreadlocks. The third had a patchy brown beard. The dog was the best groomed of the bunch.

"I understand you guys discovered a dirty campsite back in the Marcy Wilderness."

The guys exchanged a glance. "We didn't think the ranger would call the cops. We don't want anyone to get arrested, just, you know, be cool—pack it in, pack it out."

"Right," dreadlocks said. "It's not cool to leave your trash."

"There's a possibility this wasn't a careless hiker. Was the campfire still warm when you got there?"

"Yeah, as a matter of fact, it was. We could smell the smoke. He'd just kicked some dirt on it. A real fire hazard."

Frank glanced at the dog. "Was he barking as you approached?"

The guys thought for a moment. "You know, he might have been," Bandana said. "Bix flushed a grouse as we were hiking. I think it was about ten minutes before we got to the campsite."

Scruffy Beard cocked his head. "You're saying we scared someone off? Why would anyone care if they ran into us? We're totally chill."

"You are. But he's not. Where are you guys from? Haven't you heard about the escaped prisoner we're looking for?"

Bandana slapped his own head. "The dude who took those little kids hostage? Whoa—no way!"

"Do you still have the cans you picked up?"

Dreadlocks walked over to a bulging full-frame pack leaning against the porch railing. Unzipping one of the many pockets, he handed Frank three tuna cans with pull-tab tops and two plastic applesauce cups. The tuna was the same size and brand as one of the cans discarded at the Giant View house.

"That's all of it?" Frank asked.

"Wait, I found something too," Bandana said. He dug through his pockets and produced a crumpled blue and yellow bag.

Frank touched the bag with one finger. Honey Maid Teddy Grahams. A roly-poly bear danced across the package. "These are what the kids at Happy Camper Daycare had for their snack. Pam gave each kid a bag to distract them when they had to march out past Ronnie holding the gun."

The ranger looked perplexed. "How could he have something from home with him when he escaped?"

Frank shook his head. "He couldn't. Prisoners surrender everything when they're processed."

"So that means…"

"He's been getting help from his wife...or his son."

CHAPTER 26

"I CAN'T BELIEVE IT. AFTER WHAT he did to her?" Earl said when Frank told him about the incident the next morning. "She insisted she never wanted to see him again."

Frank sighed. "I've seen abused women go back to their husbands over and over again. You pull them apart screaming and kicking at home on Friday night, and by Sunday morning they're holding hands and feeding each other bites of pancake at the diner."

"Love is strange," Earl said.

"It's not love. It's some kind of sick desire for mutual destruction. I didn't think that Pam was that type."

"So maybe it's RJ. A kid would want to help his dad, no matter what."

"Psychologically, RJ makes more sense," Frank said, "but he's only fourteen. How would he get supplies to his dad without a vehicle? Ronnie has hiked ten to twenty miles a day, zigzagging through the backcountry. There's no way the kid could be doing that much hiking without anyone noticing. He hasn't missed any school since Ronnie escaped. I've checked."

"He's got an ATV," Earl offered.

"You can't drive an ATV over the Verona Range." Frank gazed out the window at the thickly wooded mountains on the horizon. "And he could never drive an ATV on the road for that many miles without someone noticing."

"So-o-o..."

Frank turned away from the window. "RJ provides the food. Someone else delivers it. What did you learn from Denny about these video games? Could one of the players be helping Ronnie?"

"I don't know." Earl tossed the burnt end of his pecan sticky bun in the trash. "Denny's a nice kid. He showed me his whole gaming system, and all the user names of the kids at school that they play Call of Duty and Dead Rising with. Then he showed me the list of the people who played

Resist or Die and it was all different user names. Denny said he didn't know who the people were."

"And you just took him at his word? Isn't there a way to verify that?"

Earl gave him a pained look. "Of course I followed up. Gamers have on-line profiles. They don't have to reveal their real names, but most of them describe themselves. Some even have a profile picture. I didn't recognize anyone as local."

"But it's not impossible. A person could put anything in his profile, right?"

"Right. To be absolutely certain, we'd have to ask to see each gamer's account, and for that we'd need—"

"A warrant," Frank sighed. "We're not at that point yet."

When the phone buzzed with an internal call from Doris, Frank assumed Meyerson was finally getting around to calling him back about the search of the Marcy Wilderness.

He snatched up the receiver. "Yes?"

"There's a lady on Line One who says her husband hasn't come home from fishing, and she's getting worried. I told her we haven't had any car crashes, but she insists she has to talk to you."

Doris knew better than to put through every call from angry wives checking up on their husbands. The guy was probably sleeping off a bender and would come crawling home soon enough. He wondered if it was the wife of one of the regulars at the Mountainside Tavern. "What's her name?"

"Mrs. Cottlemeir. That's C-O-T-T—"

"Who's that?"

"The lady whose husband hasn't come home."

"I understand, but I'm asking you if you know her."

"Know her? Why would I know her? She lives clear down near Saratoga."

Frank sat up straight. "You mean this is a tourist? Someone who came to Trout Run to go fishing and never made it back home again?"

"Yes. Exactly. She was expecting him last night. She tried to call his cell, but he didn't answer. But I told her how bad the reception can be up here, what with the trees and not enough cell towers, but those towers are real ugly so no wonder no wants them, so that doesn't mean—"

"Doris."

"Right. Well, finally she fell asleep, and now it's morning and he's still not home. So I can see why she'd be worried, I mean, I'd be worried too, if it was my husband, but I don't know what she thinks we—"

Frank punched the button for Line One, abruptly exchanging Doris for Mrs. Cottlemeir.

"Chief Bennett. How can I help you?"

Frank listened as an increasingly tearful woman explained her situation. She and her husband loved to fish. They had the use of a friend's fishing camp on Crescent Lake. She would normally have gone with her husband, but she'd been invited to a baby shower. Why had she gone to the party? It hadn't even been fun. So her husband drove up alone, and called her Friday as he was passing through Trout Run on his way to the camp. Once he was there, she knew his cell phone wouldn't work, but she expected to hear from him on Sunday as he was driving back. But he didn't call and didn't answer her calls. She went to bed worried, but telling herself he'd simply let the phone run out of juice. But now it was Monday morning, and he still wasn't back. She'd called the Saranac Medical Center. She'd called the Thruway Accident report hotline. Nothing. The story ended with a wail. "Where could he be?"

"Ma'am, as our dispatcher told you, we haven't had a report of any accidents locally, but I'm happy check the state police report. And I can ask the state police to drive out to the camp and check on your husband. Can you describe what part of Crescent Lake it's on?"

She gave him addled directions full of "turn at the place that used to be the Black Bear Campground" and "if you see the little waterfall, you've gone too far." As far as he could tell, the access road to the camp sounded like it was several miles on the far side of the village of Verona. Was it within his new jurisdiction? Possibly, but hard to be certain without seeing it on a map.

"How long will it take until I hear something from the state police?" the wife asked.

"We-e-ell, that depends on how busy the officer covering that territory is, and how far away he is from there on his patrol. Could be an hour, could be tomorrow."

"Tomorrow! I can't wait until tomorrow! Something is terribly wrong. I'd drive up there myself, but I'm babysitting my grandson for the next three days. I can't drive around the Adirondacks looking for Joe with a sick toddler in my backseat. Can't you help me?"

He heard the pleading in her voice. He also heard the warning in Meyerson's. No showboating. Stay in your own backyard. "I'm not sure it's in my jurisdiction, ma'am."

She began to sob. "Please…my husband is missing. Why won't you take me seriously?"

"With all due respect ma'am, it's not a crime to come home late from a fishing trip."

"You don't understand. Joe's not like that. He doesn't drink. He doesn't sneak around. He always calls. He would move heaven and earth to find me if I were missing. Aren't you married? Wouldn't you do that for your wife?"

She couldn't have planned her assault any better if she'd spent a month researching. Frank looked at his desk. He couldn't even claim to be busy. Every task he'd been procrastinating on, Earl had done. He'd been such a marvel of efficiency since auditioning for his promotion that all their paperwork was up-to-date, and even the dreaded Spring Fling traffic plan had been resolved. And Earl had just left, which meant the morning patrol was underway. Frank sighed. "All right ma'am. I suppose I can drive out there. Expect to hear from me in forty-five minutes."

He headed out to his truck and called out to Doris as he passed. "If Meyerson should happen to call, tell him I'm doing a personal favor for a friend."

Frank hoped he wouldn't find an empty boat floating on the pond. Mrs. Cottlemeir had insisted her husband was in good health and always wore a life jacket while in the boat. Of course, that's what he did when he was with her and what he promised to do when he was away from her.

What he actually did was no doubt another matter.

Frank left Route Nine at the erstwhile campground, turning onto two-lane paved road, and again onto a narrow gravel road with no name, and finally onto a dirt track marked by a crooked wooden arrow nailed to a tree. No doubt about it—the camp fell in the unincorporated area outside Verona, totally outside his new jurisdiction, totally off the grid. No electricity, no running water, certainly no cell service. But he was here now—no point in turning back without checking on Mr. Cottlemeir.

His truck lurched along and Frank downshifted to keep it from losing traction on the steep descent to the lake. Soon he saw the cabin—little more than a shack, really—with a concrete block chimney and just one window on the side facing him.

Frank could see fresh tire tracks, so the man had made it here. But no sign of Mr. C's truck. And Frank certainly hadn't passed it on the way in. If it had stalled or been abandoned it would be clearly visibly because it couldn't be driven more than a few feet off the road in woods this dense.

He got out of the truck suddenly intensely aware that he shouldn't have come here alone. Yet there was no good reason to leave without checking out the cabin. The forest was so silent that when a woodpecker knocked on a tree behind him, Frank jumped.

He circled one side of the cabin and looked out at the lake. A flat-bottomed fishing boat bobbed next to a rickety dock. A bait bucket sat on the shore.

Unease crept up his spine. Mr. Cottlemeir hadn't packed to leave, yet his vehicle was gone. Had he driven out to get something and never returned? Would someone eventually notice a car in the Grand Union parking lot that hadn't moved for days? A car with a man whose heart had stopped sitting behind the wheel?

Frank approached the house. There was a screen door, with the main door open behind it. Not that unusual. If anyone wanted to break into this flimsy shack, a locked door wouldn't stop him, so might as well let the fresh air in.

He stepped up on the porch and noticed a hole in the screen.

A perfectly round hole.

He breathed deeply to steady himself.

That's when he smelled it.

Fish. Not fresh. Like the alley behind a seafood restaurant on a hot day.

"Mr. Cottlemeir? Trout Run Police. I'm coming in."

He stepped across the threshold, blinking as he left the bright afternoon for the dim interior. A dark, sticky tide ran across the sloping floor toward him.

Blood. More blood than could be shed by any fish living in Crescent Lake.

Large, corrugated boot prints tracked through the blood, becoming fainter as they reached the door.

Frank paused. He needed to preserve the scene, but if there was any possibility that Cottlemeier was still alive....

He shined his flashlight around the dim interior. The cabin was just one open room. Bunk beds to sleep six on one side.

A propane-fueled stove with a rough countertop on the other.

A bigmouth bass lay sliced open on the counter.

Cottlemeir lay in a heap at the foot of the stove.

His face was gone.

Frank had to drive back out to the main road before he picked up a cell phone signal to call in the shooting. Forty-five minutes later, Meyerson arrived with a full crime-scene team. Glaring at Frank, he donned a Tyvek suit and entered the cabin, barking out orders to his men. Half an hour later, he emerged and yanked open the door of Frank's truck.

"What were you doing out here?"

"Hi, Lew. Nice to see you, too."

"Don't start with me, Bennett. Yesterday you were nosing around at the Adirondack Loj. Now, you're out of your jurisdiction again."

Frank was too tired and discouraged to get into a pissing match with Meyerson. He'd spent the last hour thinking about Ronnie, about how everyone, even he, had underestimated what Ronnie was capable of. Like John Brown, Ronnie had crossed the line from self-appointed freedom fighter to terrorist. And now, a totally innocent man was dead. "The guy's wife called me, worried about her husband. She wasn't able to describe the cabin's location precisely. Once I got out here, I realized it was outside the Verona lines, but I figured I might as well check it out if I'd already driven twenty miles. Don't tell me you would have turned around."

Meyerson scowled. "Tell me everything you know."

So Frank methodically recounted every detail of the call from Mrs. Cottlemeir and his discovery of the body. He also reminded Meyerson that the campsite where the hikers had found the trash was less than fifteen miles from their current location. He finished with, "Ronnie Gatrell is a stone cold killer."

"We won't know for sure that Gatrell killed Cottlemeir until we get the results from the CSI unit," Meyerson said. "He didn't leave us a message this time."

"I know damn well what they'll find. Those boot prints will match the size and brand that Ronnie stole from the Giant View house. The bullet they dug out of the wall will have been fired by a seven millimeter Remington just like the one Ronnie stole."

"You're probably right, but I've still got to talk to the owner of the fishing camp and to Cottlemeir's family."

"What about the truck? Do you have an APB—"

"Of course we do," Meyerson snapped. "We can't be certain until we establish the time of death, but since the victim was cleaning a fish when he died, Ronnie—or whoever—must've killed him no earlier than Saturday afternoon or evening or as late as Sunday afternoon. That means he could have driven anywhere from six hundred to fifteen hundred miles by now."

Frank's head still echoed with the cry of anguish that had come through his phone when Mrs. Cottlemeir had called him again to ask what he'd discovered and he had to tell her that her husband wouldn't be coming home. He'd said, "There's been an accident." He wouldn't, couldn't, say more. Couldn't say, "Your husband's been gunned down by a man who wanted his truck." Couldn't say, "Your husband's dead because no one took his killer seriously. No one thought he was truly dangerous."

Except me.

And I didn't do enough to bring him in.

"Man, what rotten luck—to go away for a little fishing and end up in the one cabin in the Adirondacks where an escaped prisoner wants to hide out," Earl said after Frank got back to Trout Run and filled him in on what had happened at the fishing cabin. "It's like being one of the three people out of a hundred thousand at the Boston Marathon to get hit with that terrorist's bomb."

"Yeah, what are the odds?"

Frank set his coffee cup down. What were the odds? Astronomical.

He crossed the office to stand before Earl's desk. "The Marathon bombers intentionally placed their bombs at the finish line because they knew that would be the most crowded place. What if Ronnie didn't just stumble onto that fishing cabin? What if someone knew Cottlemeir would be there with his truck and that person tipped Ronnie off? What if it's the same person who's been delivering food?"

Earl reared back as if Frank had spit in his face. "You think someone in Trout Run set up poor Mr. Cottlemeir to be murdered? C'mon—people might have sympathy for Ronnie, but no one would do that."

"Maybe they never imagined Ronnie would kill the guy. They just figured they'd offer Ronnie an ideal opportunity: remote location...one lone man...grab the truck and go."

Earl nodded slowly. "Yea-a-h, I could see that. But why did it go so wrong? It's not like they fought over the truck keys. Ronnie stood in the door of the cabin and—"

"Executed him. And calmly walked over and took the keys." Frank banged his fists together. "Whoever's helping Ronnie doesn't really understand who they're dealing with. But I do. And I think Meyerson is finally taking Ronnie seriously."

"Does he believe now that someone's helping Ronnie?"

Frank's eyes scanned the office. The straggly potted plant that Anita had commented on reproached him from its spot atop the file cabinet. Some things never changed: the office décor and Meyerson's unwillingness to ever admit Frank was right. "He's not telling me. But this murder makes the sheriff and the jail staff look even worse for letting Ronnie escape, and the state police look incompetent for letting him slip through their fingers so many times. Meyerson had his back up at the crime scene, but honestly, if we come up with some leads for him, he's going to take them."

"We need to know certain things." Earl pulled out a yellow legal pad. "One—how did the helper know Cottlemeir would be at the cabin last weekend?"

"It's gotta be someone who either knows Cottlemeir or, more likely, knows the guy from Keeseville who owns the cabin. I'd love to talk to him, see who he knows in Trout Run. But Meyerson's going to interview him. I can't go near the guy."

Earl kept his eyes on his note pad as he doodled a fat moose. "I know people in Keeseville."

Frank chuckled. "I bet you do."

Earl looked up and grinned. "I'll just keep an ear tuned to what people are saying." He wrote on the notepad again. "Okay, two—if someone knew Cottlemeir was going to be at the cabin, how would that person alert Ronnie? If someone's helping him, how are they communicating?"

Frank picked up the dying philodendron and dropped it in the trash. "If we knew that, we'd know everything."

CHAPTER 27

NEWS OF JOE COTTLEMEIR'S MURDER topped every newscast from Saratoga to Plattsburgh, but the people of Trout Run and Verona knew more about the crime than any reporter.

They say he was unrecognizable.

...nearly decapitated

I bet Ronnie's on his way to Mexico in that truck.

No, they say Ronnie's got enough weapons and food to hole up for months. If the Feds try to take him, it'll be another Ruby Ridge.

"They" was the most widely quoted source. But even though the information people traded was wildly inaccurate, Frank sensed that the tide had finally turned against Ronnie. Rollie Fister reported a rush of business from people buying new locks, and all along the school bus routes, parents waited with their kids.

Frank squinted out the office window toward Malone's Diner and finally took up a pair of binoculars. Just as he suspected, the neon green R^3 sign no longer hung on the diner's front door.

He decided to let Marge back into his good graces and eat an early dinner at the diner. If Marge was aware of Frank's recent absence, she didn't let on. His favorite table, the small booth for two near the window, was free. He settled in and studied the menu. After being away for more than a week, Frank thought everything looked good.

A repeated pinging sound made him look up. There in the back booth against the wall sat Anita and Olivia. They weren't speaking to each other. Anita gazed into the screen of a laptop placed beside her chef's salad, while Olivia was utterly engrossed in a cellphone she cradled in her hands. The phone pinged again, and Olivia's thumbs moved across the screen.

Texting! Lucy had been right. Anita had quickly gotten Olivia the phone Lucy and Edwin had denied her. Frank raised the menu in front of his face and peeked over the top. Other than the phone, Olivia looked like her usual self. He needn't have bothered being discreet. Anita and Olivia were both so absorbed in their devices that Frank could have stared at them as if they were pandas in the zoo and they wouldn't have noticed.

When the waitress arrived, Frank ordered the chicken potpie and surrendered his menu. Now he watched Olivia with no cover. Who could she be trading messages with so intently? Some boy? Why wasn't she playing board games with her girlfriends? Why wasn't she doing her homework or reading a book?

Why weren't mother and daughter talking to each other?

The waitress cleared their plates and dropped off their check. Anita closed her laptop, and still without saying a word, the two rose and headed for the door.

As they passed him, Frank looked up. "Hi, Olivia. Hi, Anita."

Anita nodded curtly, but Olivia looked happy to see him.

He scrambled for something better to say than "how's school?" The Spring Fling talent show was coming up. All the kids loved that. "Are you getting excited for the Spring Fling?"

"Yeah. I know some kids who doing a dance routine in it."

"Maybe you'll dance or sing next year, eh?"

Anita kept walking toward the door.

"Maybe." Olivia tossed her long hair before she followed.

In her earlobes, tiny silver earrings sparkled.

When the chicken potpie arrived, Frank found his appetite had vanished. He prodded at the crust, fuming. What would Anita allow Olivia to do next—get a tattoo? Follow rock bands around all summer long?

His thoughts were interrupted by a loud conversation at the counter. The Stulke brothers spouted off to anyone who would listen. "Ol' Ronnie outsmarted the heat again," one said.

"Yep, he got himself a truck now. They won't never catch him now, right Marge?"

Marge snorted. "I didn't think Ronnie had that much balls. But I guess he does."

Balls? Did it take balls to shoot an unarmed man in the back?

Frank shoved his plate across the table and stood. "Ronnie Gatrell is not some quirky folk hero," he sputtered as he turned toward the door. "He killed a man, the father of three, sneaked up behind him while he was cleaning a fish for his dinner and shot him in the back of the head.

Ronnie is a vicious, cowardly psychopath, and if I find out who's been helping him, I guarantee you that person will be looking at time behind bars." Frank started to open the door, and doubled back, pointing a finger at Marge and the Stulkes. "And I'm not eating here again as long as you tolerate people like them undermining law enforcement."

That evening when Penny asked why he was packing a bag lunch for the next day, she set off a tirade.

"Calm down, Frank. Pierced ears are not the first step on the road to a life of prostitution." Penny pulled out a can of hearty minestrone from the pantry and offered it to him. "And since when do you care what those moron Stulke brothers say about anything?"

"It's the principal of the thing. Anita is buying Olivia's love, intentionally bribing her with things that Lucy and Edwin said she shouldn't have. And I don't care about the Stulkes. I care that Marge tolerates them."

"Maybe it's not a bribe, dear. Maybe these are gifts from a mom who feels bad that she missed five years of her daughter's life. Can you blame Anita for wanting to do something to make it up to Olivia?"

"Why are you defending her when you know how devastated Lucy is?"

"I'm not defending her. It's just...well, there are no easy answers here, you know. I don't see Anita as evil. I don't blame her for wanting to mother her own child. Anita came into the library yesterday, did I tell you that?"

"No. What did she want?"

"She applied for a library card and she took out three books: Healthy Meals in Minutes, Raising Happy Teens, and The Hunger Games. That last one is a young adult novel."

"Yeah, I know. I've seen Olivia reading it."

"Exactly. I figured Anita must be checking it out for Olivia, so I told her that I knew Olivia had already read it. And Anita said, 'I know. That's why I want to read it.'"

"So you think Anita is trying to be a good mother."

"I do. I want to hate her, for Lucy's sake. But somehow I can't seem to do it."

CHAPTER 28

"DONALD AND I HUNG OUT at the Thirsty Moose last night." Earl set a cup of coffee and a maple Danish on the desk as Frank squinted at his computer screen.

"Nice."

"In Keeseville."

Frank spun around. "Did you hear something?"

"The guy who owns the cabin is president of the Ausable Rod and Reel Club. He knows everybody and everybody knows him. The kind of guy who buys strangers drinks and offers rides to hikers. He'd let just about anyone who liked to fish use that cabin."

Frank scowled. "So he might have told any number of people that Cotttlemeir would be at the cabin that weekend." He turned back to his work. "Sorry for sending you clear over there on a wild goose chase."

"No problem." Earl bit into his jelly donut. "The Moose is a fun place. Guess what someone tried to sell me at the bar."

"Weed?" Frank grinned. "Don't tell me you made an arrest over there!"

"Pills. But not the kind that get you arrested."

Earl reached into his pocket and produced a green and white bottle.

"VitaVine." Frank read the label aloud. "Is it some kind of vitamin? Did you buy them to counteract the effect of all those donuts?"

"Nah. It's not real vitamins, it's some kinda bogus supplement. My mom and my Aunt Sheila got invited to a VitaVine party." Earl swallowed the last of his donut. "They both bought a bottle—it's pretty cheap—but the real point of the party was to recruit more people to sell the stuff. The lady who held the party kept telling them they'd make so much money, they could quit their jobs and work from home."

"I hope your mom didn't quit her job."

"Nah, my mom always says there's no such thing as a free lunch. Sheila was the one who was tempted. I told her to leave it alone—it's called multi-level marketing, but it's really nothing but a Ponzi scheme. We learned all about them in fraud class."

Earl studied the label of the pills. "'A proprietary blend of minerals and herbs'. It's probably nothing but baking soda and dried up grass. Did you know the FDA doesn't regulate this stuff at all? You could make anything into a pill and sell it."

Frank held his hand out for the bottle. "And people do. But I'm surprised there's anyone willing to buy it in Trout Run."

"That's the point. The only way to actually make any money is to recruit more sellers. They all have to buy the pills they're going to sell. Pretty soon, everyone you know is a seller, and no one's left to be a buyer. And the only person to make money is the person at the top of the pyramid."

"Sounds like you really paid attention in fraud class. Did you learn about Nigerian Prince email scams, too?"

"We did! It was really interesting." A fine shower of powdered sugar fell off Earl's fingers as he lectured. "You would think that everyone knows about that by now, but they keep doing it because it still works. The slogan of the fraud squad is, 'There's a sucker born every minute. That's why we have lifetime job security.' Did you know those operators actually share mailing lists of people who have fallen for scams? If you've fallen for one scam, you're actually more likely to fall for another."

"Really? They sell lists of senile old people?"

Earl kept up his lecture as he prepared for the morning patrol. "Actually, seniors aren't the most common victims; they just tend to report the fraud more often. Younger people with financial problems and an over-confident personality are the most likely to get scammed."

"Huh. Well, there are plenty of people with financial problems around here. I guess one of them invited your mom and Aunt Sheila. What's the hostess's name?"

Earl shrugged. "I'm pretty sure the party was in Verona. So the VitaVine network has spread from Keeseville to Verona."

Frank tossed the pill bottle to Earl. "But the buck stops at Earl Davis, fraud buster."

CHAPTER 29

"MEYERSON CALLED," EARL ANNOUNCED AS Frank entered the office.

"What did he want?"

"Wouldn't say. You're supposed to call him."

Frank scowled. When Earl was a civilian Meyerson had always refused to tell him anything. But now that he was a sworn officer, surely Meyerson could get the stick out of his ass and treat Earl like a colleague, not a flunky.

Frank swallowed his irritation and dialed.

"Bennett. The CSI report on Cottlemeir's truck and the cabin are in."

Frank tapped a pencil on his knee, rocking back in his chair. "Yeah?"

"Negative."

"Negative for what?"

"Gatrell. His fingerprints are nowhere in the cabin or the vehicle."

Frank sat up. "He wore gloves. We know he stole a pair. And what about he boots? The killer tracked through the blood."

"The tread marks don't match the brand of boots Gatrell stole. And the print is approximately two sizes smaller than those boots."

"What about the bullet?" Frank could hear the desperation in his own voice.

"Different caliber—25-20 Winchester. The gun Gatrell stole was a seven millimeter."

Frank hunched over his desk and gripped the phone. "No, it can't..."

"Gatrell didn't kill Cottlemeir. I didn't think it looked like his work. He's a crackpot, not a killer." Meyerson's tone of voice changed from matter-of-fact to smug. "Looks like Gatrell's not the menace you've been making him out to be. He's just a crazy backwoodsman. If he can survive blackfly season, he might stay out there all summer. But when winter rolls around, he'll have to come in. We'll get him then."

"What's that supposed to mean? You're giving up looking for Ronnie?"

"Resource allocation. I have a murder to investigate. I've spent too much money and manpower on Gatrell. I have no choice but to redirect some of my staff. I'll keep a couple guys on the hunt for Ronnie, but I can't afford more."

Click.

Frank leaned back in his chair and kneaded his eyes. Penny scolded him for this habit, said it was damaging, but it sure felt good especially when the world he was looking at made no sense whatsoever.

He told Earl the news without opening his eyes. Earl knew better than to offer the first opinion. The silence helped him think.

How could Cottlemeir's murder be the work of someone other than Ronnie Gatrell? How many dangerous lunatics could possibly be roaming the backwoods of the High Peaks at any given time? What were the odds?

CHAPTER 30

THE NEWS THAT RONNIE GATRELL hadn't killed Joe Cottlemeir spread through the High Peaks faster than a flash flood, and with equally unpredictable results. People who yesterday had barricaded themselves in their houses because they were terrified of becoming Ronnie's next victim now said they had never believed that Ronnie had killed that guy in the first place. Cottlemeir was an outsider, a downstater, and he must've been killed by the same breed.

Frank replayed his vow to never eat at Malone's again over and over in his mind. Why had he made such a scene? How would he live this down? He drove clear to Verona to eat at the sandwich shop there, then decided to go home early and take a nap. After all, he had to come back on duty tonight to direct traffic after the Spring Fling at the high school.

Despite the relentless hammering and sawing of the workmen, Frank stole an hour's nap with the benefit of Vivaldi played through his noise-cancelling headphones. When he woke, the workers had packed up for the day, and he found Penny in the living room threading the new curtains she'd ordered onto the curtain rod.

"Thank goodness you're awake. I thought I might have to drill the holes for the brackets myself," Penny said.

Frank shuddered. Penny's tendency to eyeball instead of measure made her dangerous in the vicinity of power tools.

"I solved the mystery of why Caroline won't talk to you." Penny said, handing Frank the drill.

Frank paused in lining up the brackets. "How?"

"I called Eric at work. We had a nice talk."

Frank descended the stepladder. "How do you know Eric's work number?"

"Unlike you, I actually listen when he talks about his job. I went to his company website and found his email. I told him how concerned we were and asked him to call me when he had a moment to chat. He called seconds after I hit send."

Penny was looking smug, a quality he didn't find particularly endearing. But he was dying to know what Eric had said. He would never have called his son-in-law himself.

"And..."

Penny crossed the room and picked up the framed photo of Estelle and Caroline from the bookshelf. "Do you know where this was the last time Caroline was here?"

"How should I know? She hasn't been here since that weekend in January when they all came up to go skiing."

"We had just begun the remodeling project a few days before. Remember the day the guys used sledgehammers to knock down the kitchen wall and my favorite vase crashed off the shelf in here?"

Frank nodded. There had been some tears over that loss.

"After that happened, I packed up everything fragile that might get broken, even if it wasn't near where the men were working."

Frank gazed at the photo in Penny's hand, the last one taken of his wife and daughter. Caroline and Estelle laughing, caught in a moment of candid joy. Two weeks later, Estelle was dead. "She thought I'd gotten rid of her favorite picture of her and her mom."

"She thought I made you get rid of it, and you agreed to keep me happy." Penny smiled. "Don't forget, I'm the wicked stepmother."

"And I'm the sad old codger trying to satisfy his trophy wife." Frank set down his drill. "If only she knew, that photo made me realize—"

"What?"

"The first time I invited you here, I'd been nervous as a cat before you came, straightening up, wanting to make a good impression. I was thinking of putting that picture up in the guest room so you wouldn't have to see it. But you arrived before I had a chance to move it. When you came into this room, you went straight for the picture. You weren't uncomfortable at all. You really studied it. And you told me how beautiful it was. And that's when I knew."

"Knew what?"

"That I was falling in love with you."

Penny pulled him into her arms. "I've never felt threatened by Estelle. She's a part of you. In fact, I owe her a debt. She broke you in."

"That's for sure. You wouldn't have wanted the twenty-one-year-old me."

"Sometimes I feel her presence here. When Caroline wouldn't speak to you, I was so worried. I didn't want you to gain me if it meant losing her. One afternoon, after the workmen left, I sat in here and talked to Estelle, told her how I was trying but I couldn't seem to get anything right. Cried a little."

"Don't tell me she answered you."

Penny handed him the rod with the new curtains. "There's no need to call the mental health clinic. I'm not hearing voices. But I did feel better. And later that night when I was lying in bed, the idea just popped into my head that I should call Eric. So here we are."

Frank set the curtain rod in the bracket and reached for his phone. "So I can call her right now and everything will be all right. Eric must've told her about the misunderstanding by now."

Penny lunged for the phone. "No! Caroline will be even madder if she thinks Eric and I have been plotting behind her back."

Frank massaged his temples. "This is too much for me. I know why she's not speaking to me, but I can't act on that information?"

"You just need to be indirect, dear. How about this: write Caroline an email about something else—maybe send her an interesting article—and then in a chatty way at the end just mention how glad we are to have the remodeling almost over and Penny has been so busy unpacking the boxes of all the photos and knick-knacks she put away for safekeeping. How does that sound?"

"I don't chat in emails." Frank banged the stepladder over to the other window. "If I send her an article, I just say, 'I thought you'd be interested in the attached.' "

Penny wrapped her arms around her legs and rested her chin on her knees. "The thing I love about you is the thing that's screwing us to the wall here."

"What, my tactlessness?"

"Your honesty."

Penny leaped up. "What if I send Caroline an email and tell her that when I unpacked the photo, I noticed the frame had gotten chipped. I want to have it reframed as a surprise Father's Day gift for you. And then I can send two photo frame choices and ask her which one she likes better. Wouldn't that work?"

Frank felt two opposing waves rise up within him. One was a wave of love for his wife, who was willing to do anything to solve a mess she hadn't had a hand in creating. The other was a wave of irritation at his daughter. What the hell was wrong with her? She couldn't just say, "What happened to the picture of Mom and me that used to be here?" She had to sulk and fume and make everyone around her miserable?

He swiped the screen of his phone. "Or I could just call her right now and tell her to stop being such a silly spoiled brat."

Penny squeezed his hands in hers. "Try it my way first, dear, please."

"It's hard for her, Frank. She misses her mother. It's not fair that I get to enjoy the boys instead of Estelle."

"She said she was happy for us. She gave me her blessing."

Penny ran her hand over his forehead, smoothing back hair that wasn't out of place. "Saying it is easy. Living it is hard."

CHAPTER 31

FRANK TRUDGED TOWARD THE PATROL car as the last of the volunteers cleaned up after the annual Spring Fling. Traffic out of the school parking lot had been insane: parents stopping in the middle of the road, kids darting between cars, impatient drivers trying to pass on the right. His neon reflective vest, whistle, and color-tipped flashlight were insignificant weapons in the battle against drivers crazed to get home after three hours of tap-dance routines, feedback-infused guitar jams, and off-key renditions of Adele's latest love ballad. He slid behind the wheel and rested his head with his eyes shut to get back his energy before driving home.

Someone knocked on his car window.

Frank opened his eyes to see Anita Veech peering in at him.

He powered down the window. Strange that she was still here; he doubted she would have volunteered for the cleanup committee. And it was pushing eleven—Olivia should be in bed by now.

"Hi, Anita—car trouble?" He hoped his tone was friendly and concerned.

She shook her head, but didn't speak. Then she took a deep breath. "Have you seen Olivia?"

He bolted out of his slouch. "Seen her? What do you mean? She's not waiting in your car?"

Anita gave a half-shake of her head, more twitch than dissent. "I figured she'd be here, but she's not."

Frank got out of the car. "Start at the beginning. Who did Olivia come to the Spring Fling with?"

Anita shrugged. "She's been talking about going for days. I didn't really pay her much mind. Then I got home from work today and she wasn't home. Usually she leaves me a note or sends me a text. She didn't answer when I called. I figured she got busy makin' plans."

"Busy with plans? Since when do twelve-year-olds get to make their own plans?"

Anita looked down and kicked at the dirt on the shoulder of the road. "I figured she probably didn't want to come to this show with me. She probably wanted to be with her friends. I figured she musta got a ride with one of them. So fine. I'd just come over here and get her when all the excitement was over. Except I didn't see her come out. I saw that pack of girls she runs with and she wasn't with them. So then I figured...."

Despite the chilly spring air, Frank felt beads of sweat pop out on his forehead. "Figured what?"

"She might be with those Bates people."

Those Bates people. Those parents who love her. Those guardians who supervise her.

"You think she went back to Edwin and Lucy? Why? Did you and Olivia have an argument?"

Anita shrugged. "No fights. But I don't know what's in her head. I thought you could call them."

Frank was already punching the screen of his phone. Edwin's phone rang and rang. Of course, they were asleep by now. They hadn't gone to the Spring Fling. No need to be cruelly reminded of their childless state.

As the phone continued to ring, another thought popped into his head. Maybe they had Olivia and were refusing to answer his call.

Finally, a groggy Edwin answered. "Hullo?"

Frank's heart clenched. How could he ask this question? "Edwin, it's Frank. Is...is Olivia there by any chance?"

All signs of sleep disappeared from Edwin's voice. "Olivia? Why would she be here? Wha—? You mean she's not with Anita?"

"Uh, correct. Anita is with me now. She thought Olivia might have gone..." He caught himself before the word 'home' left his tongue. "... gone back to the inn."

"Edwin? Edwin? What's going on?" Frank could hear Lucy's plaintive voice in the background.

"I'm going to check her room," Edwin said. "The back door is always unlocked. Maybe she slipped in and went straight to her bed."

Frank could hear the scuffling of their footsteps and the bang of the bedroom door opening. Then silence.

"She's not here, Frank. Where the hell is she?"

"You said you didn't see Olivia with her friends here at the Fling. Did you stop and talk to any of them?"

Anita looked past him at the shadowy hulk of the high school. "They were with their parents. I didn't want to..."

Even through his rising anxiety, Frank felt a stab of sympathy for Anita. She still saw herself as an outcast here. Any other mother would have rushed up to the other parents, totally willing to ask for help. Anita was reluctant, afraid of their judgment. She knew the other mothers wouldn't rally round her with concern and support. More likely Anita would face raised eyebrows...pursed lips...unspoken words.

Can't you keep track of your child?

Aren't you in control?

He knew because the same thoughts were running through his head.

"What about Jenny Kellum, the girl who received your letters from prison? Did you call her?"

Anita gave a quick shake to her head. "Jenny and Olivia...they're, they're not really so tight anymore."

No doubt Mrs. Kellum had been horrified by what her daughter had done. She'd probably stepped in to break up the friendship just as Lucy had predicted.

Frank put his hand on Anita's shoulder. "Let's go back to your place so I can check it out. Then I'll go over to the inn."

"Can't you get the phone company to track her through her cell phone?" Anita asked.

Frank brightened. "You have that special GPS software that lets parents track their kids?"

Anita shook her head. "That's real expensive. We just have the basic plan. But on TV the cops can always track the location of the phone. Can't you do that?"

"That's more effective in a city with a lot of cell towers. But we'll try. Let's go to your apartment first."

Frank followed Anita back to her apartment. The entrance was up a flight of outdoor steps that led to a rear-facing deck. Anita had left the porch light on, but the dim bulb illuminated only a small circle around the door. There was no sign of forced entry. Frank shined his flashlight over the deck railing into the back yard. Hard to see much but two Adirondack chairs and a small raised bed garden plot.

"What's beyond the back yard?" Frank asked.

"The yard drops off kinda steep at the back end. Stony Brook is down below, but there's no path. You'd like to break your leg going down that way."

Maybe Anita would, but Frank had more confidence in a nimble twelve-year- old. He would check it out later. For now, he followed Anita into the apartment.

The place was tidy, but Spartan. The main room contained a beige loveseat, a mismatched green easy chair, a TV, and a dinette table with two chairs. There were shades on the windows but no curtains. No artwork adorned the walls. A counter separated the tiny kitchen from the rest of the room. One plate, one glass, and one fork rested in the dish drainer.

"Are those from your dinner?" Frank asked.

Anita nodded. "But she musta been here after school. There's a banana peel in the trash."

Frank peered into a mostly empty trashcan. "Anything else? Any sign that someone else was with her here?"

Anita shook her head. "Not that I can tell."

Frank turned down a short hall: a small bathroom; one bedroom with a twin bed, a night stand with a book and a couple bottles of medications, and a card-table and folding chair, illuminated by a glowing laptop screen. Frank took a step into the room. Meaningless letters, numbers and symbols marched across the screen of the computer—computer code, he supposed. He paused to check the bottles on the nightstand: nothing dangerous, just Tylenol and some kind of vitamins. Across the hall, another bedroom. This one had posters on the walls, a fuzzy purple pillow on the bed, a beanbag chair in the corner occupied by a menagerie of stuffed animals. Frank entered and opened the closet door. The short pole was crammed with hanging clothes. A small set of plastic stackable drawers was full of underwear and socks.

"Is anything missing?" Frank asked.

"Sure doesn't look like it. But the kid's got way more clothes than me. I've never seen her wear the same thing twice."

Frank tried to ignore Anita's aggrieved tone. Of course, Olivia had brought with her all the clothes Edwin and Lucy had bought…more, and better quality, clothes than Anita could afford. Had these clothes been a bone of contention between mother and daughter?

It soon became apparent that Anita didn't have a clue what the names and phone numbers of Olivia's friends were. Anita shared her own cell phone with him readily enough, but the string of three and four word text messages between Anita and Olivia dated over the past few days was not illuminating.

AT DINER. HOME @7
STAYED AFTER SCHOOL. WILL GET RIDE.
THERE'S NO MILK.

"Let's try to call her again." Frank pressed call. Immediately, a low buzzing noise emanated from under the stuffed animals on the bedroom chair.

Frank pulled out Olivia's phone. "Looks like she intentionally left it behind."

"I guess she watches those cop shows too," Anita said.

"We need to call the homes of all her friends," Frank said. "Lucy will have their names and numbers. I'm going over to the inn. You stay at the apartment in case she comes back here."

Anita nodded. "You think....I mean....She's just foolin' around, right?"

"The only thing I'm sure of is that no one can predict what teenagers will do. We need to find her before she gets hurt."

The inn's lights were blazing when Frank pulled up. He found Lucy and Edwin in the kitchen, Edwin pacing, Lucy already on the phone. Everything about the kitchen looked the same—cheerful mismatched china on the shelves, overgrown herbs crowding the windowsill, stacked tins full of Edwin's cookies—yet everything felt off-kilter.

"I'm sorry to call you so late, Marie, but is Olivia sleeping over with Katie?" Lucy held the phone to her ear with her left hand and scribbled furiously on a note pad with her right.

"She's already called Olivia's three best friends," Edwin explained. "No one has seen Olivia since the end of the school day. According to these kids, Olivia rode the bus home and said she'd see everyone later at the Spring Fling."

Lucy hung up and massaged her temples. "I've called every single girl in the eighth grade, even the ones Olivia never socialized with. No one has seen her. She definitely wasn't at the Spring Fling, and her best friend Ava was surprised. She texted Olivia, but Olivia didn't answer."

Now the tears spilled over. "Where could she be? She would never have missed the Fling. She's been talking about it since before....before she left us."

Edwin attempted to put his arm around his wife, but Lucy twisted away. "She left her alone. Anyone could have broken into that apartment. Someone abducted Olivia."

"There's no reason to think that." Frank sat at the kitchen table and extended a hand toward Lucy. "I've been to the apartment and there's no sign of forced entry or struggle."

Lucy twisted the sash of her bathrobe, resisting all efforts to console. "This never would have happened if they hadn't taken her away from us."

"Anita gets home from work by five-thirty every day. Olivia is only alone for a few—"

"She was never alone here. I never left her unsupervised!"

This was no time for parenting advice, but Frank suspected Olivia might have enjoyed a little unstructured downtime. And twelve wasn't too young to stay at home in the afternoon. But Lucy was clearly beyond reason. He turned toward Edwin. "Have you talked to Olivia at all recently? Do you have any idea if she was unhappy?"

"We're not permitted to have any contact," Lucy jumped in before Edwin could answer. "But her teacher told me—" Lucy pursed her lips.

"What?"

"I can't say. Ms. Elkins could get in trouble."

"We ran into Olivia's teacher at the Stop'N' Buy and she mentioned that her grades are slipping, that's all." Edwin set three mugs of tea on the table. "Hardly surprising, with all this upheaval."

"But have you talked to Olivia?" Frank turned from Lucy to Edwin, waiting for his response.

Edwin turned his back, rooting through some containers on the counter. "Olivia and I used to do most of our talking while I was cooking dinner for our guests. I still have to cook, but she's not here."

Before Frank could challenge this non-answer, Lucy started in again.

"What about Olivia's things? Was anything missing from her room?"

"Anita couldn't tell," Frank admitted. "The drawers and closet looked full, but that doesn't mean she couldn't have taken a few things with her."

Lucy slammed a glass on the counter and poured herself some red wine with a shaking hand. The tea was forgotten. "Let me go over there. I could tell you what's missing. I know every article of clothing my girl has. I know all her books, all her stuffed animals..." She took a swig of wine and choked on it, collapsing into a chair with mix of coughing and wailing.

"That's not a bad idea, but for now, let's stay focused on the friends. You said you called all the girls in her class. What about the boys? Could she have—"

"She's only twelve! She's not interested in boys. She thinks they're gross and dumb."

"Boys are gross and dumb, but that doesn't mean she's not interested.

What if an older boy showed her some interest? Any ideas?"

Lucy's eyes widened. "Oh, dear Lord—not that!" She grabbed the school directory. "I'll start calling the parents of all the boys."

"Luce, it's nearly one in the morning," Edwin objected. "Wait until tomorrow."

"She's out there." Lucy gestured to the wide outdoors. "Alone. And I won't stop until I find her and get her home safe." She began dialing. "Wherever home may be."

Frank pulled Edwin into the dining room.

"What did you two talk to Olivia about on your last night together?"

"Lucy and I sat down with her. We wanted to let her know that we weren't angry. But Lucy couldn't keep herself from crying. And that upset Olivia and she ran up to her room and refused to come out. So I ended up sitting on the hall floor outside her room, talking to her through the door. I told her how much we loved her. I told her we would always be there for her no matter what. That she could always come to us if she needed anything."

Frank forced Edwin to hold his gaze. "And has she?"

A split second of hesitation. A blink. "No."

Frank took a deep breath. "Edwin, this is difficult for me to ask, but I'd like to look around the inn—upstairs, the basement."

"What? You think I have her hidden here?" Edwin's eyes bulged. "How dare you!"

"I'm sorry, but the way you were talking when you first learned Anita wanted Olivia back, about running off to South America—I have to explore every possibility. It's my job to rule things out."

"She told you to do this, didn't she? She sent you over here because she's a paranoid nutcase, just like her old man."

"Anita thought it was possible Olivia might have returned here. She doesn't suspect you of taking her."

"But you do? My friend?"

"If Olivia doesn't turn up tomorrow, we'll have to call Trudy. She's bound to ask that question. It would be incompetent of me not to search here. This is hard for me, Edwin. Don't make me get a warrant."

Edwin spun around. "Fine. Search my home. Look in all the closets and under the beds. See if you find Olivia bound and gagged."

Frank put his hand on Edwin's shoulder. "I'm just ruling out the possibility."

Edwin shook free. "Fuck you, Frank."

The smell of coffee woke him. He'd stayed at the inn until nearly four, looking though the rooms Edwin and Lucy and Olivia occupied as their home, as well as the guest rooms, all vacant in the off-season. He went up to the attic and down to the basement, all the while avoiding Edwin and Lucy.

He found nothing suspicious.

Unwilling to wake his wife when he came home, he had stretched out on the sofa to catch a few hours of sleep. Now the sun poured through the east-facing window and Penny appeared in the living room bearing a mug of coffee. Frank sat up, massaging his stiff neck.

Penny sat beside him and offered the coffee wordlessly. After he'd drunk half of it, she began. "I feel like I should have met you at the inn last night."

Frank had filled her in with a quick phone call as he was driving to the Iron Eagle, but had insisted that she stay home.

"You couldn't have helped. It wasn't a social call."

"How are Lucy and Edwin?"

"Lucy is frantic. Edwin…." How was Edwin? Furious. Outraged.

Penny squinted without her contact lenses. "Why are you so quiet?"

He told her about the search.

Penny's eyes widened. "You thought they were hiding her there?"

"I had to rule out the possibility. I don't think she's at the inn, but that doesn't mean they're not involved."

"You don't think…it's not possible that… Edwin and Lucy arranged—" She couldn't continue.

"It's crossed my mind. Not Lucy—she was distraught at the news Olivia was missing. I know she's not that good an actress. But Edwin." Frank leaned back against the sofa and shut his eyes.

"Why? Was he acting strange?"

"No. He was consoling Lucy, trying to keep her calm. Which is what he might do if Olivia really were missing, but also if he'd taken her off somewhere and wasn't ready to let Lucy know."

"So, why…?"

"Because he didn't seem terrified, not like Lucy." Frank gulped his coffee. "And he was so furious at me."

Penny fussed with a ribbon on her nightgown. "People react differently in a crisis. You can't suspect him just because he wasn't hysterical."

In the kitchen, the theme music of the morning news program drifted from the radio. Outside a chickadee sang.

"It can't be a coincidence that she disappeared on the night of the Spring Fling." Frank spoke more to himself than to Penny. "The entire town was at the high school, including me and Earl. Anita thought Olivia was there. The streets were empty."

"But that would be a perfect situation for a kidnapper, too." Penny's worried eyes opened wide and she laced her fingers through his.

Frank squeezed her hand. "Despite all the publicity they attract, stranger kidnappings are extremely rare."

"You think Edwin paid someone to steal her? Planned it for last night? How would he do it?" Penny whispered.

"He's smart. He has resources. He used to live in Manhattan."

Penny shook her hand free of his grasp. "Edwin doesn't know people like that. He worked in publishing. How can you even think such a thing?"

Frank turned away from his wife's dismay. It was his job to think the worst about people, to think of all the crimes desperation might drive a good person to commit.

"The things Edwin said when Anita first came back—that was just talk," Penny said. "He calmed down after the hearing, once he realized—"

"Once he realized the legal system had let them down. Maybe that's when he started planning for this."

"Oh, Frank, no! He can't have done anything illegal. Not Edwin!" Penny paced around the room. "Olivia must have run off. Today she'll get scared and come home. Right?"

"I hope so."

Penny plopped down beside him again and forced him to look her in the eye. "What if she didn't run away? What are we going to do? Edwin and Lucy are our friends."

"Not we. Your job is still to be their friend. I'm the one with the problem."

CHAPTER 32

AS SOON AS HE GOT to the office Frank reported Olivia missing to the state police and to Trudy Massinay.

But Trudy already had the news.

"Edwin called me at daybreak. He says this disappearance is evidence Anita isn't supervising Olivia adequately."

Edwin hadn't wasted a moment getting that message out. "How did you respond?" Frank asked her.

"I assured him I was on top of the matter, but I had a hard time getting off the phone with him. Edwin can be very persistent."

"Yeah. Tell me about it." Frank wasn't about to share his suspicions about Edwin, but he did want her take on Olivia's disappearance. "Trudy, what do you think is going on? Were you aware that Olivia was unhappy living with Anita?"

"I don't think this episode is necessarily an indication that Olivia is unhappy with her mother. She's just very confused. She's been forced to choose between two sets of people she loves, two loyalties. It would seem she wants to get away from both of them. Unfortunately, I have no idea who she'd turn to as a neutral party." Trudy sighed. "Not me, obviously."

Frank set Earl to work filling out the paperwork to have her listed as a missing person. In the middle of the furor, Doris entered the office.

"Frank, Denise Kellum is on the phone. I told her you were real busy, but she insisted she has to talk to you."

Denise Kellum. Olivia's friend's mother. Owner of the fateful post office box. Frank snatched up the phone.

"Chief Bennett, I thought you should know. Jenny just went on Facebook and she says Olivia posted a selfie late last night and the message says she's fine and no one should look for her because they won't find her."

Earl quickly located the picture on Olivia's Facebook page.

The girl stared at the camera defiant, impudent.

"She doesn't look scared," Earl said, giving voice to Frank's thoughts. "I mean, someone could force her to post the picture, but they couldn't really force her to have that expression."

"She doesn't have her phone with her. So she used someone else's phone or computer to access her Facebook account. There must be a way to trace that."

Earl nodded. "I'll work that angle. It will take a while, though. For an adult's page, we'd need a search warrant. But since she's a minor, Facebook will consider our request without it. There are still hoops to jump through though."

"Well, start jumping."

What a day!

A cop should receive a hazardous duty bonus for interviewing middle-schoolers. He'd talked to every eighth-grader at High Peaks Middle School and every single one claimed to know nothing about the whereabouts of Olivia Veech. Kid A thought Kid B might know, but Kid B was the person who'd referred Frank to Kid A in the first place. And so it went, around and around in circles. On one point everyone—teachers and students alike—agreed: Olivia had been quiet and withdrawn since the return of her mother to Trout Run. Frank drove home with the sounds of high-pitched squealing, clanging locker doors, and garbled loudspeaker announcements ringing in his head. Someone at that school had to know something. Olivia wasn't Ronnie, living a hermit's life in the mountains. A twelve-year-old had to be with someone. Who?

He entered his house to merciful silence. The workers were gone for the day. No sign of Penny, but he didn't mind. Was tonight book club at the library? Probably. He seemed to recall Penny mentioning something this morning.

A couple hours to himself sounded good. Very good.

He changed into sweatpants and bedroom slippers, poured himself a beer, and stretched out on his recliner with his new LBJ biography.

The room grew dim as he read under the glow of the floor lamp. Eventually, his eyelids drooped and fell.

"Frank! Why aren't you dressed?" Penny stood at foot of the recliner with her hands on her hips.

"Huh?" What time was it? What day was it? Should he be at work?

"The fundraiser." Penny's normally cheerful face was a study in outrage.

"What fundraiser?"

"The Library Luau. The event I've been working on for months! I just popped home because I forgot the basket for the grand prize raffle and I figured you must already be on your way. Why are you napping?"

Frank dragged himself into a sitting position. The dropped book jabbed his leg.

"You would've slept right through the whole thing if I hadn't come home. I can't believe you forgot!"

"No, no—I just wanted to recharge before the party."

Penny grabbed her basket. "Get changed at meet me at the library. How will it look if my husband can't be bothered to come?"

His recliner vibrated with the force of the front door's slam.

What was wrong with him? Penny had been working long and hard on the Library Luau. If the party was fun and the silent auction successful, then the Luau would become a yearly event in Trout Run's social calendar, and she'd be able to count on an extra fifteen grand in the Library's budget. She was already nervous; the last thing she needed was to be irritated with her husband.

However, making small talk with Trout Run's most upstanding citizens was the last thing he felt like doing tonight. The brief nap made his desire to crawl into bed even more consuming. During the five long years of his bachelorhood, he'd missed having a partner in countless ways. But going to cocktail parties to be supportive wasn't one of them.

Nevertheless, he hauled himself upstairs, splashed cold water on his face, put on a clean shirt and pressed khakis, and headed back into town.

When Frank pulled up to the town green, the library glowed with bright lights. The daffodils Penny had planted last fall were blooming in cheery clusters beside the front walk. Why were there burning tiki lights by the front door? Oh—Luau, Hawaii. Right. Parked cars lined the street, so the party was well underway. At least he wouldn't have to make awkward conversation with the early birds.

He walked into a wall of heat and sound. The library had never been so packed with people. A teenage girl ran up and looped a plastic lei around his neck before he could dodge the assault.

"How many tickets do you want for the Tricky Tray, Frank?" Ardyth Munger asked from her table at the door. She wore a loud flowered dress and sipped from a glass with an umbrella floating in it.

Frank handed over a twenty. Ardyth's pursed lips and raised brows forced him to dig back into his wallet for a second portrait of Jackson.

"Keep the stub and put your tickets in the basket in front of the items you'd like to win," Ardyth said.

The prize table swarmed with sharp-elbowed ladies eagerly depositing their tickets, a crowd Frank had no desire to engage. Occasionally, he caught a glimpse of the prizes: big items like a power-nailer donated by Venable's Hardware and snowshoes donated by The Rock Slide, and lots of smaller items like handcrafted pottery, necklaces, paintings of Adirondack scenes, toys, fancy food. Local stores and individual craftspeople had given generously, unable to resist Penny's pitch that having an item in the silent auction would be good for their business. Frank knew he was being a stick-in-the-mud, but he didn't understand people's willingness to spend a hundred dollars on tickets for a chance to win something they could've bought for twenty-five bucks. Luckily for Penny, most people didn't share his views, because the action around the prize table got more frenetic by the minute.

He headed over to the bar table to get a glass of wine.

"You won't be able to tear your tickets with a wine glass in your hand," Gage Shelby, the bartender, warned.

"What about you? My wife's got you barricaded here, working instead of partying."

Gage handed over a full glass. "Oh, I don't mind. It's great to be part of an event that pulls together so many different people from the community."

Frank scanned the room. Gage was right—Penny had managed to attract people to the Luau who didn't normally darken the doors of the library. He spotted one of the carpenters from the remodeling team at his house and a few guys who would normally be at the Mountainside at this time of night. A small clutch of teenagers grazed around the snack table.

Alone in a corner, Frank spotted a forlorn Pam Gatrell. With her stood a young man, clearly the elusive RJ. He was a handsome kid with his father's intense dark eyes and his mother's wide smile. Frank walked up, sipping his wine. "Nice to see you here, Pam." He extended his hand. "And you must be RJ."

Like a typical young teenager, RJ fumbled the handshake and had a hard time meeting Frank's eye. "Hi," he muttered. He looked like he'd shot up recently and didn't know how to handle so much length in his arms and legs.

Pam eyed Frank uneasily, as if she expected him to start interrogating RJ right here at the party.

Instead, Frank said, "Do me a favor, RJ. Go play these tickets."

RJ looked confused. "What do you want to win?"

"Win something for yourself." Frank held out the tickets. "It won't look right if the librarian's husband wins a prize. People will think the drawing is rigged."

Frank could see longing doing battle with fierce pride on the boy's face.

"I'll try to win something for you, Mom. What do you want? A vase? A picture?"

Although her son was nearly as tall as she was, Pam ruffled his hair. "Spread the tickets around however you want, honey. Maybe you'll get lucky."

She watched him lope toward the prize table. "He's such a good boy. So thoughtful. Thank you for giving him those tickets. He really wanted to play. I didn't want to come tonight—we can't afford it—but RJ seemed to want to get out of the house, so I gave in."

Frank wondered why RJ wasn't hanging out with the other kids. Had he approached them and been rejected earlier in the evening?

"I imagine you've had a rough couple of days with the latest developments," Frank said.

Pam swallowed a slug of wine. "First the state police came pounding on my door saying they think Ronnie killed that poor fisherman and RJ is smuggling Ronnie food. They had RJ in tears with all their stupid questions. Then the next day, they're like 'never mind' and that Meyerson guy won't even answer my calls."

Frank knew this wasn't the right time or place, but he couldn't stop himself. "Pam, is there any possibility that RJ is working with someone else to get Ronnie supplies?"

For a moment he worried that she would explode right then and there, but then her face crumpled. "Look at him," she said softly.

Frank followed her gaze. RJ was tearing off the tickets Frank had given him and thinking long and hard before he deposited each one in a prize basket. Occasionally he would steal a glance at the teenagers in the corner, but turn away quickly if they seemed to be looking back at him.

"All he wants is for his life to be normal like any other kid's," Pam said. "He's so torn up inside, he can't even find the words to talk about it."

One of the guys who normally drank beer at the Mountainside wandered by clutching a tumbler of wine in each hand. "Hey, Pam—the drug store's offering a basket of bug spray and first aid stuff. Better try to win that for Ronnie!" He stumbled away, chuckling at his wit.

"Ben's an idiot," Frank said. "Don't listen to anything he has to say."

Pam's mouth formed a hard line, her shoulders pulled back in defiance. She stared out at the crowd of people she'd known all her life. "It's not just him. It's as if people blame me for what happened, but they don't blame Ronnie. They're cheering for him to stay on the loose out in the backcountry at the same time they're refusing to let me watch their babies or even let their older kids hang out with RJ. Hypocrites!"

Frank was glad he'd cheered up RJ with the tickets, but Pam fairly radiated hostility. Small wonder no one wanted to chitchat with her. He scrambled for something innocuous to say and came up short. Across the room, he spied Edwin talking to Rollie Fister. Normally, Edwin would be a lifeline in social situations like this, but everything had changed since Olivia's disappearance. Frank turned his head to avoid making eye contact with Edwin. Really, when he thought about it, wasn't it odd that Edwin was here at all? Would a father feel like going to a party when his daughter was missing? He scanned the room again. No Lucy. No Anita.

"How's the job in Plattsburgh?" Frank asked Pam as a last, desperate conversational gambit.

"Miserable. I come home smelling like a big fried chicken, and I'm away from RJ for too many hours a day. But what else can I do? We can't curl up and starve."

Finally the chairwoman of the Trout Run Garden Club wandered by with a flower blossom behind her ear and Frank asked her a question about spring cleanup day. Having gotten her started on the topic of planting spring flowers, on which she could cheerfully talk for hours, Frank was able to slip away.

Desperate to avoid Edwin, Frank slinked into the stacks. In the 800s (Biography) he encountered Marilee of the closed Honeycomb Bakery coming through the back door trying to balance two trays of mini cheesecakes and éclairs.

"Whoa. Can I take one of those for you?"

"Thanks, that would be a great help. My daughter was supposed to be here tonight to serve, but she just started a new job in a restaurant in Placid and couldn't get off."

Frank took a tray of desserts from Marilee and followed her to the buffet table in the lobby. "I'm sorry to hear about the bakery closing. Glad to see you're still doing parties."

Marilee's mouth tightened as she bent over her creations, arranging them in artistic groupings. "We were just starting to make some money with the catering. Now, we're back in debt again. If only I hadn't listened to—"

Frank followed her gaze across the room. Leon Shelby stood talking to a young couple. He had his hand on the man's shoulder. Even at this distance, Frank could hear Leon's advice. Gage, still pouring wine at the bar, kept one eye on his father. "You can't go wrong with that property," Leon told the couple. "Great location. Guaranteed to increase in value over the years."

"Huh!" Marilee said. "Those two better watch their wallets."

"Leon gave you bad advice about the bakery?" Frank asked.

"Yes. Leon Shelby was one of our best customers when we were just selling baked goods out of our house. He kept saying we should open a retail outlet, that he'd keep an eye out for a good property for us. I didn't want to take the risk, but my daughter is young. She kept telling me we had to think bigger if we ever wanted to make our dream of baking full-time a reality. She kept reading me stories about Steve Jobs and Mark Zuckerburg, and Gary Erickson."

"Gary Erickson?"

"He's the guy who makes Cliff Bars. He started out baking with his mom and now his company is worth a billion dollars." Marilee held the back door of the library open for Frank. "I told her I didn't need a billion dollars. I'd be happy with a reliable car and a new furnace for our house. I should have known better, but I didn't want to crush her dreams, ya know? Leon kept saying that property was perfect for our bakery—zoned commercial, low taxes, building in pretty good shape. All that was true, but there's no drive-by traffic there. We didn't capture any tourist business. Some days we'd be open for hours before even one customer showed up in the store. Finally, we couldn't hang on any longer. We had to close down. Now Leon says it might be months…years…before he can sell that building for us. When he was trying to get us to buy it, it was the best place in the world. Now that he's selling it for us, it's got no end of problems."

Frank set the trays down and Marilee started arranging the tiny cakes. The more she talked, the madder she got until one strawberry tartlet sailed out of her fingers and hit the wooden floor with a splat. Frank knelt to wipe up the mess. "You think Leon tricked you intentionally?"

Marilee shrugged. "I don't know. What's the expression? Cavvy, cavvy-something."

"Caveat Emptor. Let the buyer beware."

"Yeah. I should have known to beware of someone who was such a smooth talker."

Moments later, Penny announced that the winning tickets for the Tricky Tray were about to be drawn. Frank settled in a corner with a plate of broken pastries and watched as grown women shrieked like they had been crowned Miss America just because they won a basket full of Mary Kay cosmetics. The announcement of the winner of the nail gun brought a round of fist bumps from the men. A vaguely familiar young woman who won six cooking lessons at the Iron Eagle wrapped her arms around Edwin, and his startled face disappeared into her cloud of curly red hair.

Winner after winner went forward to claim a prize. Frank watched RJ anxiously checking his ticket stubs every time a number was called. Was it too much to ask that the poor kid would win some trinket? Now the big lady who'd won the cooking lessons was standing with Edwin, Pam, and RJ. Edwin said something and the boy nodded and scuffed his sneaker into the floor. Finally, with just a few more prizes left to be awarded, RJ's face lit up and he darted forward with his ticket stub in hand. The announcer handed him a pair of porcupine quill dangling earrings made by the hippie chick sisters who ran a combination organic vegetable-funky craft stand at the farmers market. The prize wasn't much, but RJ seemed elated. At least he'd had the thrill of winning something.

The Tricky Tray ended and the party began to wind down. By 11:30, only Penny, Frank, and Ardyth remained. "Whew!" Penny blew upwards to blast her drooping bangs out of her eyes. Her eyes beamed with excitement above her smudged mascara. "Lots more people came than I expected. And people bid on the strangest things."

"Yes, Carl Fisk won the selection of homemade jams and fudge, and I know he's diabetic. And RJ Gatrell won a pair of earrings."

"I think he bid on those for his mom," Frank said.

Ardyth and Penny exchanged a glance. "Boys never know what their mothers like," Ardyth said. "Pam would never wear those."

"But I think everyone had fun, right?" Penny asked.

"No doubt about it," Ardyth said. "And I've done a rough tally of the money—$18,000!"

"Oh my God—now we'll be able to afford some online subscription databases like a real library."

"You did a fantastic job, Penny." Frank pulled her into a hug. "I'm so proud of you."

Penny snuggled against his shoulder for a moment, then stretched to look around him. "What's that on the prize table? Someone forgot to take what they won?" Penny sighed. "Now I suppose I'll have to deliver it to the winner tomorrow."

"I can do it for you when I'm on patrol," Frank said, and moved to get the basket.

Ardyth beat him to it. "No one won this one. No one even bid on it." She grimaced. "I'm not surprised. One year's supply of VitaVine Nutritional supplements." Ardyth tossed the pill bottles in the trash.

CHAPTER 33

FRANK WALKED INTO THE OUTER office the next day to find Doris already on the phone with a personal call. "Yes, I see why you're worried…that does seem odd." She caught sight of Frank, lowered her voice, and swiveled her chair. "Look, I can't talk now. Maybe later."

"What's up with Doris?" Frank asked Earl once he'd shut the door behind him. "She seems to be taking a lot of personal calls lately."

"Her niece is getting married soon. Must be wedding plans." Earl spoke without moving his gaze from his computer screen. "Frank, a response from Facebook came in overnight."

Finally, some useful information. "About where that picture was posted from? What do they say?"

Earl looked up with a frown. "The ISP address of the computer she used to post that picture—it belongs to the Iron Eagle Inn."

Frank scalded himself with the coffee he was pouring. "Shit!"

Earl offered him a paper towel. "Shit, you burned yourself or shit, Edwin might be involved in Olivia's disappearance?"

"Both. Well, that explains why he was having fun at the party last night. He's not worried about her. How could Edwin be so stupid? Did he really think we wouldn't check?"

"Now what are you going to do?"

"I'm going to go straight over there and—" Frank pulled his chair beside Earl's. "You better explain this Facebook thing to me in detail first."

"Wouldn't it make more sense for me to talk to Edwin? I know more about it, and…well, there will be less emotion between us."

Frank looked at his partner. Earl was his partner now. "I should recuse myself, right?"

Earl lifted his shoulders slightly. "Probably for the best."

"Okay. Go."

While Earl went to the inn, Frank occupied himself with the morning patrol. On his way out, he again heard Doris murmuring furtively on the phone. He hoped his glare and forceful door slam would encourage her to get back to work.

Thank God his patch of the Adirondacks was peaceful today. He had no patience for fender-benders or roads blocked by fallen trees when his brain was churning with anxiety to hear what Edwin had told Earl. In an hour and a half, Frank marched back into the town office.

Still, Doris was on the phone.

This time she made no effort to conceal the call. "No, no! Don't come here." Doris rolled her eyes like a cow that knew it was on the way to the slaughterhouse. "What do you mean, you're calling from the road? No, that's not a good idea!"

Frank stood in front of her desk with his hands on his hips. "What's going on? What's not a good idea?"

Doris held out the receiver to him. "It's Helen Cottlemeir. She wants to talk to you in person. She'll be here in an hour."

With a highly excitable woman yammering in each of his ears, it took Frank a good ten minutes to figure out what was going on. Apparently, Joe Cottlemeir's widow, Helen, had befriended Doris long-distance. She called several times a day to discuss the investigation of her husband's case because the state police had grown weary of her questions. Doris, incapable of saying no to anyone, had been agreeing with Mrs. Cottlemeir that something was fishy in the investigation. And somehow Helen Cottlemeir had construed that as permission to drive all the way up from Saratoga talk to Frank in person about her problems.

"You know I'm not working on your husband's case, right?" Frank had put the call on speakerphone.

Helen's plaintive voice filled the outer office. "I know. It's just—that other policeman, Lt. Meyerson—he doesn't listen to me. And now he won't even take my calls. So I just thought…I mean, you were so nice when it, it happened, I thought maybe I could tell you this and you would know what to do."

"Oh, yes," Doris chimed in. "Chief Bennett always knows what to do. And like I always say, he's really a lot nicer than people realize."

The combination of Doris's backhanded compliment, Meyerson's refusal to take calls from the victim's wife, and the fact that the woman was about to exit the Northway in Keene Valley wore down Frank's resistance. He was sure he'd regret it.

"Show her in when she gets here," Frank told Doris, but don't bother me before that.

Finally, he was alone with Earl.

"Well, what happened?"

"I talked to Edwin and Lucy separately," Earl said.

"Good. Exactly right."

"They both told me the same thing. The computer is in the office, and the office is directly accessible from the back hall, and the back door is always—"

"Unlocked. It is. I yell at them about that all the time," Frank said.

"So someone other than Edwin and Lucy could have accessed Facebook from that computer, but that doesn't explain the photo." Earl pulled out his notebook. "This is where Edwin got kinda agitated. You see, it's possible to share photo albums in the Cloud."

Frank shut his eyes. "What the hell does that mean?"

"The picture that was posted on Facebook came from Edwin and Lucy's Cloud account. But both of them claim they never saw it before. And both of them showed me their phones and the picture wasn't on either one. Lucy let me have access to their Cloud account because she was so sure I wouldn't find anything. But there was one shared album in their Cloud account—all pictures of Olivia clowning for the camera. Once I discovered that, Edwin got agitated and told me to leave. He wouldn't say another word. He kept hushing Lucy."

"So who was the album shared with?"

Earl shrugged. "On the screen it just said 'best friends.' If I could have kept digging, I could have found the email address of the other person. Now, we'll need a warrant to search. And Edwin's probably deleting the account right now."

Frank paced around the office. What was Edwin playing at? Was he hellbent on destroying his life? Was Olivia destined to have a parent or guardian in prison throughout her life?

"You know, Frank—this might look worse than it actually is," Earl said. "Maybe Edwin is as confused as we are. Maybe he's trying to protect Olivia, not himself."

Frank stopped pacing. "How so?"

"Olivia herself could have created that shared Cloud account. I mean, Lucy and Edwin both seemed surprised when I found it."

Frank made a keep rolling motion. He still didn't know where Earl was headed.

"So whoever she shared it with is who she's with now. And that person made it look like the Facebook post came from the inn."

"Are you saying Anita did this? Did she learn hacking in prison, too?"

"That would make more sense if Anita had lost custody." Earl ran his hands over his new buzz cut. "I dunno. I'm pretty confused."

"That makes two of us. We don't have enough evidence to arrest Edwin or anyone else. I guess I have to talk to Trudy next."

But Frank made no move to reach for the phone.

CHAPTER 34

DORIS TAPPED ON THE OFFICE door and poked her head in cautiously. She seemed to expect Frank might throw a shoe at her. "Mrs. Cottlemeir is here. And Earl, there's a call on line two about a stolen truck."

"Bring her in." Frank had to admit he was glad of the distraction. Earl slipped away to answer the truck complaint.

Doris bustled in with a cup of tea and a box of tissues for her new friend. She patted Mrs. C on the shoulder, gave Frank a guilty glance, and left.

"What can I do for you, ma'am? If there's something you need to know about how the investigation is progressing, I can call Lt. Meyerson and ask."

She nodded, twisting a tissue in her work-roughened fingers. "He gave me some updates at first, but lately…" She shook her head.

"Investigations take time. I understand how hard it is to wait. Still, he should take your calls." Frank reached for his phone. Putting Meyerson on the spot wouldn't bother him at all.

"I have a question I think you can answer, but first you have to know everything so you understand why I'm asking." She started digging through her large purse. "First there's this letter, which really threw me for a loop." She handed it across the desk to Frank. "He left it with all our financial records."

My dearest Helen,

I love you so much and you are the best wife any man could ever ask for. All I've ever wanted was to take care of you and our family. Everything will be all right. You will have the money you need for yourself and the kids and for Joey. Just be patient and trust me that it will all work out. The password for all the bank accounts is gonefishing22."

Love,

Joe

The letter seemed like a pretty standard message to leave behind, except for that line Just be patient and trust me that it will all work out.

"What money is he referring to?" Frank asked. "What do you have to be patient for?"

"When I first read it, I figured he must've meant the life insurance payment from the policy he has through work." Helen Cottlemeir squirmed in her seat and gazed up at the ceiling. "Joe took care of all our finances. I never paid the bills or deposited the checks or anything. I know that's old-fashioned. But he liked doing math and paperwork, and I liked doing the cooking. He gave me money every week for the groceries, and everything else we always shopped for together. Even my clothes. Joe liked to shop."

She started to cry. "He always talked me into buying things I didn't really need. He'd say, 'Go ahead. Treat yourself. You deserve it.'"

Frank began to feel a little sympathy for Meyerson. Maybe the lieutenant had been on the receiving end of one too many rambling calls like this.

He tried to bring her back on topic. "So your husband left a letter telling you about his life insurance policy. Most responsible people have life insurance. I don't think—"

She held up the sodden tissue to cut Frank off. "I'm sorry. I'm not making myself clear. A few months ago, Joe and I had a disagreement. A neighbor of ours died very suddenly, and his wife didn't even know the passwords to their bank accounts, didn't know all the places where their retirement funds were. So I said to Joe, I don't want that to happen to me. You'd better write it all down for me, show me what to do just in case something would happen. God forbid." This kicked off another crying jag.

Frank took a steadying breath. No wonder Helen had hit it off with Doris—they both rambled like poison ivy next to a stream.

Helen gulped the now tepid tea Doris had left. "I'm sorry. I still can't get used to the fact that he's gone." She wiped her eyes and continued. "Joe got real prickly that day. He said there was no need for me to suddenly get involved in our finances when he'd been doing them for thirty years. I said I just wanted to be prepared. And he said he wasn't planning on dying anytime soon, so I shouldn't worry about it. I let it drop. I'm not a person who likes to argue."

And then Joe did die.

Helen blew her nose and continued. "So after the funeral, I went through the desk drawers hoping I could find what I needed to pay the bills. And that's when I found this, right on top."

She paused with the letter held aloft as if she'd just unveiled the Holy Grail.

Frank was not impressed. "I suppose once he calmed down, he left you the information you wanted. He didn't tell you because he didn't want to admit you'd been right all along. Men are like that. I oughta know."

Helen perched on the edge of her chair, her frizzy gray curls bobbing in disagreement. "The letter wasn't there on Thursday evening, the day before he left for the fishing trip. I know because I went into that drawer looking for a large paper clip, and there was no letter then. He put it in there late Thursday night or early Friday morning. Then he left for the trip." She gripped the tea mug and lowered her voice. "He knew he wasn't coming back."

The timing was certainly odd. Frank felt a prick of excitement. Maybe Helen really was onto something, but he wasn't ready to let her see it. He continued to play devil's advocate. "Maybe knowing you were going to be apart from each other for a few days inspired him to do the right thing."

"Then how do you explain this?" She dove into the giant purse again and produced some printed pages. "This is a printout of all our bank transactions for the past three months." Mrs. C came around to Frank's side of the desk and placed the pages before him. The heading read, "Money Manager's Plus—Combined Checking and Savings."

Every two weeks, the deposit column showed $2,576. Clearly, a paycheck.

Then in the withdrawals column there were regular cash transfers to the cable company, the phone company, and the electric company. A few other checks—nothing over a couple hundred dollars. Standard middle class finances.

Then Frank's gaze settled on a five-figure withdrawal. $5,000 in cash withdrawn on February 22. Then $7,500 in cash withdrawn on March 15. Finally, on the day before Joe Cottlemeir's death, a cash withdrawal of $10,000.

Their account had gone from over $30,000 to under $1,000 in three months.

Now Frank was really interested. Surely Meyerson had noticed this?

"And you have no idea why he was withdrawing cash?"

"When I first saw it, I figured he must've given the money to our daughter to help out with Joey, our grandson. He's three and he had to have heart surgery to fix a problem he was born with. The insurance covered the operation, but the medicines, the oxygen, the tube feeding, the special therapy—all that is extra. Our daughter had to quit her job to take care of Joey. Her husband works hard, but he doesn't make enough to pay all the medical bills. So we were helping them out wherever we could."

Helen stopped talking. Her eyes focused for so long on the wall behind Frank that he swiveled to see what was there. Just an Adirondack Scenes calendar that had never been flipped to this month.

Finally, she spoke. "I talked to our daughter. She said her father told her to just give him any bill they couldn't handle and he'd take care of it. So she did. And then last month, the bill collectors started calling her. Said that the oxygen equipment Joey needs at night hadn't been paid for and they were going to come take it away. She called her dad and he said it was just a mix-up and not to tell me or I would worry. That he'd handle it."

This sounded like a plausible explanation for at least one of the withdrawals. Perhaps the company hadn't been willing to wait for a check and Cottlemeir had gone to them to settle up with cash. But Frank could tell by the look on Helen's face that the logical explanation wasn't true.

"He didn't pay the bill?"

"He did, in part. That bill was less than a thousand dollars, and Joe paid $150—enough to shut them up for a while. My son-in-law got worried and started following up on the other bills they'd given Joe to pay. None of them had been paid in full. Joe had given the companies small payments just to keep them satisfied. He used a credit card. One I never knew we had."

This time Frank could anticipate what was about to come out of the big purse. Sure enough, credit card statements showing a Visa maxed out at twenty grand. Frank scanned the Visa statement; every charge sounded medical-related. Two pharmacies, a medical equipment supply vendor, a physical therapist, a nutritionist. The balance on the credit card had continued to climb as Joe had made only the minimum payment each month.

So where had the cash from the savings account been going? Why hadn't he used it to pay off the card? Gambling, drinking, drugs, a mistress? Anything was possible, even with a guy who seemed like the salt-of-the earth family man. Frank hated to visit more pain upon Helen, but the question had to be asked. "Did your husband gamble, Mrs. Cottlemeir?"

"A fifty-fifty raffle ticket at the church bazaar, ten bucks to join the office Super Bowl pool—nothing more than that."

That he told you. Clearly, Cottlemeir had his secrets. But drugs and alcohol didn't seem to be one of them. Frank had seen the autopsy report. Nothing had been found in Cottlemeir's system except the half a beer he'd been drinking when he died. Surely an addict all alone for the weekend would be high. That left gambling.

But if Cottlemeir had been in debt to a loan shark, the enforcer most likely would have roughed him up to scare him into paying. Killing Cottlemeir when he still owed money seemed counterproductive. The facts didn't quite hold together, but that was Meyerson's problem.

"This is certainly useful information, Mrs. Cottlemeir. Didn't you show all this to the state police?"

"Yes, I did. They've seen it all. Including this."

Back she went into the bag.

There was more? Good grief! Frank sank back into his chair waiting for the next revelation.

Helen handed over a thick envelope from the Pilgrim Life Insurance Company. He pulled out the document. Two lines had been highlighted with yellow marker:

Benefit paid in the case of accidental death: Two Million dollars.

Beneficiaries: Helen J. Cottlemeir and Joseph Cottlemeir Wilson (minor).

"Did you know he had this?"

"Yes, he told me he bought a small extra policy right after Joey had his first operation. What he didn't tell me about was the accidental death clause." The widow leaned forward and put her hands on the desk separating them. "You saw Joe with your own eyes, so I know you'll have the answer. You see, they kept his head covered when they showed me the body." She took a deep breath and gazed into Frank's eyes. "Is there any chance that Joe could have…could have committed suicide?"

Frank's mouth opened but he stopped himself from blurting out "Are you kidding me?" Clearly the poor woman was coming unglued. He and Meyerson both had made it very clear that her husband had been gunned down from behind. Ambushed, but maybe they hadn't used that harsh word. "Ma'am, he was shot in the back of the head." Frank indicated the spot on his own head.

"So he couldn't have...?" She made a twisting motion with her hand.

"No. And the weapon wasn't found. And there was no residue on his hands. I realize the money problems and the life insurance seem a little suspicious, but it's absolutely impossible that your husband could have committed suicide."

She nodded. "That's what the state police said, but I didn't totally trust them. Because I've been telling them how strange all this is, how none of it seems like the Joe I know, and they just don't listen. I guess I just needed a second opinion."

Her head drooped as if she might be praying. Then she looked into Frank's eyes "Thank you for setting my mind at rest. Because suicide is a mortal sin you know—we both believe that."

CHAPTER 35

THE LIBRARY WAS MERCIFULLY EMPTY when Frank showed up hoping to share whatever Penny had packed for lunch.

"All I brought is salad, but you're in luck. There are appetizers left over from last night in the fridge."

Frank popped a mini-quiche in his mouth and chewed. They had been better when they were hot. "I feel like I've lived a week in one morning." He told Penny about Mrs. Cottlemeir's visit. "There was no end in sight to the grandson's medical bills. Cottlemeir must've thought he'd gamble some of his savings to pay off the old bills and prepare for the new ones. But he lost it all and was doubly screwed."

"So you think someone killed him because of his gambling debts?" Penny held a forkful of salad suspended. "That seems so, so...Brooklyn."

"He's from Saratoga. There's horseracing there. Maybe there are loan sharks too. Anyway, I set her mind at ease that Joe didn't commit suicide. Now I need someone to set my mind at ease that Edwin hasn't pulled off an abduction."

Penny's eyes grew rounder and rounder as he filled her in on Earl's encounter with Edwin over the Facebook post.

"But if Edwin took her, who did he give her to? Who is Olivia with?" Penny asked.

Before Frank could answer, the library phone rang.

"Trout Run Library, Penny Bennett speaking. How may I help you?"

Frank still got a kick out of hearing his wife refer to herself as Penny Bennett, so he was gazing at her fondly when he noticed her hand tighten on the receiver.

"Hello? Can you hear me?" Penny looked at him and raised a silencing finger to her lips. Then she pressed the speakerphone button.

"Penny?" a querulous voice came over the line.

Frank leaned in. Was that Olivia?

"Yes, honey, it's me." Penny kept her voice low and soothing. "We've been worried about you, Olivia. Are you okay?"

"Yeah, I guess, but…" Her voice was so soft Frank could barely hear her. Was she scared, not able to talk? He scrawled a note to Penny—SAFE?

"But what? Olivia, are you in a safe place? Can you talk to me?"

Frank ran through his options. Setting up a trace through the state police would take forever, but Penny would be able to see what number was the last incoming call, and he could find out who it was registered to. Unless it was a throwaway cell.

"I'm not hurt, but I need— I can't— Oh, I wish I never left, but now I can't come back."

"Yes, you can, honey." Penny couldn't repress her eagerness. "Everyone misses you. Everyone wants you home. I'll come get you. Tell me where you are."

"I'm not sure."

Something rattled in the background. A sharp intake of breath. Olivia's voice got even softer. "I can't talk any more. I'll call again."

"Olivia, wait!"

The line went dead.

CHAPTER 36

FRANK GRABBED THE LIBRARY PHONE and retrieved the number of the last incoming call. "Five-one-eight area code. She's still local."

"She said, 'I'm not sure where I am.' That means someone's holding her captive." Penny's voice ascended the scale of hysteria.

"She also said, 'I wish I'd never left.' That means she ran away. Or agreed to let Edwin take her away."

Frank headed for the door. "I'll find out whose phone this is. We'll get a tap put on the library line. If Olivia calls back soon, text me."

Penny raked her hands through her long, dark hair. "But whoever she ran away with won't let her leave, won't let her use the phone. She's in danger."

Certainly, Olivia hadn't wanted to be caught on the phone. Yet Frank thought she hadn't sounded terrified, only furtive. On the porch of the library, he flipped the sign on the front door from OPEN to CLOSED and delivered one more instruction to his wife. "Don't tell Edwin and Lucy anything about this. Don't breathe a word to anyone."

While Frank was on the phone arranging for a monitor on the library line, Earl got the name of the owner of the phone number from which Olivia had called. He crossed to Frank's desk and slid a piece of paper in front of him.

Land line. Andrew and Courtney Upton.

Earl started talking as soon as Frank hung up. "Noah Upton was the little red-haired kid Ronnie held hostage at the Happy Camper Day Care Center. These are his parents. Why would Olivia be with them?"

Why indeed?

"They live on Carson Street in Verona," Earl continued. "How would she get clear over there unless someone took her? Let's go."

Frank thought aloud as he drove. "If Noah Upton was in daycare, that means the house is most likely empty all day long. We don't know who Olivia is with, or who she's afraid of."

"You think Olivia's hiding out there during the day?" Earl shook his head. "How would she know that house is empty?"

"Pam most certainly would know the status of her customer's house—"

Earl punched his palm. "So Pam is helping her husband. But what would they want with Olivia?"

Frank gazed at the road unwinding before them.

"Frank, are you listening? Maybe Ronnie is at the Uptons' house. He could be holding Olivia hostage. She hung up when he walked in on her." Earl pounded the dashboard as a slow-moving truck pulled out in front of them. He reached to turn on the siren.

Frank slapped his hand away. "The house is empty during the day while the parents work, but occupied at night. Could the Uptons be helping Ronnie?"

"Why would they help a guy who held their son hostage? And that still doesn't explain the connection to Olivia."

Frank took his eyes off the road to look at Earl. "Olivia didn't call Edwin or Lucy or even Anita. She called Penny. My wife."

"So?"

"This could be a trap."

The rain had started again, lashing against the patrol car windows. Frank focused on driving, but his mind churned with the possible ways the Uptons, the Gatrells, and Olivia might be linked. The Uptons must have been in the crowd of parents at the day care center the day of the crisis. Frank squinted with the effort of pulling specific memories from the blur of screaming and crying, fear and anger and gratitude. Some fragment of knowledge tantalized him but he couldn't pin it down. "You said Noah was the little fellow with red hair?" He spoke to Earl after several minutes of silence.

"Huh?"

Frank slapped the steering wheel. "I've got it! Noah's mom was the very emotional lady who went around hugging everyone after the kids were released. She had long, curly red hair."

"So?"

"I saw her at the Library Luau. She looked familiar, but I couldn't place her. She won six cooking lessons at the Iron Eagle Inn and she threw her arms around Edwin."

"What are you getting at?"

"Edwin. Olivia's with Edwin."

They passed the WELCOME TO VERONA sign.

"You think Edwin got Olivia to agree to hide out at the Uptons' house? And now Olivia regrets it?" Earl's voice got more incredulous with each question. "You think that call has nothing to do with Ronnie Gatrell?"

Frank stared through the windshield. He didn't want Earl to see how upset he was. How could Edwin have done this to Olivia…to Lucy… to him? In his mind he played out the nightmare scenario of arresting his good friend. Maybe there was some way Edwin could get off with probation if—

"Frank? So you think Edwin and Olivia made it look like she ran away so the social workers and the judge would think Anita wasn't a good mother?"

Frank nodded. He couldn't bear to speak. Why did Earl find it necessary to spell out every sordid detail?

"But are the Uptons in on it? Or did he just move her there for today and—"

Frank jerked the steering wheel to avoid a pothole. "I don't know! I don't know how he's planning to pull it off. Maybe Olivia called Penny because she really does regret ever getting into this scheme. Or she's just lonely there by herself. Or maybe the call is all part of Edwin's plan. He would know that Penny would tell me right away, but that there would be less scrutiny if Olivia called the library, not our office. Bad luck for him that I was there when the call came in. I heard her voice."

Earl's brow furrowed. "I still don't totally get what the plan is."

"We find Olivia. We look like heroes. Anita looks like a lousy mother. Lucy and Edwin get Olivia back. Life goes back to normal at the inn. No need to run off to South America."

"What about Anita?"

Frank's fury boiled over. "Anita is screwed. The story of her life."

CHAPTER 37

EARL TURNED OFF MAIN STREET in Verona onto Carson Street and followed Frank's order to park close to the corner. He put a restraining hand on Earl's arm to prevent him from catapulting out of the car, and sized up the scene. The Uptons' home was five houses down from the intersection with Main Street. Neither Edwin's nor Lucy's car was parked on the street or in the driveway. A big, shaggy evergreen obscured the front porch from view, and a hedge ran along both sides of the property. For a house in town, it offered a fair amount of privacy.

Because of the gloomy weather, some houses already had lights on, but the Uptons' house was dark. Frank went down the driveway of the house next door, and Earl followed. When they got to the backyard, they pushed through the hedge into the Uptons' yard. Picnic table. Swing set. Padlocked cellar doors, leading directly underground. Big flowerpot on the porch. No sign of a break-in.

Frank kept Earl behind him as they approached the house. Together, they stood at the back door and listened.

Silence.

Frank tried the door, and the knob turned. Had Edwin told Olivia to leave it unlocked to lure them in? Frank pushed Earl behind him and they entered the house through a small laundry room.

The strong scent of microwave popcorn greeted them. Someone was definitely here.

The possibility that the intruder really was Ronnie was slim, but still merited caution. Pressed against the laundry room wall, Frank shone his flashlight into the dim kitchen. The room was empty, neat as a pin, with no physical sign of the popcorn other than the scent lingering in the air.

Ronnie had never bothered cleaning up after himself in any of the other homes he'd broken into. Edwin, however, was famously tidy. Frank's tension changed from fear of a physically dangerous confrontation to dread of an emotionally dangerous one.

"Earl, stand by the door to the basement. Don't go down there alone, but make sure no one gets out this way."

Frank walked through the empty dining room into the living room at the front of the house. The big squishy cushions on the sofa looked tumbled. An afghan draped across the back of the sofa hung askew. Frank put his hand on the TV. Still warm.

Had Olivia heard them enter? Was she hiding?

He checked the front door. It was chained on the inside, so she hadn't gone out that way. He stood at the foot of the stairs. "Olivia? Olivia, it's Frank. Are you up there, honey? Don't be afraid. No one is angry at you. Everything's going to be all right. We all want you to come home."

Silence.

Frank headed up the stairs. Three bedrooms and a bath—all empty. He checked under the beds and in the closets, his heart sinking as each came up blank.

She had left before they got there. Whoever had walked in on her phone call had taken her away. If it was Edwin, at least Olivia was not in danger. Frank kneaded his eyes. But what if he still didn't understand what was going on here?

The popcorn and the warm TV taunted him with how narrowly they'd missed her.

When Frank returned to the kitchen, Earl had pulled the white plastic trash bag out of the can. "Lots of snack food wrappers and soda cans in here. We can check them for fingerprints if we need to. I also checked the browser history of that old Dell." Earl pointed to a clunky computer on a desk in the corner of the kitchen. "Facebook, Instagram, YouTube, BuzzFeed. All sites a teenager would visit. She's alone here all day amusing herself until the Uptons get home."

Was she? Frank glanced around the kitchen and the small family room adjacent. Not a sippy cup…not a Cheerio…not a toy out of place. He yanked open the fridge: no milk, no juice, no eggs, just a brown-edged head of lettuce and some condiments.

"The Uptons aren't helping Olivia. They must be on vacation." Frank turned toward the basement door. "Let's check down here."

He flipped the wall switch at the head of the stairs, but no light came on. As he fumbled for his flashlight, a sound rose from the dank cellar.

"Someone's down there," Earl stage-whispered.

Whispering was hardly necessary. They'd been thumping through the house like elephants. Certainly anyone hiding in the basement knew they were on the way down.

Why was Olivia hiding from them? The thought of a trap returned. "Stay here, Earl."

The sound came again. A rustling.

Was it intentional? A lure?

The beam of Frank's flashlight cut through the dark. He edged down the stairs sideways, his back against the rough concrete wall. A shelf full of canned goods. A tool bench. A washer and dryer.

He shined the flashlight into the corners of the basement. A flash of movement. The rustling sound grew louder. Frank flattened himself against the wall.

Two small eyes glowed in the flashlight beam.

A chipmunk. The terrified creature had figured out how to get into the basement, but couldn't figure out how to leave.

Frank's grip on the flashlight relaxed. He paced around the basement. Beside the water heater and furnace, one corner of the basement held a square of carpeting, a mini-fridge, a TV with an attached PlayStation, and a dingy recliner. Andrew Upton had a little man-cave down here where he retreated to play video games. Two empty Miller cans and a crumpled chip bag lay on the floor. Frank took one step closer to the chair.

On the nubby beige upholstery of the arm, a splodge of brownish red.

Earl appeared behind him. "Blood! She is hurt."

"Could be. Or maybe it's just spilled salsa." Frank lowered his head to look more closely. That's when he saw it. Long, pointy, beige and black so it blended with the chair. He plucked it up with his fingertips and held in in the beam of the flashlight.

A porcupine quill.

CHAPTER 38

FRANK CONTINUED STARING AT THE quill.

Earl prodded him. "C'mon—what are we waiting for? What is that thing? We need to get this blood called in to the state police."

Frank headed back to the kitchen. With a quick flick of the wrist, he dumped the garbage bag out on the counter. Popcorn bag, two empty soda cans, microwave pizza box, two Kit-Kat wrappers.

And…Frank held a yellow and blue package aloft.

"Teddy Grahams," Earl said. "Ronnie's got Olivia and he's on the run. He's slipped through our fingers again."

Frank stared at the package. Then he started to speak. "RJ Gatrell is fourteen, a freshman in high school. How might he have known Olivia? What could have brought them together?"

"I don't know. 4H has girls and guys, but RJ's not in 4H."

"Neither is Olivia. But there has to be something. Those two are friends. I'm sure of it."

Earl stiffened. "Wait a minute! That stolen truck report that I took this morning—it was Dennis Webber's. He's got an old truck in his garage that he tinkers with, fixing it up for when Denny is old enough to drive. I bet—"

"RJ took it. That's how he got Olivia over here. RJ isn't old enough to have a license, but that doesn't mean he doesn't know how to drive. He's got an ATV."

Frank kept talking as he swept the trash back into the bag and headed for the door. "Pam now works at the Burger King near the mall in Plattsburgh. When we get back to the office, call them up and find out what days and hours she's worked this week. I bet RJ has had plenty of opportunities to slip out of the house unnoticed. And I want you to find out where the Uptons work, and where they've been this week, and who knows about their schedule."

Earl hustled to keep up with Frank, who was already at the door of the patrol car. "So that's how he gets the supplies to his dad. Maybe there never has been anyone else helping Ronnie."

"Maybe," Frank said as he threw the car into reverse. "Except now RJ has convinced Olivia to pitch in. At the library fundraiser, RJ won a pair of porcupine quill earrings. I thought he got them for his mom even though Penny said they're not the kind of thing Pam would wear."

Earl nodded. "Anita let Olivia get her ears pierced. You were complaining about that."

"RJ is a good-looking kid. He's a year or two older." Frank shook his head. "A year ago, Olivia would have had more sense than to do this. Now her hormones have kicked in and she's as dumb as any other teenager."

"But if she went off with RJ, why did Olivia tell Penny she didn't know where she was?"

"Maybe she's still trying to protect RJ. Possibly she wants to sneak away from him and have Penny pick her up, but she doesn't know how to give the right directions. Or maybe—"

"Maybe what?"

Frank couldn't let go of the possibility that Edwin was somehow involved. Courtney Upton was taking cooking lessons at the inn. Frank and Edwin were friends, but he didn't know everyone Edwin knew... didn't know the many ways Edwin had woven himself into the Trout Run community. Could Edwin have made some sort of deal with RJ? Watch over Olivia for a few days and I'll help your dad?

When they got back to the office, Frank informed Trudy of the near miss with Olivia. When he got off the phone, Earl had some answer for him.

"The Uptons have been staying with her mom in Saranac Lake during the week so that the grandmother can watch Noah while the parents are at work," Earl said. "The house has been empty all week. And Courtney did mention it to Edwin at the Library Luau."

Frank and Earl looked at each other in silence.

"There's one more thing," Earl said.

Frank rubbed his eyes with the heels of his hands. "What?"

"The browser history on the Uptons' computer showed one other website—VitaVine dot com. Courtney said she and her husband had never visited it. That means Olivia and RJ were looking at it."

Frank shook himself to attention. "That stuff keeps cropping up. Don't let me forget about it. But right now, I have to call on Pam Gatrell." He pushed himself out of his chair.

"Frank."

He turned with one foot out the door. Earl's worried eyes met his own.

"What about Edwin? Should I go over to the inn and talk to him?"

The radiator clanked. Doris slammed the lid of the photocopier.

"Not yet."

Frank sped down the long driveway to the Gatrells' house. Careening around a bend, he nearly crashed into a car speeding up the drive. They both slammed on their brakes, avoiding a head-on crash by a few feet. Pam leaped out of the other car, wild-eyed.

"What happened? What do you know?" she screamed as she ran towards him.

Frank caught her in his arms. "Where are you going?"

"RJ is missing! Have you found him? Isn't that why you're here?"

"I just missed him. He and Olivia Veech were at Courtney Upton's house."

"Wha—? Why would he be there? Olivia...you mean that girl who ran away from home a few days ago?"

Frank forced Pam to sit down in the patrol car and calm down. Gradually, a coherent story emerged. She'd been working extra shifts at the Burger King all week. She and RJ had often missed each other—Pam asleep when he left for school, RJ asleep when she returned from work. Today, she'd assumed he'd gotten himself off to the school bus stop, but the high school attendance office had called to report that RJ wasn't in school. And the baseball coach said he'd missed practice all week. When she'd checked his bedroom, the bed was undisturbed, still made up with the fresh sheets she'd put on yesterday before she left for work.

"So you're telling me he broke into Courtney's house and he's been hanging out there with some girl?" Pam's knee jittered up and down. "How old is that Veech girl? Did she pick him up and drive him there?" Pam held her head in her hands and rocked. "Please God—I can't cope with a grandchild on top of everything else."

"Olivia is only twelve. I don't know why she's with RJ. How do they know each other?"

"They don't. RJ never hangs around with girls. I've never even heard him mention Olivia."

"What about Olivia's foster parents, Lucy and Edwin Bates?"

Pam shook her head until her hair flew. "What are we waiting for? Let's go get him."

Frank prepared himself to break the worst news. "Pam, Dennis Webber's old truck has been stolen out of his barn. I think RJ has been using it to take supplies to Ronnie, and then returning it. But this time it's been gone all night and day. RJ knows how to drive, right?"

"Ronnie let him drive his truck on the dirt road that runs along the brook on our property. Never out on the road." Pam's eyes opened wide and she lunged to get out of the patrol car. "Oh my God! I can't believe RJ is helping Ronnie."

Frank pulled her back into the passenger seat and steered the patrol car around Pam's SUV. "Ronnie kept supplies in your barn, right? Let's go see what's missing."

Frank pulled open the big barn door, revealing a dim, dusty interior. He pulled out his flashlight: ATV, lawn tractor, workbench, tools. He turned to face the long, western wall: cans, floor to ceiling. Tuna, beans, vegetable, fruit, soup, coffee—a fortress of non-perishables..

"Holy crap! How long did it take him to get all that?"

Pam sighed. "About a year. He'd drive all over looking for sales and dollar stores."

Frank ran the flashlight beam methodically across the shelves. The products were arranged by category, and Frank noticed holes where cans had been removed: tuna, applesauce, peaches, baked beans, and finally, Teddy Grahams. He heard a sharp intake of breath from Pam when his beam rested on that spot.

Frank turned again and his beam fell on something else. The tower of cardboard boxes that had been in Pam's hallway on his first visit had been moved out here. Now, a green logo printed on the side of each box faced him. He opened the top box.

VitaVine.

Frank took Pam back to her house and made her promise to stay put.

"We've got an APB out on the truck. RJ can't drive it for long without being spotted. Now, tell me—is there a spot where Ronnie and RJ might meet up? A favorite hunting or fishing location maybe?"

Pam cradled her head in her hands. "I don't know. I never paid much attention to where they went. I should have."

"What about this VitaVine stuff? How did Ronnie get involved in that?"

"What does it matter?" Pam snapped. "It was one of his crazy money-making schemes. Ronnie was going to solve all our problems by becoming the vitamin king of the North Country. Ha!"

"But who recruited him?" Frank pressed. "It could be important."

Pam met his gaze. Her pretty green eyes were rimmed with red but they didn't blink. "I honestly don't know."

Frank believed her.

CHAPTER 39

"RONNIE...SOMEONE IN KEESEVILLE...ANITA...RJ AND OLIVIA—THERE are too many connections for a coincidence," Frank said to Earl. "In between looking for that truck, I want to find out more about this VitaVine network."

Earl was already clattering on his keyboard. "It's a nationwide company headquartered in Wisconsin. Privately held, but they reported twenty million in sales last year. Testimonials from satisfied customers.... hmmm...'helped me recover from cancer'...'cured my depression'...'I am no longer insulin-dependent.'

"Amazing. Does it raise the dead?"

"Only if you take all seven of the products at once." Earl kept tapping. "There's a whole thread devoted to it on Reddit. 'Does it work?... Yes, it's amazing...No, it's crap.' It goes on like that for pages."

"Someone donated a basket of it to the Library Luau." Frank pulled out his phone and called Penny.

"Who donated the VitaVine?"

"Huh? What are you talking about?"

"To the Luau. Who gave that basket of pills that no one bid on?"

"Let me check my records. It's certainly not something I solicited, but once word of the Tricky Tray got out, people started dropping off donations unasked. It might have come in when one of the volunteers was manning the front desk." Frank could hear his wife scrambling through papers on her cluttered desk. "Here it is."

Long silence. "Oh my!"

"What? Who donated it?"

"Nancy Tomlinson."

Earl had never asked his mother or aunt where they'd gone to the VitaVine party. When he made the call, his mom confirmed that Nancy Tomlinson had been the hostess.

"What's the likelihood that Nancy will talk to us about VitaVine?" Frank asked Earl.

"Slim to none. Meyerson told her she didn't have to answer your questions."

Earl thought for a moment then a sly grin spread across his face. "How about if my Aunt Sheila calls her and says she's interested in selling VitaVine and wants more information? I could tell her what to ask."

"You think she can pull it off?"

"Oh, yeah. Sheila can really keep a straight face. She's the family champion at Fictionary. I'll get her prepped tonight."

The next morning, Doris came into Frank's office and stood behind his desk, craning her neck to look out the window. "It's so miserable out there. My niece Shelly is getting married tomorrow at noon. I told my sister that April isn't the best month for a wedding in the Adirondacks. But no one listens to me."

Undeniably true. Frank kept typing.

"Do you think it's going to rain tomorrow? Will it be any warmer than today?"

"You can't predict tomorrow's weather by looking out the window today," Frank said. Hell, in the Adirondacks, you couldn't predict the next hour's weather by looking out the window.

"I just wish I knew whether I'm going to need a coat. And if I'm going to be able to wear my open-toed shoes."

Frank tried taking a yoga breath, as Penny recommended. "Why don't you go on weather dot com and see what they have to say."

"Earl usually helps me with that. But it's okay—I can see you're busy."

In his rational mind, Frank knew that Doris didn't lie in bed at night plotting ways to aggravate him, but it sure seemed to be so. "Doris, Earl's Great Grandma Gert is on Facebook and she's nearly a hundred. You can Google for the weather."

"Oh, I don't want to mess up Earl's computer. I'll wait. He should be back from the morning patrol soon."

Frank pulled his cellphone from his pocket and handed it to Doris. "Just press the sun picture and the weather report will pop up."

Doris plopped into a chair with the smartphone in her hand, as mesmerized as a toddler. "Look at that—they have the hour-by-hour forecast." She began to recite the likelihood of rain and the temperature for every moment of the wedding day. Luckily, Penny arrived before Doris got to the reception outlook.

"C'mon, Frank—I can't take more than half an hour for lunch."

Frank grabbed his coat and headed for the door.

"Wait, your phone! I'm almost done. Just let me see what it says—"

"Keep it, Doris. I'll be back by one."

As Penny returned Frank to the town office after lunch, they saw Doris out on the front walk, looking up and down. "Good Lord, is she still trying to read the clouds?" Frank said.

He opened the car door and Doris charged toward him, a panicked mare running without regard to rocks, or ditches, or fences. "There you are!" She stumbled, and Frank lunged to steady her. "I couldn't reach you because I had your phone. And you weren't at the diner."

Couldn't the department get along without him for half an hour? "Isn't Earl here?"

"That's what I needed to tell you. Olivia and RJ have been spotted in a cabin on the old logging road that leads to Sunfish Pond. Earl went over there by himself. I told him to wait for you, but he wouldn't listen. I called the state police for backup, but the trooper is clear over by Schroon Lake."

Of course, Earl wouldn't have risked missing Olivia a second time. He'd done the right thing, and, for once, so had Doris.

"Here." Doris thrust his keys and his phone into his hands. "It's the cabin with the green roof. Go!"

Frank headed toward his truck as Doris chattered behind him. "And she called, but she was so wound up I couldn't make heads or tails or what she was saying, and I said are you sure, and she said..."

Why was she still carrying on like this when everything was under control? Frank slid behind the wheel of the truck. "Who saw the kids? Who called it in?"

"Pam. Pam Gatrell. RJ called her. The kids are out there with Ronnie."

Frank slapped the portable blue light on the roof of his truck and raced to toward Sunfish Pond. He had sped off so quickly he hadn't asked Doris how long ago Earl had headed out. Frank hoped, prayed, that he was only a few minutes behind Earl.

What was Ronnie intending to do with the kids? Was he planning another hostage showdown as a political statement? Surely he wouldn't hurt his own son?

John Brown's last stand popped into Frank's mind. The zealot hadn't seemed to regret that he'd led his sons to their death in the raid on Harper's Ferry.

Frank's foot pressed harder on the accelerator.

He radioed Earl and got no response. Fished out his cell phone and called, but the call immediately rolled to voicemail. Of course there was no cell coverage out there. Whatever was happening, Frank would dive into it blind. Ronnie was armed. Earl wouldn't talk him into dropping his weapon this time. Ronnie had his short taste of imprisonment. Frank knew the man wouldn't go back. Maybe this time he would force their hands, demand to be shot so he could go down in a blaze of glory, resisting the tyrannical police. What headlines that would inspire! "Cops Shoot Man Who Resisted Bank Takeover of His Land."

And what if it came down to a gun battle between Ronnie and Earl? Would Earl be able to kill a man to save his own life? Earl had been wearing a badge for barely a month. He shouldn't have to make that choice.

He sped past the OK Café and the bait and tackle shop on the way to Sunfish Pond. As the road twisted, he caught glimpses of Stony Creek, high with the winter melt, rushing furiously toward the Verona Bridge, the bridge it had taken out during the Hurricane Irene flood. If only he understood Ronnie's endgame. How had the kids ended up with him? Why was RJ bringing him the truck now? He could have smuggled it to his father right after the escape. Why wait? Frank wished he'd had the time to talk to Pam, but that wish was futile.

A quarter mile from the old logging road, Frank killed the blue light. He jolted down the gravel road for a mile, and then pulled onto the shoulder when he spied the sun glinting off the taillights of patrol car between the trees ahead. He slipped through the woods, keeping the car in his sights.

But as he crept closer, he could see the patrol car was empty. Where was Earl?

A shot reverberated through the forest. A rifle shot, not the sound of a nine-millimeter.

Ronnie, not Earl.

He heard footsteps crashing through the underbrush, gaining speed as the runner drew closer. Ducking behind a large boulder, Frank drew his weapon and kept it trained on the spot where the runner would emerge. Ronnie was armed, and Frank knew he would have only a split second to decide whether or not to shoot.

A figure raced into the clearing. Frank's finger tensed on the trigger.

"Stop! Drop your weapon or I'll shoot!"

The runner spun around, eyes wide with fear.

Olivia.

Frank lowered his trembling arm. They stared at each, too stunned to speak. Then Olivia ran to him and flung her arms around his neck. He hugged her, but there was no time to offer solace. He didn't know who was behind Olivia. Ronnie might still spring on them.

Frank pressed Olivia's face into his shoulder to hush her and listened. He didn't hear more footsteps, only the pounding of Olivia's heart.

"You're safe now, Olivia. But you have to help me. Where are RJ and Ronnie? Have you seen Earl?"

"RJ is with his dad in the cabin. Earl is in the woods." Olivia took a shuddering breath and wiped her nose with her sleeve. "When Ronnie was looking out the window trying to shoot at Earl, I ducked out the back door and ran as fast as I could."

"Where is RJ?"

Olivia's eyes filled with tears. "He's helping his dad. He won't leave him."

"How far away is the cabin?"

Olivia shrugged. "I just ran toward the woods. I didn't know where I was going."

An arrow of fear stabbed Frank's heart. Why had Earl not returned fire? Was he worried about hitting RJ? Or had he himself been hit? One part of Frank longed to put Olivia in the truck and drive her to safety. But he couldn't risk leaving Earl here without back-up. Who knew when the state troopers would arrive?

He pulled Olivia back through the woods to his truck. "I want you to crouch down under the dashboard and stay there. Don't look out the window, you understand? I'm locking you in."

She nodded.

Muttering something between a curse and a prayer, Frank yanked open the car door and pushed Olivia out of sight.

As he stepped back to slam the door, he heard a sound from the cowering ball on the floor of the truck. "What did you say, honey?"

She hid her head between her knees. Frank strained to hear her words.

"I want my Daddy."

Frank bushwhacked through the woods as silently as he could. The quiet oppressed him. No more gunshots, but also no shouting, no movement.

Soon he found a path that led uphill and hesitated. He didn't think this was the way Olivia had come. But maybe the path led to a ridge that overlooked the cabin. Then he could get a wide-angle view of the scene. He climbed quickly toward a bright area where the trees thinned out.

The path ended in a big rock outcropping. Frank flattened himself on the ground and crawled out to the edge. Thirty feet below him lay the cabin with the green roof. The patrol car stood in the drive leading up to it.

He pulled out the lightweight binoculars he'd strapped to his belt. First he scanned the car: empty.

Where was Earl?

The cabin appeared closed up, but then he focused on the right front window. Something protruded from under the sash.

The barrel of Ronnie's rifle. Frank followed the direction it was pointed. He panned across the small clearing that surrounded the house and into the woods, training the binoculars on the dense green trees. Leaves. Branches. Trunks. Rocks.

Where the hell was Earl?

Then as he strained to focus, he thought he detected a movement. A low limb trembled. Some leaves closer to him shook. There was another outcropping like this, a little lower down between Frank and the movement.

Was it Earl moving through the woods to get there? Or was the movement simply a chipmunk or a grouse?

Suddenly a flash of light in his peripheral vision and an explosion of rifle fire. The branch he'd been watching splintered and fell.

Frank scrambled back from the edge of the overlook and took cover behind a boulder. "Earl! Are you hurt?"

In response, Earl shouted to Ronnie. "Send the kids out, Ronnie. My back-up is here."

"Good! Then I can kill more cops. End the government dictatorship."

Ronnie was coming totally unhinged. His money problems were a distant memory. Now he was on a bigger crusade, seeing himself as some kind of misguided freedom fighter. Earl would never talk him down this time.

"You don't want your son and Olivia to get hurt," Earl continued.

Another rifle shot was the only reply.

The lower ridge between him and Earl offered a good angle to attempt a shot into the cabin window. Earl appeared to be moving in that direction. Frank decided to meet him there.

He crept cautiously down the trail, trying not to create any movement that would draw Ronnie's gunfire. Clearly, Earl was unaware that Olivia had escaped. Had Ronnie realized it? Would her departure infuriate him? Or make him and RJ more willing to go down together as martyrs?

"Show me Olivia, Ronnie. Let me see she's okay," Earl called.

Frank cringed. Don't ask that.

His voice was closer. They were certainly converging on the same spot. Frank wanted to call out to Earl, but didn't want to give away their location.

A shout of anger from inside the cabin.

Shit! Ronnie must've discovered Olivia's absence.

"I'm going to kill you!" Ronnie screamed. "Why weren't you watching her? Can't I trust you to do one thing right?" A crash, like the sound of the cabin door slamming.

The situation was unraveling fast. No time for negotiating now.

Frank drew his weapon and rerouted, crashing through the underbrush to get a view of what was happening. He broke through just as Earl appeared on the open ledge, just a few feet away as the crow flies.

But Frank wasn't a crow.

Ronnie was out on the cabin porch, holding RJ in a chokehold with his powerful left arm. The rifle was tucked under his right arm, pointed in Earl's direction, but hardly aimed.

A squirrel leaped from a tree and landed on the roof of the cabin. The noise made Ronnie's head jerk to the left. RJ used that distraction to wriggle out of his father's grasp.

Earl had a clear shot. He dropped to one knee on the ledge and aimed his weapon with both hands.

The guns went off simultaneously.

Frank recoiled.

He opened his eyes to see Earl airborne.

Frank reached out his arms as if to catch a fly ball.

Earl crashed to the ground fifteen feet below.

CHAPTER 40

IN THE MOMENT OF STUNNED silence that followed, RJ jumped off the cabin porch and took off running toward the patrol car and the dirt road Earl had driven in on.

Ronnie stood frozen with the rifle in his hand, staring at Earl's crumpled body.

Frank took aim and fired.

The shot whizzed by Ronnie's head and he dove for cover inside the cabin.

Frank fired three more rounds as he half-slid, half-fell down the slope toward Earl. Ronnie did not return his fire.

Frank saw a bloom of red on Earl's left leg. The wildly fired bullet had hit him in the leg and knocked him off the ridge. A chance in a million.

He reached Earl's side and dragged his limp body under the cover of the trees. Ronnie could have fired again from inside the cabin and easily hit Earl and Frank, but he hadn't. Maybe Ronnie felt bewildered that his act of bravado produced such astonishing results.

Frank's anxious fingers fumbled over Earl's wrist searching for a pulse: nothing. The leg wound didn't look that serious. Frank glanced up at the ridge. Could the fall have killed him? People had survived leaps from bridges and skydiving with unopened parachutes. Surely, Earl was strong enough to survive that drop. Then he saw more blood on the rock he had pulled Earl away from. Frank checked Earl's head and his fingertips came away bloody.

He pushed his emotion down and turned to work on Earl. He was a victim, not a friend. A victim who needed the skills Frank had been trained to provide.

He began chest compressions. On the fifth compression he breathed into Earl's blue-lipped mouth. Five more compressions, another breath. After ten cycles, Earl's color had improved. He checked Earl's pulse again. This time he found it, faint but steady.

In the distance, sirens howled. Frank leaned back on his heels and waited.

Now, the help arrived. Now, after Earl had been shot. He stared at the silent cabin. Now, after Ronnie had escaped.

Again.

CHAPTER 41

WHY?

Frank sat alone in the ICU waiting room of the Adirondack Medical Center in Saranac Lake. A TV mounted on the wall flickered silently. Meaningless announcements crackled through the PA system.

Why had one wild pot shot managed to hit Earl's leg and knock him off that ledge? Why had his head landed on a rock and not the soft carpet of pine needles just a foot away?

Frank's thoughts reeled backward in time.

Why did Doris's niece have to be getting married that weekend? Why had he left his phone with her on that of all days?

Why had he let his ridiculous feud with Marge Malone drag on so that he wasn't having lunch where Doris could have easily found him?

Why had he been so cautious pursuing Olivia at the Uptons' house so that Earl felt compelled to spring into action when she was spotted again?

Most of all, why had he persuaded Lloyd Burlingame to expand their duties to Verona? Earl could've been safely patrolling Saranac Lake today if only Frank hadn't intervened to control the future.

Why?

The door to the waiting room opened. Pastor Bob ushered Earl's gray-faced parents into the room.

Why was he alive and Earl in a coma?

CHAPTER 42

FRANK SAT IN HIS OFFICE face-to-face with Olivia. Trudy Massinay sat to one side.

In the pandemonium surrounding Earl's rescue, Frank had forgotten about Olivia, and the child had stayed crouched in Frank's truck for nearly two hours before a passing state trooper had liberated her.

RJ Gatrell had not yet been found.

Now, on the first full day of Earl's hospitalization, Frank intended to cope with his fear by doing the only task within his capability: wrenching the truth out of a trembling twelve-year-old.

Yesterday, Olivia had been treated at the scene for shock, and had become hysterical at the prospect of going home with either Lucy and Edwin or Anita. Trudy had taken the child to her own house and told Frank that Olivia hadn't spoken a word either last night or this morning.

Well, that was about to change.

"You understand the situation with RJ's father is very serious?" Frank asked. "That it's dangerous for RJ to connect back up with his dad?"

Olivia bobbed her head as if she thought a stronger gesture might provoke Frank to violence. He had always been like a favorite uncle to her. The guy who took her side in arguing for a later bedtime or a second dessert. Now she was afraid of him.

What had the child seen? What had she been told?

Frank tried to make his voice gentler, but all compassion had been sucked out of him. He'd been awake all night, staying at the hospital until the doctor announced that they had succeeded in relieving the pressure on Earl's brain. There was no way to predict, the doctor had said, how long the coma would last.

Or how serious the damage would be.

Go home and call tomorrow.

He hadn't called. Penny promised to keep him informed, for better or worse.

"Olivia, you and RJ won't be in trouble as long as you tell me the truth. The complete truth."

Again the barely perceptible twitch of agreement.

"How did you and RJ get to be such good friends?"

"Church youth group."

Of course! Why hadn't he thought of that? Pastor Bob had combined seventh, eighth, ninth, and tenth grades to get a critical mass of kids. By the time the kids were juniors and seniors, they wouldn't come at all.

"Every week, we share our joys and concerns. Kids share that their cat had kittens or that they're scared they flunked their math test." Olivia fell silent.

Frank studied the child he'd rescued five years ago. He thought he'd brought her to a place where the biggest worry in her life would be factoring polynomials. How wrong he'd been.

"And you and RJ had much bigger concerns." Frank leaned forward. "But you didn't share them with the entire group?"

Olivia shook her head. "After group, we would stand outside the church and talk until his mom came to pick him up. I could walk home."

"What did you tell him about?"

Olivia's voice dropped so low, Frank and Trudy both had to lean in to hear her. "That when I was living with Edwin and Lucy, I missed my mom. But when I was living with my mom, I missed Edwin and Lucy."

"That's perfectly normal, Olivia," Trudy said. "Everyone who loves you understands that."

"All of us," Frank agreed.

Olivia searched their faces looking for signs of duplicity. Finding none, she relaxed ever so slightly.

"And what did RJ talk to you about?" Frank asked.

"The revolution." Olivia spoke with confidence. "RJ said that soon all the banks in the world would collapse and then no one would have any money and people like his dad would come out ahead because they could hunt and fish and shoot and fix things. And people like my mom and Edwin and Lucy would be helpless because there would be no more computers and no more vacations. There would be a war. And the police and the army would be against us. But he said because we were friends, he'd help me save Edwin and Lucy and my mom."

Tears spilled from Olivia's eyes. She kept herself from hysteria by an act of will.

Frank reached out and took her hand. "Honey, RJ's dad is not totally right in the head. The things he told RJ aren't true. We're not all going to lose our money. There's no war coming." He used his other hand to gently tip up her chin. "And the police are not against you. I've always been your friend, and I always will be."

"Then why is everyone talking about it?" Olivia jerked away and her voice spiked. "RJ showed me the websites. It all made sense!"

Frank glanced at Trudy for help.

"Olivia, I'll explain Mr. Gatrell's…issues…after you answer all Frank's questions."

Frank took a gulp of the coffee Doris had brewed for him. "What did RJ do to help his dad?"

"RJ knows how to drive Denny Webber's truck," Olivia whispered. "I know that's illegal."

"We're not going to worry about that right now. What did RJ do with the truck?"

"He would take supplies to his dad."

"Why didn't RJ just take him the truck so Ronnie could get away?" Trudy interrupted.

For a moment, the familiar why-are-grownups-so-dumb expression overpowered the anxious mask. "RJ's dad never wanted to run away. He wants to stay and fight. Once the revolution comes, he can get his land back."

Frank closed his eyes and took a deep breath. Facts. Keep her focused on the facts. Trudy could deal with the deprogramming. "How did RJ know what to bring? How did he know where to meet his father?"

"They had it all planned. They picked out the spots for supply drops. That's what they did when they played Resist or Die. They practiced for the time when Mr. Gatrell would be a guerilla fighter."

Lack of sleep had splintered Frank's brain into a thousand pieces. Was Olivia telling him that Ronnie had planned for his escape before he'd even committed the crime that put him behind bars? "RJ knew his father was going to run away?"

Olivia nodded. "He knew it would come someday. He just didn't know when."

"But everyone said RJ's been very upset since his dad has been on the run."

"Before it was a game. RJ didn't know what it would really be like—that some people would be mad, and some people would call Ronnie crazy, and some people would be on his side."

A prickle of tension raised the hairs on the back of Frank's neck. "Who else was on Ronnie's side, Olivia? Who was helping him besides RJ?"

"I told you, there are thousands of people ready to join the revolution." Olivia squirmed in irritation. "They all know each other from the game."

"I mean re—" He swallowed the word "real." "I mean local people, right here in the High Peaks. Someone who might be helping Ronnie... and RJ...right now."

"I dunno. No one ever went with RJ to the drop-offs. He'd just hide the package and go. Only this last time, I went."

"And why was this time different? Why did you go?"

"I had to go with him to return the favor he did for me. He took a risk, so I had to take one too."

Frank cocked his head. Everything the kid had done since she'd started writing to her mother in prison had been risky. "What exact risk are you talking about?"

"On the night I ran away, RJ took me back to the inn. So I could see it for the last time before it got, you know—"

He didn't know.

"Destroyed. In the—"

"Revolution. Right." He felt Doris's bitter brew roiling in his stomach. Was this the moment Olivia would tell him that Edwin had always known where she'd been? "So you saw your fa—, you saw Edwin?"

She nodded. "Through the kitchen window. He was making dinner, just like always." Her eyes got shiny. "And that's when I got the idea to go in."

Frank's stomach heaved. Was it not enough that Earl was clinging to life? Did God have to make him arrest his best friend on the same day? Could Edwin seriously have let her go off with these lunatic Gatrells? "So you went in to tell Edwin where you'd be?"

Olivia produced an eye-roll dramatic enough to cause vision damage. "Of course not. I sneaked into the office and posted the Facebook message so no one would worry about me. I used a picture I'd taken a while ago that I never shared before." She stood up and stretched. "RJ was waiting in the truck at the end of the driveway. He would never have let me go in. But I didn't get caught." She turned to Trudy. "Can we go now? I'm hungry."

Frank laid a restraining hand on her arm. "You still haven't told me why you and RJ were with Ronnie. This wasn't just a drop-off, it was a meet-up."

"Yeah, Ronnie left RJ a message in their secret spot that he needed to see him."

Frank tightened his grip on Olivia's arm without meaning to. "What secret spot?"

Again the eye-roll. "I don't know where it is. That's what made it secret. They set it up as part of the game."

"Where do you think RJ is now, Olivia? Would he have met up with his Dad again after he ran away from the cabin?"

Olivia squirmed away from Frank. Like rip currents, her moods pulled her closer to Frank then dragged her away. "I think RJ took me along because he was kinda scared. But Ronnie was mad I was there. He said he needed to talk to RJ about how to save their land, but he couldn't do it with me there. And he got madder and madder until I ran away." She turned toward the door, her voice a whisper. "I don't know what RJ will do now."

Frank moved to get in front of her, forcing the girl to make eye contact. "Is RJ afraid of Ronnie or of the other people playing the game? Is there someone else helping Ronnie that RJ might turn to?"

Olivia pulled the hood of her sweatshirt over her head trying to withdraw as far as possible into her shell. "I don't know. RJ used to act like he was sure he was right about everything. But now…I just don't know."

Frank was sure Olivia did know something she wasn't telling him. But questioning a child was different than squeezing information out of a punk like Wade Cochran. He needed to take a page from Earl and be patient, take a step back. He'd let Trudy work with Olivia now, and come back to talk to the child again tomorrow.

Frank squeezed Olivia's shoulder. "Thank you, Olivia." He nodded to Trudy. "Get this kid some food."

"Let's go to the diner, and then we'll have to go over to your mother's office. I'm not leaving you home alone."

Olivia paused in her rush to leave. "My mom's not going to go back to jail, is she?"

"Don't worry, your running away won't affect her parole." Trudy headed out toward Doris's desk.

Olivia looked back over her shoulder at Frank. "She won't go back to jail, no matter what, right?

CHAPTER 43

THE RANGER CALLED JUST BEFORE lunch.

"Some fishermen called this morning to report they found a deer that had been shot and partially butchered in the field. They were angry that someone was hunting deer out of season. I thought it might be—"

"Where?" Frank demanded.

"Veazey Pond Wilderness. Deep backcountry. There are some hunting blinds out there. Lean-tos. The fishermen found the spot when they were portaging between lakes."

"Tell me how to get there."

"If you don't want to paddle, there's an old logging road that you can access on an ATV. After that, you have to backpack four or five miles."

"I have to get my gear together. I'll meet you in an hour."

Frank checked the time. The library stayed open until seven tonight, so Penny wouldn't be home to plead with him not to go. He got back to the house and swiftly loaded his external frame pack: food, water, raingear, extra layers, sleeping bag, compass, matches, first aid kit, headlamp, GPS, bug spray.

Gun. Handcuffs. Rope. Ties.

He scrawled a note and left it on the kitchen table. Have to work all night. See you tomorrow.

"Let me go with you," the ranger said.

"Absolutely not."

"But Frank, it's too risky to go in there alone with no back-up. And what if the kid is with him? It'll be two-to-one."

"I can't wait for the state police to get their asses in gear. They move like cargo ships. We need a speedboat to catch Ronnie. He's already shown he knows how to outwit their dogs and their helicopters. I won't let him slip away again. I owe that to Earl."

"You don't owe it to him to get yourself killed."

Frank said nothing. What was the value of his own life? What joy was there in making love to Penny when machines were inflating Earl's lungs? What happiness could he derive from building Legos with his grandsons when Earl's hands lay slack? What pleasure could he take from Caroline's accomplishments if Earl might never walk or talk again? Even bringing Ronnie to justice wouldn't restore Frank's happiness. All he could hope was that it would remove one brick from his load of guilt.

And if he failed and Ronnie killed him, so be it. At the very least, Frank's murder would ensure Ronnie was sentenced to life in prison with no parole. If Meyerson could manage to catch him.

"Take this two-way radio," the ranger insisted.

Frank made a face. "Just another thing to carry. It won't work further than two miles."

"Two miles is better than nothing. I'm camping right here until you get back."

Frank headed into the wood, then turned. "And don't call the troopers once I'm out of sight. If this capture goes south again, it'll be on you."

Frank set off hiking through the backcountry. Mud sucked at his boots like freshly poured cement. Newly hatched bugs, eager for their first meal, swarmed around his face and neck, drinking the tears in his eyes, taking refuge in his nostrils. If he had been hiking for recreation, he would have turned back in a quarter-mile. The image of Earl tethered to his hospital bed kept Frank placing one foot in front of the other. In the damp, gray light of the forest, time lost all relevance.

Eventually, a body of water appeared.

According to the map, this was Birch Pond, and the portage to Veazey Pond would be approximately halfway around the perimeter. There was no path, just an obstacle course of rocks, weeds, roots, and muck.

Frank's left foot sank ankle deep into cold water. Blackflies, utterly unrepelled by his insect repellent, crawled under his collar and chewed off chunks of his flesh, the better to lap up his blood. He put one foot in front of the other and tuned out his misery with fantasies of a cold beer and a hot shower.

And the vision of bringing Ronnie down with one shot.

The fantasy didn't take RJ into account. What if the boy were with his father? How would Frank capture the father without harming the son? Was RJ wising up to craziness of his father's worldview? Or was the kid still his father's staunchest ally?

The sun sank lower in the sky. If Ronnie were hunting, he would most likely come out at dusk as the animals became more active. Frank didn't want to bump into him unexpectedly. He needed to move while Ronnie was hiding, and hide when Ronnie was moving.

He trudged along the perimeter of the lake, searching for any trampled area that might indicate canoeists had carried their boats through to the adjoining pond. Occasionally, through the trees, he caught a glimpse of sunlight glittering on Veazey Pond, but the underbrush seemed impenetrable. No one had carried a canoe through here. Where was the portage?

His nose twitched. Was it his imagination eager for a clue, or did he smell something different than the scent of wood decaying in the dank mud? He inhaled deeply: rotten flesh. Something dead lay nearby.

If that was the deer Ronnie had killed, then the path must open up soon. Trees grew right up to the edge of the pond here, but further down the shore he could see a small, muddy clearing. An ideal place to land a canoe. He picked up his pace, and sure enough, he saw drag marks in the mud, broken twigs, and a narrow, overgrown path leading to the next pond.

Frank headed down the path, and the stench of rotting meat grew stronger. A small animal scurried through the underbrush—he had disturbed its meal. A twist in the path and he came upon it: a young, three point buck shot cleanly through the neck. Animals had been gnawing on its extremities, but a large piece of meat had been neatly cut out of its flank. A few days' worth of food for Ronnie and the rest of the meat wasted since he had no way to preserve it.

Frank scanned the woods for the tree stand. Only by calculating from which direction the deer had been shot could Frank discern it: just a few strips of wood nailed into a maple tree to form a crude ladder, and a tiny platform barely wide enough for a man to stand. But the location was ideal, overlooking a path the animals took to drink at dawn and dusk.

According to Rusty, the lean-to was half a mile northwest of this point. But to avoid a chance encounter with Ronnie, Frank would have to hike around Veazey Pond in the other direction and hope that he would come up on the lean-to from behind. Reluctantly, he left the relatively easy hiking of the trail to bushwhack around this much larger pond. Low branches slapped his face. He succeeded in placing his other foot into a shallow inlet, so both boots and socks were equally drenched. He kept a birch that slanted out over the pond in sight as a marker of where he'd left the trail and the tree stand. In an hour, he was directly opposite it. Time to leave the shore of the pond and head inland to look for the lean-to.

The afternoon light grew dimmer. Periodically he paused to listen for the sound of other human footsteps. But all he heard was the scuttle of chipmunks and grouse and the splash of a heron fishing in the pond.

He consulted the compass frequently. If his calculations were correct, the lean-to should be right in this area. But no matter how he reviewed the logic of his work, the lean-to refused to appear. Clumsy with exhaustion, he caught his toe on a root and nearly fell. Time to sit down and rest. He perched on a fallen log and fished a granola bar out of his pack. The forest looked different from this angle. Away from the water, there was less undergrowth. He could see twenty feet in every direction between the tall, widely spaced hardwood trees.

Green. Brown. Gray.

The lean-to would also be grayish, would blend in with the landscape.

His gaze continued to roam—right to left, left to right.

A spot of orange.

Wearily, he pushed himself up to investigate.

Just lichen growing on a log.

Behind the log, he saw it: a spent rifle shell casing. Still shiny. It hadn't been there long.

Crouched on his knees, Frank could discern a faint path descending through the trees, the natural way one would walk to avoid obstacles.

He followed this path up a slight rise. To his right, a hearty hemlock had sprouted in a tiny patch of soil on top of a huge boulder then sent its tenacious roots down to find nourishment on the forest floor.

He smelled burnt wood.

Frank edged around the boulder and there was the lean-to: a wooden platform wide enough for two men to stretch out on, framed by three rough walls and covered by a sloping roof. Although the front side was completely open, the lean-to still provided decent protection against the rain and the cold, damp ground.

Charred logs rested inside a circle of stones in front of the lean-to. The camper had rigged a bag high between two trees to keep his food supply away from bears. Signs of Ronnie were everywhere: the sleeping bag he'd stolen from the house on Giant View, the backpack he'd taken from the first vacation home. A pair of socks hung to dry over a support beam. No direct evidence of RJ, but he could be sharing this camp.

No Ronnie. No gun.

He was out on the hunt.

Frank found a secure hiding place on the far side of the boulder.

He settled in to wait.

Two hours later, a single rifle shot echoed in the distance.

No more.

If Ronnie had been successful, he'd be heading back to eat his catch. Frank took the opportunity to stretch. Then he drew his weapon and positioned himself for the best view of the lean-to.

Within fifteen minutes, Frank heard footsteps. He strained his ears: one walker or two? Certainly, there was no attempt at stealth.

Out of the twilight shadows, Ronnie appeared at the crest of the hill holding a dead possum in his left hand and his rifle in his right.

Frank held his breath and watched the trail behind his prey.

No sound. No movement.

No RJ.

Humming under his breath, Ronnie propped the rifle against the side of the lean-to. Then he sat on the floor, pulled out a knife from his pack, and began to skin the animal. Frank couldn't imagine how hungry he'd have to be to eat that.

A scruffy, reddish-brown beard covered Ronnie's face. His filthy hands shook slightly as he worked—that's how hungry he must be. "C'mon now, get outta there." Ronnie spoke to the dead possum as he scraped out its entrails. Who else did he have to talk to?

He arranged the possum on a spit made of sharpened sticks. Then Ronnie set about making his fire.

The wood was damp and the breeze had kicked up, so the spark of flame refused to catch. Ronnie became completely engrossed in his project, cursing his failures.

The target was twenty feet away. Facing Frank, yet unaware of his presence. Frank knew he could shoot Ronnie right now and then place the hunting rifle in the fugitive's hands.

Clearly, self-defense. There wouldn't even be an investigation.

Do it.

He saw Earl crumpled like a discarded doll at the base of that ledge. Saw him wired to machines and tubes in the hospital.

Do it.

Saw him patiently negotiating…saw him rescuing the kids at Happy Camper. Saw him accepting his award for Best Community Policing.

When Ronnie hunkered down over the fire with his face inches from the ground, Frank sprang.

In one movement, he kicked the rifle toward the woods. Ronnie looked up and found Frank's Smith and Wesson inches from his head.

"Lay flat on the ground. Put your hands behind you," Frank ordered.

The feral rage of a cornered animal glowed in Ronnie's eyes.

Would Ronnie resist? Would he force Frank to kill him?

Frank pressed the gun into Ronnie's temple. "It's over, Ronnie. Time to come in."

The tension drained out of him. Ronnie Gatrell stretched out on the ground and allowed Frank to cuff him.

Frank stood and studied his prey.

Could the end be that easy?

"You can't leave me here tied up overnight. That possum will attract bears." Ronnie had begun complaining within minutes of his capture. "I have grease and blood on my clothes. I'll be mauled to death."

What a fitting end for Ronnie that would be! "Don't tempt me," Frank growled. "We're hiking out of here at dawn."

Frank lit the fire and cleared away the disgusting possum.

"Hey, I'm hungry. I wanted to eat that."

Frank said nothing, just continued to set up the camp. He unrolled his sleeping bag on the platform and threw Ronnie's over him as a blanket where he sat tied to the post.

"This ain't warm enough," Ronnie complained.

Frank stepped out of the circle of firelight and relieved himself against a tree.

"Hey, untie my hands for a minute. I need to pee, too."

Frank spun around. "Piss down your leg. You never get to choose again, understand? Earl can't feed himself. Earl can't take himself to the bathroom. Earl can't cover himself. So now you get to live like that too. That's your future, Ronnie."

Ronnie squirmed against his restraints. "I didn't mean to shoot him. It was an accident."

Frank crouched down two feet from Ronnie's face. "When you shoot a gun in the direction of a police officer and the bullet hits him, that's assault with intent to kill. The law doesn't care if you took careful aim or not."

"I only hit his leg. It's not my fault he landed on his head when he fell." Ronnie whined like a ball-playing child claiming a lamp had leapt to its own demise. "A good lawyer can get me off."

A lawyer? Ronnie sounded like every other two-bit punk Frank had ever arrested. Where was the revolutionary? "I thought we were on the brink of war," Frank goaded. "When the banks collapse and the new world order begins, won't your Resist or Die comrades liberate you from jail?"

Ronnie laughed, an ugly sound that morphed into a hacking cough. "Had everyone going pretty good with that one, didn't I?" He wheezed and spit into the bushes. "Money is the only thing that liberates anyone. Don't you worry, my liberation is coming."

"So the game was just a way to get RJ and other people to help you?" Frank stood over Ronnie and prodded him with his boot. "You know your son is out here somewhere looking for you?"

"Stupid kid shouldn't have brought that girl with him. I told him, bitches mess with your head. I wouldn't be in this fix now if he'd'a listened to me and done things right."

"Done what right? Who's helping RJ?"

Ronnie curled on his side. "You talk too much, Bennett. You better get your beauty sleep if we're hiking out at dawn."

A mix of adrenaline and anger kept Frank awake all night, but he didn't feel sleepy when he loaded his backpack for the hike out. He rousted Ronnie, shoved a granola bar in his mouth to silence his complaints, and set about instituting the plan he'd developed to control his prisoner on the hike out. He loosened the rope binding Ronnie's legs just enough to allow the prisoner to take short, shuffling steps. Then he looped a rope around Ronnie's waist and tied it to his own waist with five feet of play in the line. He fastened it with a slipknot. If Ronnie tugged, the rope would tighten, but if Frank pulled the short end the knot would quickly release.

The prisoner had to lead, so Frank strapped the headlamp to Ronnie's head. Slowly, they made their way down the trail in the dim light. Ronnie stumbled frequently and twice fell to one knee, howling in protest. Truthfully, it was hard to hike without being able to use his hands for balance, but Ronnie had proved he couldn't be trusted. If the hike out took twice as long as the hike in, so be it.

When they reached Veazey Pond, Frank figured the hike would get easier. Yesterday, he had bushwhacked around the far side of the pond to get to the lean-to, but today they could stay on the marked trail keeping the pond to their right. He checked the map and estimated they had only two more miles to go. They trudged along in silence, Ronnie finally accepting his fate.

Half a mile further on, Frank's ears pricked at the sound of rushing water. He hadn't encountered that on the way in. They climbed a short hill, and the stream came into sight, tumbling headlong down the slope to their left and eventually emptying into the pond. In the summer, you could probably cross the stream by stepping from rock to rock, but the spring rains and snowmelt had swollen it to a raging torrent. All stones except one large boulder were submerged in the swift current.

Ronnie turned and grinned at Frank. "Now what, boss?"

Slightly downhill from where they stood, a large tree had fallen across the stream, its trunk about a foot above the surging water. Using this log as a balance beam was the only way to cross the stream. The alternative would be to backtrack and circle the pond, adding two more miles onto the hike.

Ronnie must have passed this spot multiple times on his way to the tree stand, so he knew they'd encounter this obstacle. He hadn't warned Frank because he wanted to put him in this bind. Risk the crossing or endure the long detour.

"I can't walk that log with my hands tied behind my back." Ronnie shook his tied wrists. "Untie me until we get across."

"Not an option." Frank studied the log, reviewing everything that could go wrong. Only ten steps across, but a stumble would be disastrous. He couldn't cross tied to Ronnie and risk being pulled into the water if Ronnie fell. If he untied the rope that joined them without untying Ronnie's hands, Ronnie could try to run on the other side while Frank crossed. But he couldn't run fast, and Frank was armed. The bigger worry was that once across, Ronnie might kick the log to knock Frank off.

They should turn around.

Frank knew this, but he couldn't bear the extra miles. Two more miles of bugs. Two more miles of hunger. Two more miles of exhaustion. He wanted this over.

Ronnie would cross that log with his hands tied and wait on the other side or Frank would blow his head off. Simple as that.

Frank untied the rope from his waist, leaving it dangling from Ronnie's. He drew his weapon, using it to direct Ronnie. "Walk across and wait for me by that rock next to the trail. Don't try anything stupid."

Ronnie's eyes met his. For a long moment, he didn't say anything. The petulance and defiance had drained out of him. Ronnie nodded, turned, and started across, the rope trailing behind him like a long tail.

Frank stood on the bank holding the rope loosely so it wouldn't trip his prisoner. Ronnie stepped onto the log, swayed, righted himself. Wisely, he didn't look down but kept his eyes focused on a tree on the other side.

Three steps. Four. He was out in the middle now, the water roaring just inches beneath his feet. Five more steps and he'd be across. Once Ronnie moved away from the log, Frank would toss the rope across and make his own journey, keeping his weapon drawn.

Ronnie took two more steps and the rope grew taut. Frank had misjudged. He might have to let the rope go before Ronnie reached the far bank. Frank took a step closer to the log and draped the rope along it.

Ronnie stopped.

"What's the matter?" Frank called, but his words disappeared in the roar of the water.

Ronnie turned ninety degrees.

Then Frank heard it. "Dad? Dad!"

Ronnie went into the water.

CHAPTER 44

FRANK LUNGED FOR THE ROPE he'd just laid down. It ripped through his fingers as the brutal current swept Ronnie downstream. Jumping in after Ronnie was pointless. No one could swim in surging whitewater. Frank crossed the log so quickly he didn't have time to feel nervous.

As he stepped onto the bank on the other side, RJ emerged from the woods.

"Where's my dad?" Filthy, cold, scared—the kid looked half his fourteen years.

No time or energy for explanations. Frank pointed to the rushing stream and raced down the trail toward the pond. As the raging water coursed beside him, he caught one flash of Ronnie's green jacket tumbling past.

His mind churned as quickly as his legs. Had Ronnie jumped? Is that really what he'd seen? In the split second before Ronnie had left the log, Frank could have sworn he saw Ronnie bend his knees to push off.

Or had Ronnie lost his balance because Frank had made him walk across the log with his hands tied? Or because RJ had startled him?

Maybe Frank simply wanted Ronnie to have jumped.

Would Ronnie be drowned by the time the stream deposited him in the calmer water of the pond? Drowned because of Frank's irresponsibility? Or was this Ronnie's last crazy bid for freedom in front of his son? Could a man in a drenched down coat, heavy boots, and shackled legs pull himself out of the water?

Maybe a man couldn't, but what about a cat with nine lives?

Frank reached the mouth of the stream. Ripples fanned across the pond. Two loons swam by. No sign of a body. No sign of footprints on the bank.

Frank spun around. Where was RJ? Hadn't he followed Frank down the trail?

"RJ? RJ! Come here."

The only sound was the water surging into the pond.

Is this how the long chase ended? What if the police divers never found Ronnie's body? Would he live on as a folk legend out here in the back-country, people whispering that Ronnie Gatrell still roamed the forest? Roamed it with his son?

A wave of rage surged up in Frank's gut. He shut his eyes and screamed.

CHAPTER 45

FOR ONCE, FRANK HAD TO agree that Meyerson's anger at him was entirely justified.

"You went after Gatrell with no back-up, lost him again, and now his kid's missing too."

"Ronnie's gotta be dead. Even if he made it out of the water, he'd die of exposure with no dry clothes," Frank said, trying to convince himself.

"He's got secret stashes everywhere—the kid said so." Meyerson cracked his knuckles as he paced the room. "I could decide to ignore Ronnie, but I gotta find the kid. His mother's going crazy. RJ doesn't have his father's backwoods skills. That means more men on overtime, thanks to your grandstanding."

Frank looked at his clasped hands, covered with bug bites and scratches. "You're right. I screwed up. My conduct was inexcusable."

A long silence hung in the air.

Frank felt Meyerson's hand on his shoulder. "How's Earl?"

"No change."

Their lives had taken on a grim rhythm. Earl's parents took turns keeping a vigil by Earl's bedside all day. His aunts and cousins and Penny came after work. That left the early morning hours and late evening hours for Frank.

"As Queequeg and I are now fairly embarked in this business of whaling; and as this business of whaling has somehow come to be regarded among landsmen as a rather unpoetical and disreputable pursuit; therefore, I am all anxiety to convince ye, ye landsmen, of the injustice hereby done to us hunters of whales."

Penny paused in her reading as Frank entered the room.

"Any change?" he asked, although he could see damn well there wasn't. Earl still lay there wired to blinking, chirping machinery.

"Nothing the doctor finds significant, but I don't know…when I stop reading, I sense that he notices. He stirs a little, like he wants me to go on."

Frank yanked out a chair on the other side of Earl's bed. "You're imagining things." He could tell that Penny was wounded by his harshness, but he didn't care. He'd had enough of cock-eyed optimism and the power of prayer and the will to live. Earl was gone. The body in the bed wasn't him. It was an Earl-shaped turnip, a vegetable replica of the funny, sensitive, brave young man he'd once worked with. The first time he came to the hospital and saw Earl, the hot rage he'd felt against Ronnie, and the people who'd helped Ronnie, and Meyerson, had energized him. He'd channeled that rage to capture Ronnie.

And what good had he done?

Possibly Ronnie was dead. But certainly Earl was condemned to exist like this for years until some infection carried him off.

And RJ, another mother's beloved child—was he slowly dying of starvation or exposure? Was he looking for his father, afraid to come home?

For the first time since Earl had been injured, Frank cried. Once the first tears slipped down his cheeks, he found he couldn't stop. His shoulders shook and he sobbed, wailed. Penny came to his side of the bed and held him without saying a word. A nurse popped her head in the room and quickly withdrew.

When the fit had passed, he sat drained and limp.

Penny took a deep breath and spoke. "I know you don't believe in my intuition and my feelings, but I sense that Earl is with us." Her gaze turned to the pale form in the bed. "Our Earl is in there, I know he is. He wants to come back to us. We have to show him the way. We can't give up right before we're about to succeed."

Cold despair pinned Frank to his chair.

Penny stood. "I'm going down to the café to get a cup of tea." Before she left, she reached across Earl's inert form and placed Moby Dick on Frank's side of the bed.

He sat with his eyes closed, the incessant thrum of the hospital playing like elevator music. Where did Penny get her optimism? Where did Bob get his faith? He felt hollow, as empty inside as an old oak brought down by the wind.

The staticky screech of a loudspeaker announcement summoning some doctor jolted Frank's eyes open. The gray brick of Moby Dick mocked him from the white blanket. When Frank opened the tome to a random page, the words swam before his bloodshot eyes. He took a deep breath and began,

"Next: how shall we define the whale, by his obvious externals, so as conspicuously to label him for all time to come. To be short, then, a whale is a spouting fish with a horizontal tail. There you have him."

Sweet Jesus, this was one dull book! Why had Penny chosen it? Frank paused and poured himself a glass of water from the pitcher on the bedside table.

Earl's hand twitched.

He'd done that before. The nurses said it didn't mean anything, just an involuntary spasm.

Frank resumed reading, but he glanced up more frequently. Why had Penny set him up to feel this pathetic tickle of hope? Earl couldn't hear him any more than the bouquet of fading flowers on the nightstand could.

"By the above definition of what a whale is, I do by no means exclude from the leviathanic brotherhood any sea creature hitherto identified with the whale by the best informed Nantucketers—"

A sound—less than a cough—emanated from the bed.

Earl's lips, dry from a week with no food or water by mouth, attempted to come unstuck.

"Earl?"

His eyelids flickered.

"Earl! Earl!" Frank jumped up and ran to the door. "Nurse!" he bellowed into the hall. Then he ran back to the bed.

Earl's eyes were fully open now. He blinked blearily. His mouth moved, but was too parched to make a coherent sound. Frank grabbed the water glass and dribbled some liquid across Earl's lips and down his chin.

"Why..." Earl whispered.

"You're in the hospital, Earl. Ronnie Gatrell shot you in the leg, and you fell and hit your head, and you've been unconscious," Frank babbled, clutching Earl's hand. "Are you in pain?"

"Why..."

Frank lowered his ear to Earl's mouth to hear better.

"Why have you been talking about whales?"

CHAPTER 46

"GUESS WHO CAME INTO THE library today?" Penny threw her arms around Frank's neck and danced with him around the finally finished kitchen.

"If you're this happy, I'm guessing J.K. Rowling dropped by."

"No, silly. Earl's mother. She came in to get him some audiobooks. He's been released from the hospital and he has to rest at home quietly for another week."

Doctors and therapists had kept Earl busy every day since he'd come out of the coma, and Earl's mother had shooed away all visitors in the evening so her son could get his rest. "Am I finally allowed to see him?" Frank asked.

"Yes, Earl's been asking for you. Mrs. Davis said you can stop by tomorrow as long as you promise not to talk about work."

Frank found Earl enthroned on his mother's plaid couch, a North Country sultan attended by a bevy of flannel-shirted handmaidens.

Despite his partially shaved head and splinted leg, Earl looked remarkably well. Frank would have been happy to sit and stare at the kid for half an hour, but Earl had something else in mind.

"Mom, could you fix me a cup of tea and some of that date bread Grandma made? Toasted. And put the cream cheese on it. And Carrie, could you go up to my room and find my other audiobook? This one is kind of dull."

The two women jumped to do his bidding, and as soon as they left the room, Earl hiked himself up and grabbed his laptop from the coffee table. "I've been working on something. I have a lot to tell you."

"You're not supposed to be working. You need to—"

"I'm so bored. I can't stand watching another episode of Judge Judy. Or listening to another audiobook. So pay attention."

Earl dropped his voice. "Aunt Sheila met with Nancy Tomlinson about selling VitaVine." Earl tapped a key and Secrets of VV Sales appeared on the laptop screen in bold red type. "Sheila acted real interested, so Nancy would call her every day. Finally, Nancy said Sheila had the talent to be a high-potential seller and she was going to give her advice that she didn't give to anyone else. She was going to turn her on to some targeted prospect lists and special sales techniques on this website, so she could make a killing selling VitaVine."

"Let me guess. If she paid for the honor."

"Exactly. See, VitaVine itself is a legit business. It uses multi-level marketing, but that's not illegal. And it sells supplements that are probably useless, but that's not illegal either. But this," Earl tapped the screen, "this website doesn't show up on a Google search for VitaVine. The words VitaVine don't appear anywhere on the site—just the initials VV. You wouldn't find it unless you had the website address." Earl paused for dramatic effect. "Because you're being let in on the secret techniques. And once you're there, it offers you the first bit for free. Then this sales video ends on a cliffhanger, so you have to pay ten bucks for the next bit of information. And you probably get something worthwhile, and you make some sales. And then I bet it asks you for more...and more."

"Until you're in over your head."

"Right. I can't keep going further into the website to see how it works without paying money." Earl looked at him hopefully. "Do we have a budget for that?"

"No!"

"Yeah, I figured we didn't. Anyway, I bet it makes you think you're just not working the sales system quite right. But if you pay for more instruction, then you'll bail yourself out and make a fortune on top of that."

"And you think that's how Nancy and Ronnie both lost so much money?" Frank asked.

"Yep. I don't know which one fell for it first, but one pulled in the other."

In the kitchen, the teakettle whistled. Frank glanced over his shoulder. "So, is the Secret of VV Sales site part of the VitaVine company?"

"No, I think it's separate. Someone developed it because they saw the potential."

"Potential for....?"

"Being duped. Because if you're dumb enough to think you can make money selling VitaVine, you're dumb enough to fall for this scam."

Earl slapped the laptop shut as his mother appeared bearing a tray. "I'm sorry, but I didn't make any for you, Frank. Earl needs to take a nap after his snack."

"Of course, I don't want to wear him out. May I stop by again tomorrow?"

Mrs. Davis beamed. "I think you cheered him up. By all means, come again."

Sitting in Earl's living room, Frank had found it easy to get caught up in his partner's enthusiasm. How great to see Earl back to normal, his brain fully functioning! But back here alone in the office, Frank wasn't entirely sure what to make of Earl's theory. The kid was simply speculating on how a scam might work. Maybe it wasn't a fraud at all, just a self-help website set up by a fellow VitaVine salesman. And if the Secrets of VV Sales website really was a fraud, it might be run out of Russia or Nigeria or Silicon Valley. Definitely out of his jurisdiction.

Regardless, Earl was right about one thing: Ronnie and Nancy had come together through VitaVine. If he worked to prove the connection, he might yet get Nancy arrested for facilitating Ronnie's escape. But did he care? All that really mattered now was finding RJ.

And what could he do to help? The Department of Environmental Conservation Search and Rescue team had joined the search for RJ, but no one had found a trace of him in the woods. Nor had there been any break-ins. Frank worried that the kid had died of exposure although his mother hadn't given up hope. She called Frank, Meyerson, and the DEC rangers every day begging for updates.

He hated not having anyone to bounce an idea off of. No point going home early—Penny was off at a librarians' meeting in Placid. He'd just called Caroline and the kids yesterday. Pastor Bob was at a weeklong retreat. Even Doris was otherwise occupied preparing for the town-wide spring cleanup. This was the kind of evening when he would have taken himself to the inn. Popped in the back door to see what Edwin was cooking and finagled a dinner invitation.

But that was out of the question. Olivia was back to living with Anita although under closer supervision from Trudy. Frank didn't know how the child had resolved her longing for her foster parents; Edwin and Lucy were still furious at him for suspecting them of being involved in Olivia's disappearance.

Frank paced restlessly around the office. A week ago all he did was bargain with God to let Earl live. He would give anything, everything.

And God had granted his wish.

Now, here he was unhappy.

Humans were never satisfied.

His stomach rumbled. It looked like tonight was the night to patch things up with Marge and eat dinner at Malone's Diner.

The place was nearly empty, but Frank sat at the counter. Nothing made Marge madder than having to walk clear across the dining room to wait on a singleton.

"Evening, Frank." She handed him the menu instead of slapping it down in front of him. "Beef stew special tonight. But take your time deciding."

Take your time deciding? Had he entered the Twilight Zone?

"Beef stew is my favorite. I haven't had it in a while. Quite a while."

Marge hugged the menu to her ample bosom. "Look, Frank. I'm sorry. Seems you were right about Ronnie all along. If Earl had died or, or never woken up, I—" She shuddered into silence, her mouth agape.

Frank watched in fascination. He'd never before experienced Marge at a loss for words.

"Well, I wasn't entirely right. Ronnie didn't kill that fisherman after all."

Another customer entered and ended their awkward apologies.

How quickly life went back to normal! His feud with Marge over, Frank basked in the familiar charms of the diner—the hiss of the coffee urn, the brief blast of country music audible when the door to the kitchen opened, and most of all, the flavor of the stew. Ah! He hadn't enjoyed Marge's stew since…

…since that day when he'd been sitting in this exact seat, next to the vegetarian girl who had pissed Marge off so much.

"Hey, Marge," Frank asked when she came to refill his coffee. "Remember that day you yelled at the flaky vegetarian girl and told her to go eat in Keene? Who was that, anyway? A tourist?"

"Nah, I would never talk like that to a tourist. She was the girl who worked for Gage Shelby before he hired Anita. She'd come in here every blessed day asking about what on the menu was vegetarian. There are only three vegetarian entrees." Marge held up three fat fingers. "I told her that, but still she'd ask questions about every single item every day. Finally, I blew up. I felt kinda bad about it later, 'cause she was a friend of Darrell's."

"Darrell?"

Marge waved in the direction of the kitchen. "My morning grill guy. The one with the nose ring. Nutty but reliable."

"Darrell didn't forgive you?"

"Oh, what I did turned out not to matter. Gage fired the girl for the same reason she bugged me. She never stopped asking questions."

CHAPTER 47

ON FRIDAY, FRANK WENT FISHING.

A lot had happened between Thursday evening's stew with Marge and Friday morning's maple cruller coffee break. Penny had verified that Gage said all his previous coders had quit of boredom. She also reported that Gage had finished editing the John Brown video. Darrell the grill guy had denied having a contact number for his question-asking vegetarian friend, but Frank's phone had rung with a call from her twenty minutes after his chat with Darrell.

The girl had a lot to say, much of it expressed in acronyms and jargon Frank didn't understand. But he grasped the bottom line: the project she had been coding for Gage had nothing to do with a hiking smartphone app. When she'd confronted him with that knowledge, Gage had encouraged her to find another job. Quickly.

All of which brought Frank to Gage Shelby's office on a fishing expedition.

Gage had a charming stone house with a view of Trout Run's covered bridge. A nicely crafted wooden sign over the side door read BRIDGE TO THE FUTURE APPLICATIONS. Frank walked up a flight of stairs to a loft area above the garage and knocked on the interior door.

"C'mon in," a male voice called.

Frank entered a sunny room filled with three desks, several monitors and keyboards, and the video equipment he'd seen at the reenactment.

No Anita. Maybe she was out getting coffee.

"Penny told me the video is finished. I was wondering if the husband of the star could get a preview."

If Gage was annoyed by the interruption, he certainly didn't show it. In fact, he seemed delighted by his guest. "Sure! Sit right down. I was just cleaning up a few little glitches before I upload it to YouTube and the Historical Society's website." Gage pulled up a chair for Frank near a large computer monitor. "You won't even notice the blips. I'm a crazy perfectionist."

Despite his suspicions of Gage, Frank found himself quickly caught up in the video. Penny could give any PBS narrator a run for her money, and Gage had even managed to make the guy playing John Brown sound convincing.

"Outstanding! Honestly, when Penny and I were at the reenactment, I had my doubts about the guy playing John Brown. I heard Ronnie Gatrell did a better job last year."

"Yeah, too bad I didn't shoot this video before Ronnie went off the rails." Gage fiddled with some controls on his equipment. "People say Ronnie's dead. You saw what happened to him. What do you think?"

"Not sure." Frank watched Gage. "Seems like his body should have washed up by now. And Ronnie is a survivor, I'll give him that. You know what his last words to me were?"

Gage rolled his desk chair to an adjacent computer. "No, what?"

"He admitted all that government conspiracy, revolution stuff he spouted was BS. He said money was the only liberation, and he expected to be liberated."

Gage arched his eyebrows. "Well, Ronnie always has been a talker."

"You've known him all your life?"

"Used to watch him play baseball and basketball for the high school when I was a kid. He set some records."

"Yeah, Ronnie must be about the same age as Anita." Frank looked around the empty office. "Where is Anita, by the way?"

Gage gave the empty desk a careless glance. "She doesn't work here anymore."

"You fired her?" This was not the information Frank had expected to reel in. "Have you told Trudy Massinay? This job is part of her custody agreement."

"Anita quit this morning. And no, I didn't tell that government bureaucrat. I never bought into being part of the social welfare system's Big Brother team."

Gage had claimed Anita's predecessor quit, and that hadn't been true. "Why would she quit? She'll never find another job like this in Trout Run."

Gage shrugged. "These coders are all the same. No loyalty. She seems to think she's found something better in Glens Falls."

"Glens Falls! That's too far away to commute."

"Who said anything about commuting? She and the kid are moving there."

Gage's bombshell drove out any interest Frank had in uncovering the exact nature of Bridge to the Future Applications.

He called Trudy, but rolled to her voicemail. So Frank went straight to Anita's apartment. Olivia would be at school. At least, he hoped so.

Anita answered his loud hammering. After a moment, she stepped aside to let him enter. Three large cardboard boxes stood in the middle of the living room.

Neither of them spoke.

After what seemed an eternity, Anita lifted her chin and said, "I hear you've been talking to one of the other girls from Break Out Coding."

The surprises kept coming. "You know the girl who worked for Gage before you? You were in jail with her?"

"Tanya never did time. Pretty young girl like her they sent to rehab and a diversion program. She learned coding same as me, and she went to the same follow-up group. You know, to keep us on the straight and narrow."

Was Anita on the straight and narrow, or was she blowing out of town just in time to save her skin? Had Tanya been feeding him a line about being forced to quit? They'd both learned to code alongside a bunch of other criminals. How had they put their talents to use? Frank swallowed his rising excitement. Wouldn't that be convenient? Arrest Anita for fraud and Olivia would go back to Edwin and Lucy and all would be right in his world.

"Tanya has a drug problem?"

"Used to be addicted to pills. Now it's vegetables. Addicts have to stay addicted to something."

For sure, Anita had a keen eye for other people's frailties. "Your friend claims Gage fired her for asking too many questions about the business. Gage says she quit, and you quit too. Your decision seems a little...impulsive."

Anita dropped a stack of books into a box. "Gage thought me and Tanya were both too stupid to understand what we were working on. It didn't take me more than a week to figure out what I was coding didn't have nuthin' to do with a hiking app. But what did I care what Gage was really doing to make money as long as I was getting paid to do work I liked? After all, Breakout Coding placed us in that job, so Gage had to be legit. I figured maybe Gage needed a cover story to keep his idea secret until he was ready to launch. He didn't want anybody to steal it—developers are like that. I figured I wouldn't make the same mistake as Tanya and get myself fired for asking questions. I put my head down and stuck to coding, but I kept my eye peeled for a better job."

"And did you figure out what he's really doing?"

Anita grimaced, revealing her prison-issued dental work. "I didn't study computer science at MIT, remember. But I did find a better job, now that I have some experience."

Was Anita simply trying to improve her circumstances? Only one way to find out. "Let me give you a hint, Anita. Is Gage running an Internet scam? Something to do with sucking people in over their heads selling VitaVine supplements?"

Anita stepped back from him, stumbling over her packing boxes. Clumsy or scared? Frank remembered what Olivia had asked. "Will my mom go back to jail?" At the time, he thought the child had been concerned about the effect of her running away. Maybe Olivia knew more than he imagined.

Anita quickly regained her composure. "Look, Break Out Coding placed me in that job," she repeated. "If you got a problem with what Gage is doing with his business, you should take it to them. I didn't think the Trout Run PD had an Internet fraud squad." Again, that unpleasant grin.

Something clicked in Frank's brain. Something was suddenly making him think about the clerk he'd paid to inform on Wade Cochran. About the useless description the clerk had offered of Wade's visitor: not fat, not thin; not tall not short; light brown hair; and one last useless detail that Frank had nearly forgotten.

A weird smile.

"You're right, Anita. I'm not really qualified to investigate computer fraud. I am, however, very interested in solving another crime: how Nancy Tomlinson helped Ronnie Gatrell escape from jail."

Anita shrugged. "Can't help you with that."

"Ah, but you can. See, you don't just code for Gage. Sometimes you run errands for him, like you did at the re-enactment."

Anita narrowed her eyes. "So? That's not illegal."

"I have a witness who saw you hand an envelope over to Wade Cochran, a payment for his part in the escape."

Anita met his gaze and didn't blink. "If you say so. I drove clear over to Newcomb for Gage, but I didn't know what was in the envelope or why I was delivering it."

Not rattled. Either she honestly knew nothing about Gage's business, or she had nerves of steel—Frank wasn't sure which. He changed course. "Does Trudy know you're moving to Glens Falls? You're not allowed to move Olivia without her permission."

"I've talked to her about making a fresh start away from Trout Run. There's too much baggage here, for me and Olivia both."

Baggage. Is that what Edwin and Lucy were?

"I put in a call to Trudy," Frank warned as he headed to the door. "I don't want you leaving until I hear back from her."

Anita gestured to the mostly empty boxes. "Olivia and I still have a lot of packing to do."

Frank descended the stairs from the second floor apartment. Despite the early infusion of information, the morning hadn't developed the way he'd hoped. A school bus rumbled by and stopped at the corner. A pack of kids got off, but Olivia wasn't among them.

Above his head, a window opened. He looked up to see Anita leaning out.

"Why is the bus so early?" she asked.

"Early dismissal today," Frank answered. "Something to do with testing."

He kept walking toward the office.

Behind him, the kids laughed and shouted. He heard footsteps running and a hand grabbed his arm.

Frank spun around. Anita's eyes were wild with fear.

"Olivia got off the bus at the covered bridge. She thought I'd be working with Gage. She doesn't know I quit."

Frank didn't understand the problem. A simple mix-up. Anita could drive over to get Olivia, or the kid could walk home. It wasn't far.

Anita clutched both Frank's arms and gave him a shake. "Olivia knows about the VitaVine. I'm afraid of what she might say. I'm afraid of him. Come with me to get her."

CHAPTER 48

ANITA'S CAR WAS PARKED AT the curb, so Frank drove it to Gage's office while Anita texted Olivia.

"She's not answering." Anita's voice shook.

"Was Gage angry when you quit?" Frank asked.

"I know stuff about him. He knows stuff about me. We called it a draw."

Mutually assured destruction. But somehow Olivia tipped the balance.

Frank hoped Anita was simply over-reacting, that they'd soon see Olivia's long-legged figure loping up the hill from the bridge. "What makes you think Gage won't just send her home?"

"He asked me a million questions about her this morning. About what she knew from the time she spent with RJ."

What did she know? Frank had intended to talk to Olivia again, but in the commotion surrounding Ronnie's plunge into the water and Earl's miraculous recovery, he had never done it. He focused on Anita. "What has Olivia told you about RJ and Ronnie?"

"She doesn't like to talk about it. But Gage thinks she knows stuff, think that I told her stuff, too. I convinced him she was clueless. I told him if anything happened to Olivia, you'd never rest until you figured out who did it. I convinced him it was best to let the two of us leave town and forget we ever knew Gage Shelby."

"But Olivia..."

Anita turned to him. "If Gage starts asking her the questions he asked me, she'll never be able to lie her way out. He has too much at stake. He'll kill her."

The bend in the road to the bridge made it possible to park Anita's car out of sight of Gage's house. Gage's SUV was in the driveway, so at least he hadn't taken Olivia anywhere. Anita jumped out of the car, but Frank blocked her from running toward the office.

"Does Gage have a gun in the office?"

"I've never seen one in the office, but he has hunting rifles in the house."

"Is there an internal door that connects the office to the house, or just the external door?"

"Internal too. It leads from the back wall of the office into a bedroom on the second floor. But he keeps it locked. Probably worried that I'll sneak into his house and rob him."

Frank peered up at the office windows, but the bright sunlight made it impossible to see if Gage and Olivia were in there. He held out his hand for Anita's phone and programmed his own number into her speed dial. "Go up the office stairs and listen. If you hear Gage talking, you press the button to call me. Don't say anything. Don't go in unless you have to. I'm going to go in through the house."

Unlike most Adirondackers, Gage actually kept his doors locked. But with a quiet tap, Frank was able to crack one pane of a window, break out the pieces, and let himself into the house. As soon as he got inside, he felt his phone vibrate.

Anita.

Gage must be in the office.

Frank slipped upstairs and quickly found the bedroom closest to the office loft. The wooden floors in the old house creaked as he crossed the room to the wall with two doors.

One had an old dull brass doorknob and the other a shiny deadbolt lock.

Frank held his breath and listened in front of the locked door.

"Mom! What's going on?"

Frank winced. Anita had obviously made noise climbing the steps. Either that, or she hadn't been able to restrain herself from entering because of something Gage had said.

"Be quiet, Olivia. I'll handle this."

Frank drew his gun and waited. He would have to shoot the lock out if he needed to enter. He wanted a sense of where each of them stood in the room. Most of all, he wanted to know if Gage was armed. Would Anita be shrewd enough to give him a hint?

Or was Anita entirely wrong? Would Gage send mother and daughter on their way?

"Olivia and I were having a nice little chat," Gage said. "She was telling me about RJ and his dad."

"I was not!" Olivia's voice sounded the faintest, as if she might be near the window. Anita should still be near the external door. That meant Gage was closest to Frank. Good. Stay that way.

"Well, you were about to tell me, when your mother so rudely interrupted us."

"Like I said this morning, she doesn't know anything. C'mon, Olivia—let's get out of here."

Olivia emitted a sharp cry.

"Put that thing away, Gage," Anita said.

Frank's hand tightened on his gun. Two questions answered.

"Now, tell me where RJ is hiding." Gage's voice. Calm, determined.

"I don't know. But even if I did, I wouldn't tell you." Olivia's voice. One hundred percent bratty pre-teen. Did she have to provoke him?

Olivia kept talking. "You're the one who convinced RJ's dad to kill that fisherman. Now his dad can never come home."

What? Ronnie had killed Cottlemeir? At Gage's command?

"You little brat!" Footsteps and Anita's sharp, "No!"

"What are you going to do—blast your office full of holes and carry our bodies out in broad daylight?"

Jesus—nothing like a twelve-year-old for bravado.

Frank shot off the lock.

CHAPTER 49

THE WEEKEND PASSED IN A blur.

Gage's arrest. Anita's interrogation. RJ's return.

Through it all, Frank remembered one promise he'd made. "Your mom won't go back to jail."

Before Anita spoke to the state police, he made sure she had a lawyer.

A good one, not the public defender.

Now, on Sunday night, he collapsed onto his sofa. Penny handed him a tumbler of scotch.

"I know you're exhausted. Just answer this: is Anita in trouble?"

"No. She didn't commit any crimes. She didn't even witness any crimes. She just knew a lot from keeping her eyes and ears open. And she didn't obstruct an investigation because no one ever asked her any questions until after Gage was arrested. She's back home right now with Olivia."

"Why didn't she just come and tell you what she knew?"

Because she's Anita. Because she's been an outcast all her life. "At first, she didn't want to lose the job. Later, she worried she'd be implicated somehow."

"But Gage is in jail, I hope?"

"Yeah, the bail hearing didn't go his way. Judges don't like people who threaten witnesses. Especially twelve-year-old witnesses."

"And RJ?"

Frank took a hefty slug of the scotch. "Turned up on his mother's doorstep yesterday. Twenty pounds lighter and two toes black with frostbite. I think he gave up looking for his dad when they started to rot."

"Eeeew! But how did he last as long as he did?"

"He and Ronnie had supply caches hidden all over the backcountry. Just a big game to Ronnie, but poor RJ took it seriously. The kid's going to need years on a shrink's couch."

"And what about VitaVine and Mr. Cottlemeir?"

Frank rattled the ice cubes in his empty glass. "I thought you were only asking me one question."

"Well, you've come this far. Why not finish? I'll get you another drink."

Frank accepted the drink and pulled Penny into an embrace. This was the saddest part of a sad and sordid tale. "Only Gage, Ronnie, and Joe know all the details. But this is what we've pieced together from information Anita and Olivia provided. Joe met Ronnie, probably when he was up here on a previous fishing trip. Joe must've told Ronnie about needing money for the sick grandson, and Ronnie convinced Joe that selling VitaVine was the answer to all his problems. And then Joe got sucked into Gage's scam and lost even more money."

"Back up. Did Ronnie know Gage was a scammer? Or was Ronnie a victim too?"

"Ronnie started out as a victim, but soon Gage brought him into the scam. Those two had a lot in common. They both were trying and failing to living up to their fathers' successes."

"I think it goes even deeper than that," Penny said. "They both like being puppet masters, controlling people, the way Ronnie did with that crazy game. And the way Gage likes directing those videos—making everyone play a part."

"Except Ronnie wasn't pulling strings when he took the kids hostage. He really did flip out. And Gage was nervous that Ronnie would start talking in jail and give away the VitaVine scam. So he arranged the escape through Nancy Tomlinson."

"Another one of his VitaVine victims."

"Once Ronnie was out of jail, he became even more of a loose cannon. Ronnie really did care about saving his land more than anything. He needed money to pay off the bank, but now he wasn't able to recruit more people into VitaVine. So Gage came up with a way for Ronnie to get part of Joe Cottlemeir's life insurance money."

Penny lifted her head from Frank's shoulder. "How?"

"Ronnie would kill Joe so the accidental death clause would kick in." Frank knocked back the last of the scotch. "Joe would have the money to save his family. Ronnie would have the money to pay off the bank."

"Wait...you're saying Joe was a willing victim?"

"Yep. Joe must've known his time was coming that weekend; that's why he left the letter for his wife. Ronnie sneaked up and dropped him with one shot."

Penny shuddered. "But Meyerson said Joe wasn't shot with the gun Ronnie stole."

"He wasn't. Gage provided a different gun. And RJ brought him boots that fit better than the ones Ronnie stole. Anita thinks the gun could be one from Gage's house. We can only hope that cocky bastard has tripped himself up."

"How were they going to distribute the money?"

"The executor of Joe's estate was some lawyer his wife had never heard of. Young guy."

"Let me guess—he knows Gage Shelby."

Frank heaved himself off the sofa. Two quick glasses of scotch made the room tilt a bit. "Your buddy Gage was at the center of everything."

Penny collected the glass and fluffed the sofa cushions. "You never did like Gage. And you always thought Ronnie was dangerous. I feel like a fool for being so trusting."

Frank switched off the lamp, throwing his cozy living room into the shadows. "Believe me, there's a downside to being suspicious. Look what it's cost me with Edwin."

CHAPTER 50

SINCE THE COMPLETION OF THE kitchen remodeling project, Penny had remained true to her vow to never use the microwave again. Delighted with her new appliances, she had become a born-again Julia Child, Googling recipes for oven-roasted pork and sautéed chicken. Unfortunately, her procurement abilities hadn't kept up with her new cooking skills, and she had once again sent Frank on a suicide mission to The Store to find urgently required ingredients.

He was digging through cans of mushrooms trying to find one that hadn't expired during the Bush administration when a familiar face appeared on the other side of the aisle.

Frank rubbed his dusty hands on his pants. "Hi, Pam. How're you doing?" She looked better than the last time he'd seen her, right after RJ had two toes amputated. Her eyes were brighter, her face less haggard.

"A few families have called me about babysitting their kids. After Ronnie's body washed up, I guess they figured they had nothing to fear."

Once the weather had warmed up, Ronnie's bloated body had risen to the surface of Veazey Pond. His legend had finally died. Frank was relieved although without Ronnie's testimony, Gage Shelby might beat the conspiracy charge in Cottlemeir's murder.

"How's RJ?" he asked.

Pam exhaled a deep breath. "A little better. Still depressed, but Denny and his dad are a good influence." She dropped a box of Sugar Pops into her shopping basket and Frank thought their conversation had ended. But she reached for Frank's hand, and her eyes searched his. "Tell me—did Ronnie jump, or did RJ startle him into falling?"

Frank didn't know the truth, but he knew the right answer. "He jumped. He knew we'd have to cross that stream. He didn't want to end his life in jail."

After Pam left, Frank moved on scrutinize The Store's meager selection of spices: cinnamon, chili powder, garlic salt. None of the tarragon he'd been sent to find.

"Hey, you busy?"

No one could construe him as that.

"I need to talk to you." Anita Veech had materialized beside him, holding a liter of Diet Dr. Pepper and a loaf of whole-wheat Wonder bread.

Frank turned to face her. "I'm listening."

"Not here." She looked around for eavesdroppers although The Store was completely empty except for the girl at the register. "Meet me at my place. It won't take long." Anita retreated down the aisle then hesitated. "Please."

Anita opened the door just as he raised his fist to knock. She ushered him over to the dinette table and waved him into a chair with no pretense of hospitality. With Gage in jail, Anita had no need to rush the move to Glens Falls. Trudy insisted that they wait until the school year ended, so the little apartment was no longer being packed up.

Anita sat down across from Frank. "I want you to work something out for me."

"Oh?" That one word expressed all his ambivalence about Anita: sympathy for her miserable upbringing and grudging admiration for the way she'd managed to start over, mixed with suspicion of her motives, and the conviction that she couldn't be the kind of parent Olivia needed.

Anita looked down at her folded hands on the table. "I figured you're the only person I can tell about this."

What was this meek bashfulness? It seemed most un-Anita-like. But Frank played along. "Of course you can tell me. You've got a problem?"

Anita didn't raise her eyes. "I've had lots of problems. It starts way back."

Frank stretched out his legs and dropped his plastic shopping bag. He'd played a lot of roles recently: medic, forest ranger, housebreaker. Why not add shrink to the list? "Start wherever you need to start."

"Remember I told you that when I first got arrested, I was kinda relieved to be away from Pap. But there was one thing about prison that I couldn't adjust to. I was never alone. Not one minute of the day. Not even in the bathroom. People talking all day, all the time. I thought I'd go crazy. Then I started taking the computer class, and they discovered I was good at it. They changed my job from working in the laundry to working in the warden's office. I put together spreadsheets and reports for her all day. They gave me a little desk in the corner and no one talked to me ever, six hours a day." Anita looked up and smiled. "I loved it."

Of course, the enforced intimacy of prison would be hard for anyone, but especially for Anita, who had spent her life living under the thumb of the paranoid, reclusive Pap Veech, rarely interacting with anyone outside her extended family. But where was she going with this? Frank couldn't help suspecting this story about the trauma of prison life was simply an attempt to soften him up for some big favor.

"Yes, I can see how that job in the warden's office would improve your circumstances. So once you got settled…." He nodded for her to continue.

"Then the days weren't so bad. But at mealtimes, and after work, I still had to deal with the stories."

"Stories?"

"That the other girls told. Some of them, they said their kids got taken by the social workers and put in foster care. Some of them had been in foster care themselves when they were young. They wouldn't shut up about it." Anita shook her head. "They said it was bad. It was always bad."

Frank glanced around the unadorned little kitchen, so different from the cheerful clutter of the kitchen at the Iron Eagle Inn. What horror was coming?

Anita slid to the edge of her chair. "At the custody hearing I said I never got any of those first letters Olivia wrote me. That wasn't exactly true."

So that made it exactly a lie. He'd always suspected Anita's tale of prison neglect was just a fabricated excuse. "So you did abandon your daughter," Frank said.

"I didn't! Maybe this doesn't make sense to you, but when you're inside, you're totally powerless. What if Olivia told me she was getting hurt? What could I do? I wouldn't be able to help her, and that would be worse than not hearing from her at all. So when I was in there, I didn't want to think about Olivia too much. I just shut that part of my brain down."

Frank recalled his college psych courses. There was a word for this… compartmentalization. You shut the bad thing up in a corner of your mind so you could manage to go on living. He'd done it himself with Estelle's death, kept the door locked on his grief so he could manage to drive a car or buy a quart of milk.

Anita took a deep breath. "But I couldn't get her totally out of my mind. Because the other girls were always talking about how wrong it was that their kids got taken away. Some of them were inside 'cause their boyfriends or husbands had been selling drugs or whatever and gotten the girls involved. They felt like they got screwed over twice: once by their men, and once by the courts. Just like I got in trouble because of Pap and my brother. And they said when they got out, they were going to take back what was rightfully theirs. So hearing them say that I thought, yeah, me too."

Great. Was Olivia just a pawn in a game of tit for tat? He didn't like the turn this conversation was taking. Anita sounded too much like Ronnie Gatrell—blaming everyone but himself for what he had lost.

"Then I got out." Anita stood up. "You've sent a lotta people to jail. You ever been with one of them on the day they got out?" She answered her own question before he had a chance to. "Probably not. Being a cop is like working at the beginning of an assembly line. You don't get to see the final product."

She went over to the fridge and poured herself a glass of soda without offering him one. "Lemme tell you—it's weird. The whole world looked different, smelled different. The colors of the leaves in the sunshine were so bright it hurt my eyes. I kept thinking people were trying to start something with me when they looked me in the eye and smiled. I was only inside for five years. People who are in for twenty, thirty years and get out? Geez, no wonder they commit another crime so they can go back."

Anita returned to the table with the soda, oblivious to her rudeness.

"The prison counselor asked me where I was going to go when I got out. I didn't have to come back here to Trout Run—Pap and my brother and our old house were all gone. But where else would I go? There was nothing for me anywhere else. There was nothing for me here, either—except Olivia.

"Coming back to Trout Run, all I could think about was Olivia. How I had to have her back. Because she was mine. The only thing that was mine. And they had no right to keep her. I got the job with Gage and he said I should fight for Olivia. I never fought and won anything before. It was a good feeling."

Anita's dentally enhanced smile expressed something other than joy. "But once I had her back..."

Suddenly Frank could see where this was headed. The story of every guy who married the beautiful model. Who landed the prime job. Who took the trip of a lifetime. Who moved into the McMansion. The long-sought dream crumbled. The chase was better than the capture.

Anita rattled the ice cubes in her empty glass. "We were together every day. Every single day in this little apartment. The weekends were the worst...her looking at me like 'now what?'. And then she ran away."

Anita stared at the blank beige wall. The only sound was the wheezing of the old refrigerator's compressor.

"I was worried something bad might've happened to her, but at the same time—"

Anita was relieved to be alone. He could see it in her face. She didn't have to say it.

"But when Gage threatened her, you were genuinely worried, terrified," Frank said. "You love Olivia."

"In my own way. But there's something wrong with me inside," Anita whispered. "I can't relate to other people."

Frank's suspicion wavered. Clearly, it was costing Anita a lot to ask for help. He tried to meet her halfway. "I understand. You need some counseling, but you're afraid if you talk to Trudy about it, she'll take Olivia away. I'm willing to talk to her for you."

Anita tipped the last ice cube in the glass into her mouth and crushed it. "No, you don't get it. I want to give Olivia back to those Bates people."

CHAPTER 51

FRANK PUT A HAND OUT to steady himself. The apartment pitched like a boat in high seas. "Give her back? After the way you fought to keep her? After the way you risked your life to protect her?"

Anita's face flushed a mottled red. She started to stand.

Frank felt like kicking himself. This was the moment they'd all longed for. He shouldn't be making Anita feel bad for her decision. He'd been so shocked, the remark just slipped out. He wasn't sure why Anita trusted him in her hour of need, but she did. He'd better step up and deliver some compassion.

"Sit, sit. I'm sorry—I didn't see that coming. You said you wanted me to help you work this out?"

Anita sank back into her chair. "I know it's me. I'm not trying to push off the blame. But Olivia is feeling the strain too. I talked it over with her. We both decided it's for the best that she go back. But I want to be able to visit her sometimes. She wants that, too."

This was the moment when he should reach out to Anita—squeeze her hand, pat her arm. But Anita exuded a force field that repelled any gesture of intimacy. "It takes a lot of courage to do what you're doing, Anita. I admire that." That much was true.

"I'll make this work out," Frank continued. "I know I can."

That part was bull.

CHAPTER 52

FRANK STOOD OUTSIDE THE BACK door of the Iron Eagle Inn. How many times had he walked right in, not even bothering to knock? Sometimes he found Lucy in her nightgown drinking tea, or Edwin cursing at a sauce on the stove that refused to thicken.

They hadn't minded.

They never turned him away.

Now he took a deep breath and knocked. No answer, but he could hear them moving around, hear the radio playing.

He tapped louder.

"What's that sound?" Edwin asked. "Is that damn woodpecker pecking on the shutters again?"

Frank pushed open the ever-unlocked door. "Hey. It's me," he called from the back hall.

Lucy and Edwin held hands and crept closer. They looked at him as if he were a wolverine, ready to pounce.

"Can I come in?" Frank asked.

Edwin pulled Lucy closer. "Why?"

Lucy shook herself free. "Of course you can come in, Frank. Have a seat."

But he didn't sit. Because Edwin kept standing.

He had rehearsed his speech, even going so far as to role-play with Penny. But when he opened his mouth, no words came from his paralyzed throat.

"What's wrong?" Lucy asked. "Has something happened to Olivia?"

This gave Frank an opening. He spat out his news in one breath. "Anita and Olivia have talked things over, and Olivia wants to come back to live with you. Anita will give you full custody, but she wants visitation rights."

Lucy's face lit with joy.

"NO!" Edwin screamed. "How dare you? Get out! Get out of my house!" His hand picked up the first object it found, a cast iron pot lid.

"Haven't you caused enough damage?"

Frank scurried out as the airborne lid took a chunk out of the doorframe.

Back in his truck, he sat with his head against the steering wheel. Could he have screwed that up any worse?

The passenger door opened, and Lucy slid in beside him. "Don't worry, Frank. He'll come around."

"No, Lucy. He shouldn't have to come around. Edwin feels manipulated. I don't blame him. I'm no better than Gage Shelby, pulling people's strings to make them jump. I'm sorry I came here and caused you more pain."

Lucy rested her head against his arm. "Oh, Frank—you've always wanted what's best for Olivia. Even right now when he's so mad, Edwin knows that's true. He's mad because he's worried about me."

"I'm worried about you, too. I hurt you once, and now I'm doing it again."

Lucy took his face in her hands and turned his head. "Do I look hurt?"

Frank had to admit, her eyes were twinkling.

"Frank, this time away from Olivia has actually been good for me. Before, I wanted so much to be her mother. It was a constant tug-of-war between us. Now, I've let that go. Anita is Olivia's mother—always was, always will be. And me, I'm her Lucy. And that's okay. I'm fine with it. I really am."

Lucy took a deep breath. "But Edwin, Edwin's her daddy. The only one she's ever had. And I'm okay with that too."

Frank looked up and saw Edwin illuminated in the bedroom window, making no pretense of the fact that he was watching them. "Will Edwin ever forgive me for suspecting him of taking Olivia?"

Lucy snorted. "I told him he has no one but himself to blame. You don't tell a cop you're thinking of running off to South America with your foster child, even if that cop is your best friend."

Frank rested his head against the seat and closed his eyes. "I miss Edwin."

Lucy squeezed his hand. "He misses you."

EPILOGUE

THE GYM SMELLED OF OLD sweat and new perfume.

"I'm so hot. Let's get this show on the road," Penny complained.

Frank yanked his tie loose. "When I was a kid, we didn't even have eighth grade graduation."

"Me either," Edwin agreed. "It's not like going to high school is optional."

"I can't tell which one is Olivia." Lucy squinted at the dais. "The girls all look alike in those white mortarboards and robes. I think she's the third one from the left."

"No," Anita corrected. "Olivia's the fourth from the left. See how one shoulder is higher than the other? She always stands crooked like that."

"You're right," Edwin said. "I tell her she's going to grow a hump."

Finally, the principal began to read the names of the graduates. There were only forty-two eighth graders in High Peaks Middle School, so it didn't take long to get near the end of the alphabet.

"Olivia Veech," the principal said.

Frank and Penny and Lucy and Edwin and Anita cheered.

Later, the graduates mingled with their friends and relatives in front of the bleachers. A smiling Olivia spun from one embrace to another. Frank turned to congratulate Rollie Fister's grandson. When he rejoined Penny, he saw Olivia holding a small wrapped box and Anita walking across the gym floor.

"Isn't Anita coming to the party at the inn?"

Penny shook her head. "Edwin invited her, but she said it's a long drive back to Glen's Falls."

Olivia watched her mother pass through the gym door into the dark night. She slipped her hand into Edwin's. "Let's go home."

THE END

THANK YOU FOR READING FALSE Cast. To help other readers discover this book, please post a brief review on Amazon or Goodreads. I appreciate your support!

Receive a FREE short story when you join my mailing list. You'll get an email whenever I release a new book. No spam, I promise!

Like my Facebook page for funny updates on my writing, my travels, and my dog.

Follow me on BookBub for news of sales.

Meet me on Twitter and Goodreads, too.

HAVE YOU READ ALL THE BOOKS BY S.W. HUBBARD?

FRANK BENNETT ADIRONDACK MOUNTAIN MYSTERY SERIES

Take the Bait
The Lure
Blood Knot
Dead Drift

PALMYRTON ESTATE SALE MYSTERY SERIES

Another Man's Treasure
Treasure of Darkness
This Bitter Treasure

ABOUT THE AUTHOR

S.W. HUBBARD IS THE AUTHOR of the Palmyrton Estate Sale Mysteries, Another Man's Treasure, Treasure of Darkness, and This Bitter Treasure. She is also is the author of four Police Chief Frank Bennett mystery novels set in the Adirondack Mountains: Take the Bait, The Lure (originally published as Swallow the Hook), Blood Knot, and False Cast, as well as a short story collection featuring Frank Bennett, Dead Drift. Her short stories have appeared in Alfred Hitchcock's Mystery Magazine and the anthologies Crimes by Moonlight, The Mystery Box, and Adirondack Mysteries. She lives in Morristown, NJ, where she teaches creative writing to enthusiastic teens and adults, and expository writing to reluctant college freshmen. To contact her or read the first chapter of any of her books, visit: http://www.swhubbard.net.

Made in the USA
Columbia, SC
14 April 2023